W9-CHY-621

Astra

*Also by Grace Livingston Hill
in Large Print:*

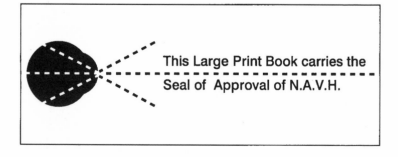

This Large Print Book carries the
Seal of Approval of N.A.V.H.

Astra

Grace Livingston Hill

1865 - 1947

Thorndike Press • Thorndike, Maine

Published in 1999 by arrangement with Munce Publishing.

Thorndike Large Print ® Candlelight Series.

The tree indicium is a trademark of Thorndike Press.

The text of this Large Print edition is unabridged.
Other aspects of the book may vary from the original edition.

Set in 16 pt. Plantin by Minnie B. Raven.

Printed in the United States on permanent paper.

Library of Congress Cataloging in Publication Data

Hill, Grace Livingston, 1865–1947.
    Astra / Grace Livingston Hill.
      p. cm.
    ISBN 0-7862-1985-8 (lg. print : hc : alk. paper)
    1. Large type books. I. Title.
    [PS3515.I486A92   1999]
    813'.52—dc21
                                 99-14895

Astra

 **1** It had begun to snow as Astra boarded the train just east of Chicago, but only in a desultory way. A few stray sharp little flakes, slanting across the morning grayness, as if they were out on a walk, looking around. Not at all as if they meant anything by it. A few minutes later, after she was settled in her place in the day coach, one suitcase stowed in the rack above her, the other at her feet, she withdrew her gaze from the unattractive fellow travelers to look out of the window again, and the flakes were still wandering around, seemingly without a purpose. She watched one or two till they glanced across the warm window pane and vanished into nothing. Only an idle little crystal drifted down from the eternal cold somewhere, and gone. Where? Into nothing? What a lovely idle little life, thought Astra, as she settled back into her stiff uncomfortable seat, with her head against the window frame and tried to turn her thoughts to her own perplexities. She was very tired for she had gotten up early after a sleepless night and hurried around to get ready for the train.

And so, idly watching the aimless grains of snow snapping on her consciousness from the window pane outside, her eyes grew weary, her eyelids drooped, and she was soon asleep.

A little later she roused suddenly as the conductor drew her ticket out of her relaxed grasp and punched it sharply, passing on to the next seat briskly. It came to her to wonder vaguely why he ever selected the job of conductor. To go through life in a dull train, far from home, if he had a home, and doing nothing but punching tickets. What a life! Only dull strangers, uninteresting people he didn't know, to vary the monotony.

Idly she drifted away into sleep again, putting aside her own disturbed thoughts about personal matters, for she really was very weary. When she awoke again the snow was still coming down. The flakes were larger now, and more purposeful as if they meant business.

She sat up and looked out. They were going through small towns and villages. People were passing along the streets with brisk steps, bundles in their arms. In market places there were rows of tall pines and hemlocks displayed for sale, and a bright cluster of red and silver stars, holly wreaths and Christmas trimmings.

Christmas! Yes, Christmas was almost here!

She drew a soft quivering breath of desolation. Not much joy in the thought of Christmas for her any more! Going out alone into an unknown world, with very little money and without a job!

The train swept out of the town where it had lingered for a few brief minutes just opposite that market with its rows of Christmas trees, and then the increasing snow drew her attention. The flakes were larger now, and whiter, giving a decided whiteness to the atmosphere. The next small town that hurried into view ahead showed up a merry string of lights along the business street. They brought out the whirling flakes in giddy relief, as if flakes and lights were in league for the holiday season, bound to make the most of their powers.

People about her were ordering cups of coffee and eating ham sandwiches that were brought around in a basket for sale. Others were drifting by toward the diner. But Astra wasn't hungry. However she bought a sandwich and stowed it in her handbag, against a time when she might feel faint, and not be able to get the sandwich so easily. Then she sat back again watching the twilight as it crept through the snowflakes. Gradually the landscape was taking on a white background from the falling snow, and soft plush flakes were melting on the windows and blurring into one another. It was becoming more and more difficult to see the landscape as it whirled by, to discern the little towns with their holiday trimmings, and more and more Astra's thoughts were turning inward to her own problems and her own drab life.

She had friends of other days, of course, friends of her childhood and young girlhood, friends of her mother's and father's, and she was hastening back to them. After all it was only two years since she had left them and gone to live with Cousin Miriam who had been almost like an older sister to her in the past when Miriam used to spend so much time at holidays and vacations from school and college with Astra's mother.

But Miriam had married into wealth and fashion, and was very much changed. The standards on which both she and Astra had been brought up were no longer Miriam's standards. She laughed at Astra for continuing to uphold them. She told her that times had changed and one couldn't continue to be dowdy and old-fashioned just because one's mother was that way. One had to do what others did, in company, even if there were things called principles. It wasn't done in these days, to have principles. One couldn't "get on" and have principles. One had to smoke and drink a little. Everybody did. To "get on" was in Miriam's eyes the end and aim of living.

Astra couldn't get away from the thought of how ashamed her mother would have been of her cousin, for Astra's mother had practically brought up Miriam from the time she was a schoolgirl of twelve, at least as much as one could do that important act within the limits of vacations and holidays.

In addition to Miriam there was Miriam's daughter, Clytie, badly spoiled, and very determined in her own way, which was the way of a changing world that Astra did not care to adopt.

Astra had stood the differences as long as she could, and then during the absence of the cousins on a western trip in which she was not included, she had written a sweet little note of farewell, and departed.

And now that she was on her way she was tormented continually by the fear that perhaps she had been wrong to go. Perhaps she should have endured a little longer. But in a few days now she would be of age, and would have a little more money to carry on quietly. To secure one of her mother's old

11

servants perhaps to stay with her, or something of that sort. It had seemed so reasonable and easy to make the transfer now when she was about to come of age. And when she considered returning before her cousins got back, and trying to live the life from which she had just fled, it seemed utterly impossible.

The twilight was deepening, and the snow outside the window was gathering thick and soft on the glass, obscuring the view. Suddenly the lights sprang up in the car, and banished the gloom of the winter world, bringing out the faces of the tired discouraged people, the grimy car, and the sharp outlines of the hard seats. All at once the world that Astra was starting out to conquer for herself looked ahead unhappily, menacingly, with appalling unfriendliness. Suppose she shouldn't be able to get a position anywhere? Suppose her small allowance should run out and she have nowhere to go? Suppose her father's friends were dead, or moved away? A lot of things could happen disastrously during a two years' absence. Whatever could she do? Not go back to her cousin's house! Never! She *must* find something to do. She could not go back to the cousins who would jeer at her, and treat her with all the more condescension, and find more and more fault with her.

"Oh God," she breathed, "please, please find me a job! You have places for other people to work, couldn't You find a little place for me? Couldn't You please do something about it for me, for I don't know how to do it for myself. I haven't money enough for very long, You know. Show me what to do."

Her head was back against the seat, her forehead resting against the coolness of the window frame, her eyes closed. She could hear the soft plashing of the big flakes that were falling now, as she rode on into the whiteness of the winter night, and prayed her despairing young prayer in her heart.

Then suddenly the door at the front of the car was flung open and a man's voice spoke clearly with a young ring to it that must have appealed to all who heard it.

"Is there a stenographer here who will volunteer to take dictation of a very important document from a man who is dying?"

Astra sat up at once, stirred to instant attention, filled with a kind of awe at this strange swift call from a man in distress. She was the kind of girl who was always ready to help anyone who needed it.

There were also two other girls standing, hesitantly, prompt and alert to answer a call from a good-looking young man anywhere. Yet they stood only an instant listening to his explanation, calmly chewing their hunks of gum. Then they slumped slowly back in their seats.

"Oh! *Dying?* Not *me!*" said one of them, pushing out her chin as if he had offered her an insult. "I don't like dying people. Excuse *me!*"

The other of the two girls shook her head decidedly. "Nothing doing!" she said with a shrug. "I'm on a vacation, and I wouldn't care ta handle a job fer a dead man!" Then they both giggled for the edification of the other travelers. But Astra walked steadily down the aisle to the young man.

"I am a stenographer," she said quietly.

She had taken reams of dictation, the notes of her father's lectures and articles; she knew she was master of the requirements.

The young man's eyes appraised her with approval, and he said:

"Thank you! This way please!" Then he turned and pointed the way through the next car, courteously helping her across the platform.

"The second car ahead," he said. "He was taken with a sudden heart attack. Fortunately there was a doctor at hand, and he is

14

doing all he can for him, but the sick man is much distressed because he knows he may go at any minute and there are important matters that must be recorded before he dies. You — are not afraid?"

Astra looked at the young man gravely.

"Of course not," she said quietly. "I'll be glad to help."

He looked his approval as they moved swiftly down the aisle and came to the small stateroom in the next car where the sick man had been laid.

He was lying in the narrow berth gasping for breath, the doctor by his side, and a nurse preparing something under the doctor's direction. The sick man looked at Astra with pleading eyes.

"Quick!" he gasped. "Get this!"

The young man who had brought her handed Astra a pencil and pad, and she dropped down on the chair by the bed and began to work swiftly, the young man watching her for an instant, relieved that she seemed to understand her job.

The sick man spoke very slowly, deliberately, his voice sometimes so low that the girl could scarcely hear him.

There were a couple of telegrams on business matters addressed to business firms, putting on record definite arrangements the sick man had completed during his journey. Then there was a briefly worded codicil to his will, concerning certain large properties the man had acquired recently, which were to be left to his son by his first wife. This codicil was to be sent to his lawyer at once, observing all the formalities of the law. All this was spoken with the utmost difficulty, gasped slowly, detachedly, as his breath grew faint, or his drifting intelligence faded and then flashed back again. It was heart-breaking, and Astra forgot her own perplexities in making sure she had caught every syllable that the troubled soul uttered.

When the dictation was completed the sick man sank limply into his pillow, relaxed for an instant as if he had reached the end. Then he roused again and feebly pointing at the papers in the girl's lap gasped:

"Copy! Quick! I — must — sign —"

Astra gathered her papers together and stood up with an understanding look in her eyes.

"Yes, of course," she said in a clear businesslike voice. "If I only had a typewriter it would take almost no time at all," she added in a low tone.

The young man stood at the door.

"Come right this way. I have a machine ready for you," he said, and led her down the aisle to another car, and into a small compartment where was a typewriter, and plenty of paper.

"It will be necessary to have two copies," said the young man. "Here is carbon paper."

Astra sat down and went expertly to work, and in a very short time she had a sheaf of neatly typed papers ready.

The young man was back at the door as she finished.

"Fine! That was quick work. I didn't expect you'd be quite done yet," he said. "We'll go right back. The doctor has given him a stimulant hoping to make these signatures possible. We'll have to be witnesses of course."

The patient lay with bright restless eyes on the door as they entered, and a relieved look came into his face as he saw them.

The doctor and nurse arranged a bedside table, tilted so that the patient could see what he was writing, and they placed the papers one by one upon it, and watched the trembling hand trace feebly the name that had been a power in the business world for many years.

It was very still in the little stateroom. Only the noise of the rushing train could be heard. Astra glanced at the windows, covered thickly now with snow, shutting out the darkness of the outside world, with only

17

now and then a faint fleeting splash of color, red or yellow or green, as the train flashed through a lighted town.

And now the signatures were finished, the last few strokes evidently a tremendous effort, as the lagging heart sought to keep the muscles doing their duty to the end, and then the poor brain fagged as the last stroke was made, and the man slumped back to the pillow, the limp hand dropped to his side, the grasp on the pen relaxed, and the pen snapped away to the floor, its duty done.

The young man recovered the pen, Astra dropped down in her chair where she had sat for dictation, and began to get the papers in shape for the witnesses.

The doctor, with his finger on the sick man's pulse was giving attention to his patient, the nurse removing the bed table, straightening the covers.

Then the sick man's eyes opened anxiously, as if there was one more command he must give. His lips were stiff, but he murmured with a wry twist one word "Witnesses!" He tried to motion toward the papers, but his hand dropped uselessly on the bed. He looked at the doctor pleadingly and the doctor bowed.

"Yes sir! I'll sign as a witness!" and turning he stooped over the little table that had been placed beside Astra, and wrote his name clearly, hastily, on each paper. The sick man's glance went to the others, and one by one they all signed their names, Astra, the young man, and the nurse. Then the sick man drew a deep sigh and closed his eyes with finality as if he felt he had done everything and was content.

The doctor and nurse did their best, but a gray shadow was stealing over the man's face. He scarcely seemed to be breathing.

Astra, after signing her name as witness, gathered the papers up carefully, laid them together on the table, and sat there watching that dying face, a little at a loss to know just what was expected of her next. The young man and the doctor had stepped outside in the corridor and were talking in low tones. The nurse was mixing something from a bottle in a glass. Then suddenly the sick man opened his eyes and looked up and they were full of anguish.

"Pray!" he murmured, almost inaudibly.

The nurse was on the alert at once with a spoonful of medicine.

"Pray?" she said snappily. "You want someone should make a prayer? Well, I'll ask the doctor to get a preacher."

She stepped to the door and murmured something to the doctor, but the sick man cast an anguished glance toward Astra.

"Can't *you* — pray?" he gasped. "I can't — wait — !"

His breath was almost gone and the girl sensed his desperation. Swiftly she dropped back to the chair again and bent her head, her lips not far from the dying man's ear and began to pray in a clear young voice:

"Oh Heavenly Father, Thou didst so love the whole world that though all of us were sinners Thou didst send Thine own dear Son to take our sins upon Himself, and die on the cross to pay our penalty, so that all who would believe on Him might be saved. Hear us now as we cry to Thee for this soul in need. Give him faith to believe in what Thou has done for him. May he rest in Thy strength, and know that Thou wilt put Thine arms around him and guide him into the Light. Give him Thy peace in his soul as he trusts in what the precious blood of Jesus has done for him. Make him know that he has nothing to do but trust Thee. We ask it in the name of Jesus our Saviour, Amen."

"A-*men!*" came a soft murmur from the dying lips.

Then suddenly a loud disagreeable voice boomed into the solemnity of the little room, where the voice of prayer still lingered.

"Well, *really!* What's the meaning of all this? George Faber, what are you doing in here, I'd like to know?"

Astra looked up and saw a tall imposing woman, smartly turned out, and groomed to the last hair. Lipstick and rouge and expensive powder combined to give her a lovely baby complexion which somehow only made her look older and very hard. She was looking straight at Astra with cold hostile eyes.

Yet so sacred had been the scene through which Astra had just passed that she did not at first take in that this hostility was directed toward herself.

The doctor had suddenly arrived, with a warning hand flung up for silence, but the woman paid no heed and boomed on.

"I go into the diner to get my dinner, and leave my husband in his seat because he said he didn't want any dinner! Just stubbornness that he wouldn't eat! And then I come back and find him *gone!* And when I at last track him down I find him in bed with a whole mob around him! And this designing young woman — who *is* she? — whining around and putting over some sort of a pious act. Who *is* she? — I demand to know!"

But the last of the question was smoth-

21

ered by the doctor's hand firmly laid across the woman's lips, as he and the nurse grasped her arms and forced her out of the room into the corridor closing the door sharply behind her.

After that things were a bit confused. The sick man's eyes were closed. He looked like death. Had he heard that awful voice maligning him?

Astra stood at one side, the papers with the dictation grasped in her hands, her frightened eyes on the sick man. Was he living yet?

Then the door opened and the young man beckoned her to come out. The woman seemed to have disappeared for the moment.

The young man drew Astra over to an unoccupied section and made her sit down.

"Shall I take these papers for the time being?" he said, and she surrendered them thankfully. He slipped them inside his brief-case.

"Mr. Faber seemed to be anxious that no one else came in on this. He told me that before I came after you," he said in explanation of his care.

"Now will you sit here for a few minutes until I can scout around and find out the possibilities? I suppose these telegrams ought to get off at once. There's a Western Union man on board. Just stay here and I'll see what can be done. I won't be long."

He hurried away and Astra sat there staring at the great white flakes that were coming down like miniature blankets lapping over each other on the window panes. The warm train seemed so protected from the darkness that had come down while she had been busy. There seemed a great quiet sadness all about her, as she sat thinking of the little tragedy in which she had had a part. And now as she thought about it she had a strange feeling that God had been in that stateroom while she had been praying for the dying man, and He had heard her prayer. She seemed still to hear the echo of that whispered "A-men!" as if it were the heartfelt assent of the man's passing soul. And it seemed a strange thing that it had been so arranged that *she* should have been the one to answer that cry from a dying man.

She wondered, was he gone yet? It surely had seemed like the end. Her own sorrowful experience when her father died had taught her to know the signs. And it had really seemed to give him relief to leave those messages behind. She was glad she had been able to help.

Then she heard a door open sharply at the extreme other end of the car, and footsteps, silken stirrings, sounded down the corridor. Suddenly there was the smart lady coming stormily toward her, battle in her eyes.

She sighted Astra almost at once and fixed her cold blue gaze upon her, coming on with evident intention to do her worst.

Now she was upon her, standing in front of her with the attitude of an officer of the law come to bring her to justice.

"Who *are* you?" she demanded, and her voice rose again. "And what were you doing in my husband's stateroom, you shameless creature, you?"

 **2** Astra looked at the woman with surprise, growing into dawning comprehension, and then a quick glow of protest.

"Oh," she said pleasantly, "you didn't understand what happened, did you? I didn't go in there of my own accord. I was asked to go."

"Indeed!" said the woman arrogantly. "Who could possibly have asked you to go? Who had a right to do so? Who are you, anyway?"

"Oh," said Astra with a quiet calm upon her and the hint of a smile through the gravity of her expression, "I am just a stenographer they asked to come and take some dictation for a man who was dying."

"Nonsense!" said the woman impatiently. "*Dying!* He's not dying! He gets these spells. He'll come out of it. He's most likely out of it now. And who, may I ask, presumed to take my husband into a stateroom and bring a strange doctor and a strange nurse and stenographer, and make such an ado about it all? Why did anybody *think* he was sick?"

"I really don't know, madam," said Astra coldly. "I was asked to come, and I came."

"Well, *really!* This is *very* mysterious! Who

presumed to ask you?"

"A young man who was in there when you came. I don't know who he is. He came into the other car where I was sitting and called out to know if there was a stenographer there who would come quickly and take some dictation."

"Well, of all absurd ideas!" said the woman snapping her eyes at Astra. "Who is this young man? Some friend of yours?"

"No," said Astra, and her own voice was somewhat haughty now, "I never saw him before."

"What is his name?"

"I don't know, madam. You'll have to ask him."

"Well, it shows what kind of a girl *you* are, going off with a strange young man to take dictation from a *stranger!* Well, what important dictation did you take? Let me see your papers! I'll take charge of them now."

"I haven't the papers, madam."

"Where are they?"

"I don't know. I presume they have been taken care of as your husband directed."

"Well, what did the papers say?" demanded the woman.

Astra looked at her with wide surprised eyes.

"Why, that wouldn't be my business to

tell," she said. "A stenographer is only supposed to do her work, and then forget about it."

"Oh, *really?* And you have the impudence to say that to the wife of the man whose dictation you took?"

Then Astra saw the young man coming toward her, and she looked up with relief.

"I'm sorry," she said quietly to the irate woman. "It was a matter of business, you know, sales he had completed on his trip, I think. I don't suppose it would interest you. And I have not intended to be impudent. A stenographer is not expected to give attention and remember the matters which she transcribes, she is only a machine while she is at work. At least that is what I have been taught."

Then she rose and stood ready as the young man reached her side, and the woman turned and stared at the young man, giving Astra opportunity to escape toward the door.

The young man soon followed her.

"I thought," he said as he reached Astra's side and opened the door for her, "that perhaps we could go in to the diner and get some dinner together. There we could have an opportunity to make a few plans about those papers. That will give us comparative freedom from interruption. I don't fancy having that woman interfering, do you? She may be his wife, but she has no idea what happened, and from what he told me, I don't think he wanted her to have. He had evidently seen his son, and had an interview with him. Now, you haven't had your dinner yet, have you? Will you go with me?"

He led her into the dining car, chose a table where he could watch anyone entering at the other end, and where they would be far enough from other diners so that their conversation would not be heard. After the preliminaries of ordering were over the young man leaned across the table and began to talk quietly.

"Now," he said with a pleasant business-like smile, "my name is Charles Cameron. My business office happens to be next door to the office of G. J. Faber, our sick man. I know him personally only slightly. We meet occasionally. By reputation I know him well. He is highly respected."

Cameron studied the face of the girl before him as she watched him while he talked. He decided she was taking in every word he said and comparing it with her impression of the sick man.

The waiter arrived just then with their order and there was no more conversation for a few minutes till the waiter was gone.

"Mr. Faber got on the train at Chicago," went on the young man, "with his wife and a lot of luggage. He had the section opposite mine. He looked up after he was settled and nodded casually to me, as he always does when we meet. After that we didn't pay any further attention to one another. His wife was occupying the center of the stage and there was no opportunity. I was reading. I dimly realized that they were having some kind of a discussion, though she did most of the discussing, and presently she went off in the direction of the diner. That seems a long time ago to me now. But I fancy she took her time. And then, too, she would be one who demanded a good deal of service in a diner, which explains her long absence during our most strenuous time."

The waiter came back to refill their water glasses, and when he left Cameron went on:

"The wife hadn't been gone but a very few minutes before Mr. Faber reached over and touched me on the arm. He said he was sick, would I help him? He wanted a doctor and a stenographer. That is how it all began. The porter said there was a rather famous doctor on board, and he brought the nurse. Now I ought to tell you that I'm afraid there is a little more involved in this than just copying

29

those notes. We've probably got to appear before a notary and swear to all this, you know. That is, if he dies, and the doctor seems to think there is no hope for him. But I thought I had better prepare you for the next act. Are you game?"

He watched her somewhat anxiously, and she suddenly smiled.

"Of course," she said gently. "Would it be likely to take long? But that wouldn't matter. I was planning to stay in the city for a few days at least. And my time is not important just now."

"Well, that certainly is accommodating of you. You know of course that this won't be any expense to you, and there will be some remuneration for your services. Mr. Faber gave me money to cover all such items when he first asked me to help."

"But I wasn't expecting remuneration," said Astra. "I was glad to help someone in distress."

"Well, that makes it nice," said Cameron, "but there will be remuneration. And now, may I know your name? It might be convenient, you know, before we are through with this business."

"I am Astra Everson," said the girl. "And perhaps I ought to tell you that I am not a regular stenographer. Although I've had

30

lutely sure about if you have accepted Christ as your personal Saviour," said Astra. "We have God's definite promise for that. He that believeth *hath* everlasting life, and *shall not* come into condemnation, but *is* passed from death unto life."

"Well, I've heard that verse of course," said Cameron, "but I never thought of it as being a definite personal assurance of salvation. Do you mean that if I have an intellectual conviction that Jesus Christ once lived on earth, and died on the cross for men, that I have a right to feel that that covers everything? That I am saved through all eternity?"

"Oh, no, I wouldn't dare to say just an intellectual belief would save. It has to be an active belief, trusting in what He has done for you personally as a sinner."

He studied her with interest.

"How did you come to the knowledge of all this?" he asked at last. "You must have had a remarkable father."

"Yes," said Astra with a tender look in her eyes, "I did. He taught me to study the Bible."

Then there came the old colored porter from the car behind and touched Cameron on the shoulder. The young man looked up questioningly.

good training, I have never done that work for anybody but my father."

"I don't see that that should make any difference," said Cameron. "You evidently are a good stenographer. One could tell that by watching you work a few minutes. Your father is most fortunate to have such an able assistant."

Astra flashed a pleasant look at him.

"Thank you," she said gravely. "But my father died almost two years ago. I've been living with a relative since. But I've come away from her home now, and I'm on my own. I haven't thought out my plans definitely yet."

"Yes?" said Cameron. "Well, could you perhaps give me an address where mail would be forwarded to you?"

Astra thought a moment and then gave him the address of an old friend of her father's.

"I shall keep in touch with them," she said, "and leave a forwarding address there if I should go away."

"Thank you. I'll be remembering that," said Cameron. "I feel that you have done a great piece of work today. I doubt if there is another person on this train that could have covered the need of that dying man as perfectly and as comprehensively as you have done. I hesitate to speak of it because I was not supposed to be in the room, and it seemed too sacred a thing for one to intrude upon. I mean you prayer. I don't know a girl in my whole list of acquaintances who would have had the courage to pray for that dying man, or would have known how, under such circumstances. Undoubtedly some of my friends pray in private, or at least I suppose they do, but I wouldn't be sure that one of them would have done it aloud, or would have known what to say if they had tried."

Astra lifted wondering eyes as if to make sure he had understood.

"But, he asked me, you know."

"Yes, I heard. And it certainly was a genuine request. I never heard such pleading in a human voice, only one word, but it told all his need. Such anguish in human eyes — dying eyes."

"I know," said Astra with a shaken voice. "I wished — someone else were there. I wished you had not gone out in the corridor. He needed some last message so much."

"Well, I'm ashamed to say that I wouldn't have been able to give that man such a message as you gave. It seemed — well — really inspired! You touched on so much. It was the kind of prayer that I would have liked to

have prayed for me if I had been that man, a hard, lonely business man who never had had time from making money to think about God or the Beyond."

Astra's eyes were upon her plate, but she lifted them slowly as she spoke.

"I think," she said as she looked thoughtfully into his eyes, "that when God sends a duty like that for which one is utterly unprepared, the Holy Spirit also gives the words one should use, don't you? I wouldn't have known how unless I had trusted Him to do that."

The young man looked at her in wonder.

At last he said with awe in his voice:

"You must know God then very intimately, if you can expect a thing like that."

There was question in his voice and his eyes were still upon her. She was almost at a loss just how to answer him. Was he a Christian, or not?

"Why," she said with some hesitancy, "of course it is the privilege of all saved people to know God intimately."

"Is it?" he said after a moment of silence. "I never thought about it in that way. I am a church member, since boyhood, but I never exactly thought of myself as saved. I — *hope* to be, of course."

"But that is something you can be abso-

"De doctah say, will you please come to him. De old gemman seem to be dying, and de doctah needs you to send some telegrams, an' help make 'rangements."

"Of course," said Cameron, throwing down his napkin and springing to his feet. Then turning to Astra he said:

"You'll excuse me, I know. I want to help, of course. No, I don't think it will be necessary for you to come. You had better go to your own car for the night and get a good rest after your strenuous evening. Besides, it will be just as well for you to avoid the unpleasant old lady. When I left the car she was still storming all around the place, determined to discover what you had written. You had a reservation, had you not? Can you find your way? Shall I take you there?"

"Oh, no, that's not necessary. I can get back to my seat. But if there is any way that I can help I'll be glad to do it, even if she is unpleasant. Her words can't hurt me."

"That's good of you," said Cameron. "If there is anything for you to do I'll send for you, or come for you. But I'm sure it won't be necessary. You had better have your berth made up and get some rest. Or, *had* you a reservation? There will probably be plenty to do in the morning and you need to get a good sleep."

"No, I didn't have a reservation. It was late when I got on the train and I didn't bother to hunt up the conductor to get one. I can always curl up in a day coach and get a good rest."

She smiled reassuringly, but Cameron looked determined.

"No, that's no way to rest. I'll speak to the conductor for you, and send you word. But go on back to your seat now. Your baggage is there, isn't it? I should have looked after that for you, but it slipped my mind. However, go back now and I'll look after everything. If I find I can't get away myself I'll send this porter. You'll know the lady, won't you?"

The dignified porter nodded his head.

"Yassir! I know de lady!"

Astra smiled, and they went on their way together, while she found her way back to her seat in the day coach, feeling a little as if she had been off the earth for a while and had suddenly been dropped back on her own again.

Her seat was there, vacant as she had left it. Her two suitcases were there, one on the floor, the other in the rack above. The two reluctant stenographers were curled into separate seats, sound asleep, one with her hat hiding her face, the other with her face in full view, her mouth wide open, audibly snoring. Astra half smiled as she passed them, glad that they were not awake. They looked to her like girls who would have asked a lot of questions, and she would not have wanted to answer them.

The windows were thick with snow now. There was no looking out on lighted towns, even if there had been any towns. They seemed to be going on endlessly into the night, and Astra was back where she had been several hours ago, looking into an unknown future, wondering what the next day, and the next, would bring forth in her life. Was she going to be sorry that she had left the shelter of her cousin's uncongenial home? Or was she just going into another more uncongenial atmosphere perhaps?

She was glad after a few minutes to see the kindly face and dignified bearing of the old porter coming down the car toward her.

"Yassum, Miss," he said importantly. "We have de berth for you now, three cyars ahead. Dese yore baggage, Miss? Just step out in de aisle. I'll get it."

With the ease of long accustomedness he swung the suitcases out and started on. Astra was glad that almost everyone in the car was dozing or asleep and not interested in her going. Somehow she felt a sudden shyness after having been called out of there a few hours before in such a dramatic manner.

She was glad to arrive in a quiet car where most of the berths were made up, a long aisle of drawn curtains, the people behind them asleep.

She found her own section was a lower berth made up, the upper not even let down. She had a passing gratitude for the thoughtfulness of the young man who had ordered it.

Then the porter handed her a folded paper.

"Gemman send this," he said.

Astra glanced at the note. It was a few words about where he would meet her in the morning.

She smiled at the porter.

"Tell him all right. I'll wait there till he comes," she said, and handed him a bit of silver.

Then she was glad to lie down and sink into a deep sleep that left her no opportunity to try and figure out the way ahead, nor even go into the way behind to see if she had done wisely in coming.

 **3** If Astra Everson had not made up her mind that she simply could not stay in her cousin Marmaduke Lester's house any longer, she would probably never have taken the definite step of going back to the old home to find her father's friend, Mr. Sargent, and discover for herself just how her finances stood.

Three years before when her father was in his last illness he had talked with her one day about her future. He told her that he was leaving her plenty to keep her comfortable as long as she lived. She wouldn't be what people called wealthy, but she would have enough, and would not need to worry about money. He had arranged her inheritance in such a way that she would be safe from ordinary financial depressions. He had so invested the money he was leaving her that it would not be likely to depreciate in value, that is, as far as the human mind was able to estimate possibilities. And he had put the whole estate in charge of this honored friend, Mr. Sargent, whom he trusted as himself, or even more, because he was a wise conservative business man who did not believe in taking chances. He would be as honorable with money entrusted to his care as if it were his own, perhaps even more so.

Her father gave Astra a little book in which all the facts were set down, and warned her not to let it pass out of her hands. He had gone over each item and hoped he had made it plain to her, and he had told her to read over these items once or twice each year, so that she would never be without absolute knowledge of her own affairs.

But Astra had been so overwhelmed that her father would speak of the possibility of his going from her that the financial matters seemed of very little account then. And even when later he went back to tell her about things, she had so dreaded to think of the day when he would be gone that she did not give her mind to considering her fortunes very seriously. Although she had taken in the fact that even before she was of age money need not worry her. Her usual modest allowance would come to her regularly, increasing a little each year, to meet her own modest needs.

But of late there had been many extra expenses that her cousin Miriam considered necessities, and had insisted upon since she was living with them; things like visits to the beauty parlor, and the continual purchasing of fashionable high-priced garments, many evening frocks, and even a new fur coat when her old one was still perfectly good. Her allowance was growing more and more inadequate to meet the requirements, and she scarcely had enough to buy little things for herself that she really wanted, like books, and tickets to hear fine music. She was reluctant to spend her money on a multiplicity of garments which her cousin Clytie wore oftener than she did herself, especially the fur coat and the evening dresses. In fact Clytie had borrowed the fur coat and several of the evening dresses to take to California with her.

Once before he left her her father had said: "Of course your natural home after I am gone would be with your mother's niece Miriam, I suppose, if she is still living, and wants you. But I have never quite trusted her husband Marmaduke's judgment in financial matters, and that is why I am explaining your financial affairs to you so carefully, even though you are so young and the days when you will come into your property are so comparatively far away. Of course Cousin Duke may be all right. I haven't known him long, you know, but I have an instinctive distrust of his business methods, and his standards of right and wrong, so I want you to be able to handle

41

your own affairs yourself, with advice of course from Mr. Sargent, who will be in charge of your affairs and be a real guardian to you. I don't want you to have to be dependent upon Duke's advice or assistance in any way. I think you will always find Mr. Sargent ready to help.

"Also I have made ample provision that you may be able to pay a reasonable sum for your board wherever you stay, after I am gone."

The time had come all too so on, and almost in a daze she had let Miriam and Duke take her back with them to their home.

As she thought over these things her father's words, which had been almost forgotten, seemed clearly voiced in her ears again. She began to feel that she had been very wrong and careless to let her affairs go in such a slipshod manner since going to live with her cousins. She had spent far too much on showy apparel that she seldom used. Cousin Duke had been kind of course and she had almost come to feel that if her father were here now he would change his ideas about him. He had been almost more kind and helpful to her than her cousin Miriam. Yet now she realized that he had been the one who had encouraged Miriam to buy expensive garments, to join clubs and dress in a showy way, and on several occasions he had told Astra that as she lived with them she must dress accordingly. He didn't want people to think that she had to scrimp in her wardrobe. He said it wouldn't be good for his business to have people think that.

There was another thing that had greatly troubled Astra, and that had been the constant differences of opinion between herself and her young cousin Clytie, which also brought on differences of opinion between herself and Miriam.

Clytie Lester was three years younger than Astra, but old for her years, and badly spoiled. Whatever she had wanted all her life had been given her by her parents if they could possibly manage it, and she had wanted a great many things. When it was not possible for her parents to get what she wanted, Clytie had ways of getting most things for herself, and one of those ways of late had been to borrow money of Astra.

As time went on, a good many of the things Clytie wanted were not things that Astra considered right, and therefore Astra's problem about lending money to her young cousin had been growing more and more complicated, and her conscience was more and more harassed about what she ought to do. She did not wish to inform upon Clytie. It was not her idea of good ethics. But Clytie was constantly putting her into situations where it was either necessary to do so, or else to actually lie about things when she was questioned.

Cousin Miriam was not gentle, unworldly and conscientious, as Astra remembered her own mother to have been. She was pretty and flighty, and rather inclined to be worldly and have easy standards of living. But she was very strict with regard to certain forms and ceremonies, and her ideas of what Clytie should or should not do were not at all Clytie's ideas. It followed therefore that Clytie did many things in direct disobedience to her mother's commands, and got away with it in the main, often from behind the screen of an unwilling Astra.

"Now Clytie," her mother would say, "I want you to go straight to the library and get those books you say you have to have for your school work, and come right home! I don't want you lingering to talk with anyone, or to take a walk or anything. I want you at home inside of an hour to try on the dresses that the dressmaker has been altering. Astra, you walk down with her and see that she gets back on time. Just remind her, won't you?"

Clytie would frown behind her mother's back, and make a mouth of annoyance at Astra, but Miriam would see that Astra went.

Always Clytie had her plans, as Astra had known she would have, and instead of going into the library herself to pick out her books, she would send Astra in, telling her she simply couldn't stay in the house, she had such a bad headache, and needed a bit of air.

"I'll meet you right here on the step, Astra," she would say, and settle down serenely on the bench beside the door. So Astra would go. For Clytie was well versed in ways to make her suffer for it if she didn't. Clytie knew how to create a scene at the dinner table afterward, and show how unaccommodating her cousin had been, when she had "such a blazing headache," and Astra would be left to bear the disapproval of both mother and father, while poor Clytie would be pitied and petted. So Astra often did things of which her conscience did not approve. It seemed the only way.

And when she would come out from the library with her arms full of the books Clytie had ordered, there would be no Clytie sitting on the bench, neither was she to be seen either up or down the street.

Astra would settle down at last, knowing full well that all this had been planned for her undoing. She knew that Miriam would blame her if Clytie was not back at the proper time. Nearly two years' experience had taught her this only too well. It was a little thing perhaps, but she would be filled with vexation as she watched anxiously, meantime glancing at her watch. It was fully an hour since she had left Clytie on the bench, and she wasn't back yet. Was it conceivable that Clytie had grown weary of waiting and gone back home without her? Should she dare go to the telephone and call the house to see? But if Clytie was not yet home what kind of a storm would that raise? She could well conceive the light in which she herself would be placed.

So she would worry along for another fifteen minutes, and then just as she rose with her armful of books to go and telephone, she would sight Clytie's coronet of pink roses which she called a hat, tilted over her right eye, as Clytie sauntered leisurely down the street surrounded by three young men! That was just about what she had always to expect of Clytie. It had happened too many times. And there was nothing for Astra to do but turn and follow the hilarious young gang down the street like a humble minion, till they reached the corner where Clytie always parted with what her mother considered "undesirable escorts," and hastened on home.

"Clytie, where in the world have you been?" her mother would ask. "It is two full hours since you left the house, and I told you to come right back! What on earth have you been doing all this time?"

"Why, mother dear, I hurried just as fast as I possibly could," Clytie would respond. "Didn't I, Astra? You know, mother, it takes the *longest* time to get waited on in that library. I simply *implored* that woman to wait on me at once, but she said she couldn't show preference, and there was a long, long line of people waiting for books. School children you know, and all that."

And then her mother:

"Clytie! That's perfect nonsense! What were you doing? Who were you talking to in the library?"

"Not a soul, mother dear," Clytie would chirp blithely. "Was I, Astra?"

Cousin Miriam's quick glance would give a passing search to Astra's face as she turned away to lay the books down on the table, and then look back at Clytie.

"Now look here, Clytie, you must have

been doing something more than just getting those books! With whom did you walk up the street and talk?"

"Not a soul, Mother, I didn't meet anyone I knew at all this afternoon. Did I, Astra?"

But for once, this last time it had happened, Astra had escaped up to her room before an inquisition, though she still had a faint fear that it all might be brought up again, later in a full family conclave, and she be made to tell all she knew of the afternoon. The trouble was that Astra had been taught not to lie, even when she was in an unpleasant situation, and they all knew it. They knew that when she admitted a thing it was so, and there was no disputing it. But they also had their ways of punishing her for it if the truth put the adored Clytie in an unpleasant light in her parents' eyes. For often when Astra had been forced to tell the truth about some ill-advised action of Clytie's, it was Astra who was treated as if she were the offender, and Clytie went scot-free.

So the days had been going by, each one a problem in itself, and Astra had been growing heartsick and sad.

Moreover Clytie's borrowing habit had increased lately, until it had come about that there was scarcely enough in her allowance check after board was paid and Clytie had dipped into it, to cover Astra's actual needs in the way of clothing, stationery and so forth.

Astra had worried a lot about this, for she felt guilty letting it go on without the knowledge of Clytie's parents, and yet if she told them there would be a terrible row, and she would inevitably get the name of being stingy. So clever was Clytie that she knew just how to work it this way, without having the situation reflect in the least upon herself. Astra had prayed about it, and had come to the conclusion that she must not let this go on, no matter what might happen to herself.

And so, when it was arranged that the Lesters were to go to California to visit Duke's mother and father, and attend a cousin's wedding, a cousin who was not related to Astra; and as she was to be left at home she decided the time had come for her to think this thing through by herself, and work it out somehow so that life would be livable, and she need not feel continually condemned.

Then the very day before the Lesters started, Astra's check arrived. Astra cashed it at once because she wished to pay her board before they left. After that was done she put the remainder in a safe place, a *new* place, where she had not kept money before. A little carved wooden box with a spring lock, and she put the box carefully away among her least used garments, in her lower bureau drawer and locked the drawer, putting the key on a ribbon around her neck.

She wasn't just sure why she did all this, but of late she had a suspicion that Clytie did not hesitate to go to her purse if she were in need of a trifle. Yet she had no proof of that, and she felt almost condemned for locking that drawer.

But locks meant nothing at all to Clytie. Nothing indeed was sacred when Clytie wanted something.

Clytie came to her as usual. She spoke nonchalantly, as if she were somehow conferring a favor on Astra.

"How about a little loan, Astra darling?" she said. "And could you make it a little larger than usual? I spent more than I meant to on that wedding gift, and I'm afraid I'm going to run short before I get back."

Astra was ready for her this time however. She looked up pleasantly from the letter she was writing and gave a faint smile:

"Sorry, Clytie, but I can't possibly spare anything this time. I'm getting some new clothes and I have a few plans I want to carry out while you are away. Besides, I'll be entirely on my own and have no one to borrow from, so I have to be economical. You haven't paid me back yet what you owe me, you know."

"Why, the ridiculous idea!" sneered Clytie. "Why should I pay you back those little trifles when you're living here in our house, just making a convenience of us? You haven't any expenses, you know you haven't. And anyway you can charge new clothes. You know Mother always says you can. Besides, you don't need any new clothes when we are away. There'll be nobody here. What would you want new clothes for? And you never want to go to parties."

"Well, I'm sorry to disappoint you, Clytie, but I really can't let you have any money this time. Why don't you ask your father for some? I think that would be better, don't you? I can't always spare it. And Clytie, I always pay my board, you know. My father arranged for that, and this time I paid for the time you are to be away. So I haven't as much as usual. No, really, I mean it. I can't spare even a dollar."

Clytie with her most unamiable expression stared in affront at her cousin.

"Well, I think you are the most unaccommodating —"

And just then Clytie's mother called.

"Clytie, why don't you come? I'm waiting for you to measure this skirt. Hurry!"

Clytie turned away hurriedly, and murmured in a fierce anger,

"Well, I'll see that you're good and sorry for this!" and slamming the door hurried down the stairs.

It was a busy day, and Astra had little time to think about her money. There were so many little last things that Cousin Miriam wanted done. There were hems to be shortened, collars to be washed out, stockings to mend. The items seemed endless, and Astra took them all up to her own room to do, out of the hurry and turmoil of downstairs. So there was no chance for Clytie to annoy her, for Clytie was sent on several errands herself, and as usual did not return soon.

Astra sat up very late finishing the mending for Miriam, and all day she had kept an eye on the third story stairs which led to her room; she was sure Clytie had had no chance to get up there without being seen.

For Clytie had a way of mauling over Astra's ribbons and collars and gloves, and calmly appropriating anything that was to her liking, and it wasn't in the least unlikely that she would attempt such a raid at the last minute. So Astra lay down to sleep the night before they left with relief, knowing nothing had been attempted that night at least, and there would be very little time for anything of the sort in the morning.

They were all at breakfast when Clytie entered with a frown on her brow.

"Mother, did you see those lovely new Pullman slippers I brought home yesterday? I thought I took them up to my room to put in my suitcase, but I can't find them anywhere. Astra, did you take them away? If you call that a joke I think it's a poor time to pull it off, just as we're starting."

"Clytie, that's no way to speak to your cousin," said her father, albeit with an indulgence in his voice that did not trouble Clytie.

"Well, I can't help it. I want those slippers, and I intend to have them! You might at least come upstairs and help me find them, Astra!" She darted an angry look at Astra and dashed out of the room and upstairs.

Astra listened and heard her footsteps going up the second flight, then she half rose to follow.

"No," said Miriam, "don't go, Astra. Eat your breakfast and then run down to the shoe shop for me. I left a pair of shoes there to have the heels straightened, and I need them."

"But Miriam, you haven't time to go after things. It's almost time we started," said her husband.

"Oh, I think we have. Hurry, Astra, you can make it, I'm sure. They are the only really comfortable shoes I have for walking."

"Well, why didn't you attend to them before?"

Astra swallowed the rest of her breakfast in haste and got herself down to the shoe shop in a hurry. When she came rushing back with the shoes the car was already at the door, and her cousin Duke stood impatiently beside it looking anxiously up toward the house.

Miriam came out presently, and after a sharp call from her father Clytie at last emerged, a sullen look upon her face. Her farewell to Astra was vengeful. But there was no time to say more for the car door shut with a snap and they were on their way, Miriam calling out last directions to Astra, something about the house, and some mending she might attend to while they were gone.

But Astra scarcely heard her. Her eyes were full of dismay as she watched the car disappear around the next corner, and realized how alone she was in the world now.

Slowly she went into the house, picking

up as she went, things that had been scattered, her thoughts almost bitter at the look Clytie had given her. How unfair Clytie was! Somehow she didn't believe those Pullman slippers had really been lost. She felt that Clytie had only been carrying out her promise that she would be sorry about not lending her money. Nevertheless, she went into the rooms that looked so much as if a hurricane had struck them, and quietly, carefully put them in order, searching as she went. If she found the slippers she would send them on after them. But no slippers came to light. If there really were any slippers, Astra thought to herself, they were probably stowed carefully in Clytie's suitcase, whence they would conveniently turn up when they were needed.

So at last, worn out with the last few hurried days in which she had so willingly sacrificed her own ways for the family good, she climbed to the third floor, thinking to sit down and read a little while and get rested before she did anything else. But when she opened her door such chaos met her gaze as drove the thought of rest entirely from her mind.

All the bureau drawers were pulled out and set about on the floor, their contents scattered hither and yon. The bed was pulled to pieces. The pillow cases were peeled off and flung in a crumpled heap. Even the pillows had been ripped at one corner and a few feathers were drifting about as Astra walked around excitedly. Her frightened eyes searched the room seeking the contents of her lower bureau drawer. And then suddenly she saw it. The little carved box that she loved so much because it had been one of her mother's precious treasures. Long ago when Astra's mother had first given it to her, it had been the place in which she kept her little string of coral beads that her grandmother had given her. Her jewel chest she had quaintly called it. But later, when she grew older, and had put away her little hoard of childish treasures all together in a larger box, this little box had been carried about with her as just a treasure in itself. Always closed and locked with the tiny key on the little chain in the secret hiding place under her watch in her watch case.

But now to her horror she saw the little box wide open, upside down, and yawning among clothes and stockings and hairpins and strings of beads. The hinges were bent back, and one was broken away, hanging free and loose. She felt as if someone had struck her with a sharp knife. With a little cry like the sound of a hurt bird, she dropped to her knees in the tumult of clothes and collars and dainty fineries, and took it up gently, as if it were human and could be hurt. And now she saw that the box had been forcibly opened, perhaps by flinging it to the floor, or striking it with a hairbrush, or a heavy bottle. That was it! Her witch hazel bottle! It was standing on the bureau where she never left it. It belonged in her little bathroom on the shelf. And the bottle was cracked. The witch hazel was seeping out. Yes, the box had been first flung on the floor, and then pounded with the bottle. She could just see the face of the determined angry girl as she did it. She had forced the box open, and there it lay ruined, broken. But where was the money? It was gone!

Astra searched wildly, then carefully, through everything in the room, but there was not even a single dollar left! Yes, Clytie had her revenge.

As she searched through the wreckage with the tears drenching her face, Astra could see in memory the angry look on Clytie's face as she cried out "You'll be good and sorry!"

At last after a long careful search through her entire room, hoping that perhaps Clytie had only played a trick, and might have repented at the last and left her at least a little of her money, Astra dropped upon her knees and buried her hot tear-wet face in the cool length of a sheet that had been flung across the head of the mattress and trailed down upon the floor. She knelt there and sobbed softly to herself, for even now in her despair she was aware that she was not alone in the house. The old housekeeper was still there, and the waitress, and they must not hear her weep, and perhaps report on it to her relatives.

After softly sobbing for some minutes she at last got quiet enough to bring her heart to a little pitiful prayer, remembering her father's words during those last days when he knew he was going to leave her:

"Don't ever forget," he had said, "that nothing is too small to bring to God in prayer. No trouble is too small for Him to notice, and to give you comfort when you are distressed. Just get in the habit of bringing everything to Him. Say, 'Lord, here's something I can't do anything about. I'm afraid of what it is going to be, so won't You please take it, manage it, and bring it out the way You want it to be'!"

She had remembered that many times in lesser situations than this, and it had comforted her to pray. It seemed to take out of her that burning desire to rush at those who had caused her trouble and demolish them, tear them limb from limb. It seemed to bring calm in the midst of the tempest in her heart.

So, after a little she was able to lay the whole matter before her Lord and ask guidance.

When she arose from her knees and went patiently about clearing up that room and putting it in perfect order once more, she seemed to be waiting for God to tell her what to do.

Before the lunch bell rang for her solitary meal she had so far recovered her equilibrium that she had washed away the signs of tears and smoothed her hair, and peace was upon her brow.

For more and more the conviction had been growing within her as she worked, that this was not the place for her to be living any longer. This trouble was not something she could bring out in the open and have cleared up. There would always be bitterness between herself and Clytie, for Clytie resented her presence in their home, and would always be jealous of everything that was done for her, every favor granted. It was hopeless to try to do anything about it. She must go away. And surely her father, if he were here now, would agree with her.

And of course this would be the time to go, while they were all away and there could be no discussion about it. Just write a nice note to Cousin Miriam, and thank her and Cousin Duke for their kindness in opening their home to her when she was first left alone, tell them that now she felt it was time to relieve them of the burden of her continual presence, that it would be better for Clytie too; and then just go. By the time they got back and realized that she had really meant it, and they got around to protest, she would have found a place for herself where she was comfortable and wanted to stay, and they would finally subside. She felt she knew those cousins well enough to be sure that none of them would mourn very much for her absence, or have pains in their conscience for allowing her to stay away, and she would be on her own and could make a new and tolerable life for herself.

But, there was one almost insurmountable objection to her going now. Her money was gone! Absolutely! *All* of it! Her careful search through her room had revealed only a fifty-cent piece, five dimes and two quarters. How was she to go away anywhere with only a dollar and a half?

As she idly ate the unattractive lunch that the two maids had provided for her she was puzzling her brains as to how she could get money to go away, and if she had the money where she would go? When she finished her lunch she hurried upstairs to look over what she owned and see if there was anything she could sell that would bring her enough to pay her for parting with it.

It was the memory of all this, and the anguish of the few hours before she started on this journey, that came flashing into Astra's mind when she awoke in her berth two days later. It was like a picture of a former life that seemed very long ago. It was hard for a moment or two to struggle back into the present and remember. Why had she ever started on this journey, and what was there for her to do this morning that would start in a few minutes now, in this new life she had come into?

 **4** Cameron had asked Astra to wait for word from him in the morning, and she was scarcely dressed and ready for the day before the elderly porter of the night before came ambling down to her section.

"De gemman say he 'bliged ta he'p wid de 'rangements, en' take de ole missus out ta her cyar when we 'rive, an' he say would yoh let me ordah yoh breakfus sent to yoh right hyeah? He says that will be least trouble ta yoh."

"Oh, why yes, of course. Thank you. Just orange juice, buttered toast and coffee. That's all."

And presently she was sitting there eating the pleasant simple breakfast, and looking at the thick patterns of frosty ferns and mountains that now decorated the windows. The snow had come in good earnest, and she was glad. It was nice to have a real winter and to feel free from the constant espionage and bickering of her cousin's home. She wondered what her father would have thought about it if he had known just what she was to go through. Surely he would have tried to make some other arrangement for her than to stay with Miriam.

But the sun had come out and was lighting up a glorious white world. It was almost Christmas and there was snow! She remembered her childish delight at snow for Christmas which had lasted through the years. That was something to be glad for, anyway, even if she was alone.

Then her thoughts went back to her hectic preparations, and her wild search for something to turn into money.

There had been answers to prayer all along the way, and a sure indication that she was right in going away. She had begun her search by asking the Lord to please provide the money if He wanted her to go. And then she had started that systematic search.

She had got out a box of old trinkets, scarcely hoping that any of them would be profitable. But first of all she came upon a heavy gold chain, and a pair of bracelets to match that had been given her by a queer old lady who had an apartment near theirs one winter while they were staying in New York. She hadn't liked the old lady very much. She was always asking inquisitive questions about her father's writing. And Astra never liked the jewelry, though she had to be polite about it of course, but it was utterly unsuitable for so young a girl to wear, and she had no tender memories of the old lady, who was all too evidently trying to attract the attention of Astra's father. But the old lady seemed to have plenty of money and likely the chain and bracelets were worth something. There was no reason in the world why she should not sell them. Their marking showed they were solid gold, not plated.

She went on searching through the jewelry, finding a number of gold trinkets, gold collar buttons, a couple of old watches with no sentimental value to them, some gold spectacles belonging to her father's old uncle, some outmoded bits of sterling silver. There was quite a handful of things. Perhaps they were not all sterling, but it might be she could get something for them. She remembered hearing her cousin speak of a good place to take such things, where they were paying highest prices for old gold and silver.

When she had gathered these things together she went to her wardrobe and looked it over. There were two garment bags containing some evening dresses. One her cousin Miriam had sent up for her a little over a week ago, insisting she should have it for the Christmas party they were expecting to give. That was before they suddenly decided to go to California for Christmas instead.

It wasn't a dress that Astra particularly liked, but Cousin Miriam said it was smart, and that was what she wanted her to have, so she had finally succumbed and bought it. She had bought it herself, paid for it with her own money. It wasn't a gift from the family, and so Astra felt free to get rid of it.

Carefully she folded it, and laid it in a suitbox, the very box it had come in. And then she gathered out a few unnecessary embroidered silk trifles of underwear. They were all bought about the same time, and had not been worn. They probably were all returnable.

Breathlessly she folded and boxed them, and at last she had quite a little assemblage that she hoped would bring her at least enough to buy a ticket back to her home town. For surely, once there, there would be some of her father's old friends who would lend her enough to get her through until her next allowance was due. She could probably go to her father's friend, Mr. Sargent, and ask him to advance her a little. Perhaps she could tell him that someone had stolen her money in the absence of her cousin. Well, at least, she would go step by step, as the day's need became evident.

Telling the maids that she was going

down town to attend to some errands, she boarded a bus with her array of bundles and went first to the stores where she hoped to return her dresses. There was great relief in her eyes when in response to her request she was merely told to go to a certain desk and her money would be refunded. Then, with a roll of nice crisp bills in her purse, and a burden that was much lightened, she went on her way to sell her old gold.

When she finally got back to the house, she had enough money to buy a ticket, enough over for incidentals, and a night's lodging at least when she got there. So she felt that it was right for her to go. There would surely be some friends when she got to the city that was still home to her, who would help her out until she could find her father's friend, Mr. Sargent.

She paid little heed to eating that day. She had too much to do. She went to the trunk room and got out her trunk and suitcases. Then rapidly she began to pack. She wanted to waste no time in getting started. As she folded her garments and stowed them in the trunk and suitcases, her mind was going over and over what she ought to do. There were some books and pictures, and things that were dear to her heart. If she left them there Clytie would make short work of them, and there was little likelihood that she would ever see them again unless she took them with her. So she went down cellar and found a box, which she smuggled up to her room while the maids were out on their own errands. She packed her things carefully, and even nailed up the box securely. She didn't want to waste money paying a man to do what she could do herself.

But while she was packing her books she came across a few that she did not care to keep, and realized that she might get a little more money from them. Also, there was a whole lovely set of her favorite poets, done in fine binding. She had bought them only a short time ago. Could she get the man to take them back and give her the money? She hated to give them up, but she could surely get them again somewhere, sometime, when money was not so scarce, so she ventured to telephone and found that the book dealer would take them back if they were still in good condition.

So she took her books down to the dealer, and got a little more money for her journey, which made her feel much easier in her mind, and quite satisfied that God was helping her.

That evening, tired as she was, she wrote a note to her cousin.

Dear Miriam:

I hope you will not disapprove when you get back home and find me gone. I have been thinking about this move for a long time, and I really feel that it is right and good that I should go. I hope you will agree with me.

It does not seem fair to Clytie that she should have to share her home and her parents with me. I feel sure she will be a great deal happier with me gone, and it is right that she should have her place in her home.

Besides, Miriam, I am not a little girl any longer. I am old enough to look out for myself; and not to be lonely if I am on my own. It will really be good for me, and help me to be more independent. So I think you and Cousin Duke, who have been so exceedingly kind to me in my sorrow and loneliness, have a right to be relieved that you no longer have me as a burden, since in many ways I cannot be quite congenial.

You need have no worry about me. I have many friends in the old place where my father and I lived so long together, and as soon as I get definitely located I will write and give you my address.

So I am sending you my heartfelt gratitude for what you have done for me, and many wishes that you may have a happy winter.

Wishing you all a Merry Christmas, and a Glad New Year,

Lovingly,
Astra.

It was very sketchy sleeping that Astra did that night, because there were still so many details of her hasty journey not yet thought out. But she was awake early the next morning and at the telephone, calling for the expressman to take her trunk to the train, calling a drayman to take her box to the station, calling the station to find out train schedules. And when she went down to breakfast she had everything pretty well in hand, and her heart was filled with a great relief.

After breakfast she told the maids.

"I am going back to my old home, Hannah," she said. "I've been planning to do that for some time, and now I think it will be pleasant to be with my old friends at Christmas time."

Hannah eyed her in amazement.

"Does Mrs. Lester know?" she asked coldly. "She didn't say anything to me about it."

"No, she didn't know. I decided since she left. But I've written her all about it, so I suppose you will hear from her soon as to any directions she may have since I am not to be here. I think you said she usually left you here in charge of the house before I came, didn't she?"

"Oh, yes," said Hannah loftily. "Every summer when they go away to the mountains, I and Nannie stays and cleans house."

"Well, then I guess you won't miss me. And here are two little packages I got for you two for Christmas. I'm sure I hope you will have a very happy time."

The two prim maids eyed the prettily wrapped boxes that Astra handed out to them, and then the doorbell rang, and Nannie hurried away to answer it.

"That must be the men I sent for," said Astra. "They said they would come early."

So there was little time for further talk. Astra had taken things firmly in hand, and the two maids felt relieved that they were not called upon to be always staying at home to be company for Astra.

Soon Astra was riding away to the station in a taxi, and the two maids stood at the door and waved a prim good-by, the while they fingered the crisp bills that Astra had given each. She had felt she could ill afford to spare them, but yet she knew she must. It was her idea of what was right.

But in spite of the fact that she was really glad to get away, she yet felt a lump in her throat at the thought that she was going into the world, with no one behind to wish her Merry Christmas, and no one ahead waiting to bid her welcome and make a happy holiday for her.

So that was what Astra was going over as she finished her breakfast, and sat forlornly staring out through the lace filigree of frost on the window pane, into a wide white world that seemed so strange and unfriendly now after her experiences of the night before, and the uncertainties of what the morning was to bring forth.

5

Astra was seated in a big rocker in the Ladies' Waiting Room with her baggage at her side, comfortably established there by the old porter from the Pullman. How he got away from his duties on the train she did not stop to question. He seemed somehow to have taken over the protectiveness of the young man, who evidently felt himself responsible for Astra, at least until their mission in behalf of the dead man was completed.

The old porter shuffled away and brought back the morning paper, and asked if there was anything else she would like.

"No thank you," said Astra with a smile. "You've been very kind. I shall be quite all right now."

"De gemman say please stay here till he come. He may havta take de old lady to her house befoh he can git away."

"Yes, of course," said Astra, "I understand."

She handed the porter a tip, though she rightly guessed that he had already had that attention. But he went away with a smiling face, ready to do a good turn to the next one that asked him.

From where she sat she could get a

glimpse of the door that led to the street, and she thought she saw the young man going out in the wake of the more than straight back of the domineering widow of the dead man. They disappeared toward a line of cars, and he did not return at once so she decided he had had to attend the widow to her home. Not a congenial task, she imagined.

Then suddenly she had a feeling that she was very much alone in the world, and she must decide what she was going to do next. She had expected to have all day yesterday to do that in, but yesterday had brought unexpected duties, and now she had arrived at her journey's end, with no definite idea of plans for the future. Of course she had been crazy to come off in such a scatterbrained way, but she had been so panic-stricken at the idea of having her cousins return before she had done anything about getting away, that she had just got out of the house, and left her plans to the future. Now in a few minutes the young man would return, and whatever he had for her to do that required her assistance and signature would likely be over soon. Then she must not seem to be uncertain about where she was going. This young man was a stranger, and she must not make him feel that she was alone and forlorn. He was polite and kind. He had already done more for her comfort than she should have allowed in exchange for the small services she had given him, and for a business that was not his own anyway. He was being philanthropic to a man who was a semi-stranger to himself, therefore she must be philanthropic too, for the sake of a general interest in humanity.

But, what should she do?

Well, she probably ought to go at once to her father's friend, Mr. Sargent, and put the matter plainly to him whether he thought she should accept a job right away if she could get one, or whether he thought her father would have preferred her to take a course in a school somewhere. But in preparation for what? Her father had often talked it over with her. He had felt she might do a sort of writing for which her life and training with him had fitted her.

She looked across out of the window near her, and could just get a glimpse of a sign she remembered. A Christian Association Home for young women! Well, perhaps that would be as good a headquarters as any for a few days, at least until she was sure that this work for the dead man was done, and she would not have to be called upon again in the matter.

Then she began to go over in her mind the list of her old friends. It gave her a forlorn feeling to realize that Christmas was almost here, and she would be absolutely alone. But then she would have been just as much alone if she had stayed at her cousin's home, and there was no point in sitting down and feeling sorry for herself. She must cheer up and try to make a pleasant day of it somehow. What difference did a special day make anyway? Christmas was like any other day if one didn't try to get sentimental about traditions. She simply must not get to thinking about it. God would have something for her to do somewhere, and as for a holiday alone, why, it would be a lovely time to read, and perhaps to think out some nice plans for the rest of the winter.

She gave a slight shake to her shoulders and sat up straighter. She was a little tired in spite of her good sleep. Yesterday afternoon and evening certainly had been exciting.

She thought of her old acquaintances, schoolmates, and college friends. Some of them were married. There was Nesbitt Halliday, such a merry amusing girl! It didn't seem possible to think she had settled down to keeping house and taking care of babies like a normal married woman. She had been such a heedless girl. Sometime she would go and see her, and see if she really *had* settled down. But there was no use in calling her up now. She had a tiny house and would be involved in Christmas doings for her children of course. And she simply must not intrude on family Christmases anywhere, even if the people were old friends. Perhaps there was someone who was lonely whom she could comfort. There was Mrs. Pomfrey, who had a big house and plenty of room to take her in if she wanted to. But she was such a pill, always fretting and fussing. No, she didn't want to get involved with Mrs. Pomfrey, kind as she was sometimes. And there was old Janet Crumb. She was always cheery. Perhaps she would be willing to take her to board for a while until she got her bearings and knew what she wanted to do. Of course Janet Crumb had a very tiny house, with only one bathroom, and it might be crowded there. If she was going to try to do that writing that her father had suggested she ought to have a comfortable place where she would not feel constricted. Idly these thoughts drifted through her mind as she sat there waiting, and one by one her old friends were considered and dropped for the time. She would call them up later of course, but not before Christmas. Oh, yes, some of them would be glad to have her for the holiday season, but somehow she did not want to go among them until she had thoroughly considered what she was going to do and could tell them. There would be too many suggestions given, and some feelings hurt, perhaps, if she did not accept what suggestions they offered. No, she must make a definite decision about what course she would take before she saw them.

At any rate, the first one must be Mr. Sargent. She must get in touch with him before she decided anything. She was in different circumstances now, not just boarding with a relative. And she had a dim recollection that her father had said something about her allowance being larger when it came time for her to provide a home for herself.

After a little she put her head back and closed her eyes, just to get away from thoughts, and then the events of last evening became vivid again, and the disagreeable wife who had so insulted her came sharply into the foreground. The thought of her made her restless, and she opened her eyes and began to study the people around her. Some tired little children, dirty and forlorn, breakfasting off soiled dejected bananas, squabbling over them on the station floor. A worn out young mother with an even dirtier baby in her weary arms. How many people there were in the world who were tired and unhappy!

Then her eyes sought the distance and she saw Cameron coming across the outer room of the station, his hat in his hand, his overcoat unbuttoned, a tired look on his nice face, as if he had had very little sleep last night. Poor man, how many unpleasant duties sometimes came in to make and spoil a day for a gentleman. He certainly couldn't have enjoyed taking that disagreeable woman back to her home.

He came on straight toward the open door, and Astra couldn't help thinking how well he walked, with a long easy stride.

Then suddenly the view of him was broken by a vision in a glamorous mink coat, one of the kind that fairly shouts how new and expensive it is.

It was worn smartly, on a frame that was both youthful and full of grace and poise, and the small smart turban that topped it was also trimmed with mink and very chic, tilted over the right eye.

The mink coat had stopped to greet Cameron, and Astra could see his pleasant smile, his easy attitude. The girl must be one of his close acquaintances. He paused and they talked together. The girl was evidently telling him something that surprised him. She lifted a wide mink muff heavy with tails, and gesticulated with it. Astra could see that the young man looked startled, was asking a question or two, gave a glance at the clock, talked another minute or two earnestly, and then with another glance at his watch, bowed, and hurried toward the room where she sat.

But as he came on Astra was conscious that something had changed, and the mink coat had done it! How absurd! This young man was nothing to her of course, just a passing stranger who had commandeered her for a bit of work. But there had been a pleasant exhilaration in seeing him come toward her a moment ago which had vanished with the advent of the mink coat. And with a glimpse of the startlingly handsome face of the girl who wore it, as she turned to go away through the door labeled "TAXIS." Somehow the whole attitude of things seemed to have changed, now that there was a girl like that in the offing. Astra berated herself. What was *she?* A foolish little romantic fool? Why should she care? Of course he would have women friends, and it only showed that she had rated him adequately, that he should have friends like that. Anyhow he was nothing to her. Why had she wasted idle thoughts on a stranger who had merely been kind? She would probably never see him again after this business was over, and she hoped it would be over soon. It was perfectly sickening that she should so pity herself for being lonely, just because it was almost Christmas, and she had no place to go.

But when Charles Cameron entered the doorway where he had asked that Astra await him, her fine patrician face was lifted indifferently, almost a bit haughtily, and she greeted him most distantly.

If she had known that Cameron was mentally comparing her to the brilliant beauty with whom he had just been talking, and thinking how sweet and unspoiled Astra seemed in comparison, she certainly would have been amazed.

"Are you all right?" he asked, and there was a pleasant friendly concern in his voice that surprised her, and dissipated the dignity in which she had been trying to envelop herself.

She gave him a quick look and saw that there seemed to be real interest in his eyes. She answered his searching glance with a bright smile.

"I? All right? Why yes, of course," and she

gave a light surprised laugh, and then suddenly she felt as if she were going to cry, at the almost tender concern of his tone. If she hadn't laughed she would have cried, she was sure, for it was such a sudden relief from her own lonely feeling, sitting there pitying herself as she thought of the approaching empty Christmas.

And then because the feeling of quick tears hadn't quite left her she went on to say brightly:

"I think it is yourself who should be asked if you are all right. From all I hear from the old porter your morning has been filled with tasks that couldn't all have been congenial. If the old lady was as irate as she was last evening it certainly couldn't have been a pleasant trip taking her home."

Cameron's face softened into a grin, and he said with a sigh:

"No, not too pleasant. It was mainly occupied in her attempt to extract information from me. Where had her husband known me? When did he speak to me and tell me he was sick? Why didn't I send for her at once to the diner? What was *your* name, and how did I become acquainted with *you?* How long had I known you, and was I sure that you were honest? Why didn't I take the dictation myself, and what was it about anyway?"

"Oh! I'm sorry you had to bear that!" said Astra. "She started in on me like that, only she took a different line. She assumed that I was the offender, daring to take an interest in a sick man to whom I hadn't been introduced!"

"Yes, I know," said Cameron with a contemptuous grin. "She tried to convince me that I didn't understand human nature or I never would have selected a good-looking, stylish, forward girl for a stenographer for a respectable dying man. Well, poor soul, she's in a trying situation, and she is taking it out on whoever comes along. But I had the satisfaction of telling her plainly that she was very much mistaken about you. That I knew of your family, at least your father, and that she must positively stop talking about you, that you had been most kind. Then I began to ask her questions about whether her husband had been well during the past weeks, and whether he had ever had symptoms of heart trouble before. That took her mind off other things, while she tried to convince me that he had never been sick, but he had just worked himself up over everything, and got to thinking he was an invalid. She raked up a few tears to convince me, and by that time we had reached the palatial mansion of which she is now mistress. But I certainly pity the servants over whom she reigns. I may misjudge her, but it doesn't seem to me that she is greatly grief-stricken over the death of her husband. Hers is more the attitude that it is his own fault he died. She declares that if he hadn't insisted on coming home from California this week instead of next, just because he got word that that good-for-nothing son of his by his first wife was going to stop in Chicago over night, and he wanted to see him, he would have been alive today! So, that's the story. She evidently hates that stepson, and that's why he was so anxious to get this transfer of that property he had bought, arranged before there was danger of her hearing of it. Well, I guess that poor man is glad he's in Heaven today instead of still living to be nagged by her. For I do think he's in Heaven after that prayer of yours, and his heartfelt 'Amen'! I think it meant a lot to him, and I believe you'll get your reward hereafter for coming to help the poor soul at the end. I'm sure neither the doctor nor I would have been able to make it all as plain as you did."

"Oh, I'm glad if you think I was any help to him," said Astra quietly with her eyes downcast.

Cameron, too, was speaking embarrassedly, but with great earnestness. He was looking down at his gloved hands, as if he were not accustomed to speak of sacred things so intimately. And then they were both silent for a moment.

"Well," said Cameron, "I suppose we had better get on with our job, that is, if you feel all right. For the old man seemed to want this part of the business settled at the first possible moment, and I think myself it had better get finished before the old lady has time to do any more inquiring. By the way, did you have a good breakfast? We may be detained at lunch time, you know. Wouldn't you like to go and get a little more to eat before we go into action?"

"Oh no, thank you," laughed Astra, touched again at the thought of this stranger's care for her comfort. How foolish she was getting, a strangulation in her throat from a mere passing kindness. "I had a fine breakfast, and I can last till a very late dinner if necessary."

Cameron smiled.

"Well, you won't have to do that, I'm sure. Just wait here a moment, please, while I find out if the lawyer is in his office yet."

Astra watched the young man as he went over to the telephone booths. He was good-looking, yes. She hadn't had much time before to take cognizance of the little things that make up appearance. He was very good-looking, yet in a quiet unobtrusive way. He didn't seem to have spent a great deal of thought on his appearance, and yet he was perfectly groomed. There was nothing ostentatious about him. He was just a gentleman, the pleasant kind that one would like for a friend.

And while he was telephoning she made up her mind. She would go over to that Christian Association and see if she could get a room there, and make that her headquarters for a few days, till she could look over the ground and see what she ought to do. As for Christmas, she wouldn't try to arrange anything. Just get some good reading, go out perhaps to an oratorio, or some good music somewhere, maybe to a church service, and wait until Christmas was over before she got in touch with her friends. They needn't even know she was in town. They would all be busy in their own homes. It would be easy enough.

Then Cameron returned.

"Well, the lawyer will be in his office in three quarters of an hour. We won't have much time to spare. What if we get you settled somewhere first. Had you decided where you want to go? Were you going to friends, or a hotel?"

"No," said Astra quickly, "I'm not going to friends till after Christmas. I thought I would see if I could get in over at the Christian Association. I used to hear that it was a nice place, and it would be convenient for the present I should think."

"Yes, it's a very nice place, I understand," said Cameron. "Suppose I telephone to see if they have any rooms, and then we can take a taxi over. I think you'll be more comfortable during the morning, to know that you have an abiding place, even if you decide not to stay there but a few hours."

They found a pleasant room looking out on a little park, and Astra was quite pleased at getting the matter arranged so easily. Then they took a taxi and started out to get the business over with.

The lawyer was late, and they had to wait, and while they waited they talked. Cameron called her attention to a magazine article concerning some of the devastation that had been wrought in Europe, and Astra said she had been in that very region with her father three years before. She described the loveliness of the scenery around the old cathedral, and how much she had enjoyed a view she could see from her window in the old pension where they had rooms. She quoted one or two things her father had said about the mighty structure, and said she felt as if an old friend had died when she read that the building had been bombed.

More and more as she talked freely, forgetting herself, and losing her shyness, Cameron saw what a fine mind she had, and how well she talked. But most of all he noticed the sparkle of her face in conversation, the deep intelligence seen in her choice of language, the fine judgment, and thoughtful opinions she had formed, not only concerning things political in Europe, but toward all general questions of the day. She was well-informed, and ready with an answer, that was not merely a childish conclusion of a youthful mind, but showed thought, and a consideration of past history.

"You and your father talked things over together, didn't you?" he asked as he watched her interestedly.

Her vivid face had a flash of radiance.

"Oh yes," she said with a wistfulness in her voice. "We had wonderful talks together, even when I was quite a little girl. But we didn't always agree."

"You didn't?"

"No. We often had long arguments about things, continuing over several days. Dad was teaching me to think things out, I guess. He said he wanted me to be able to think things through and form wise judgments. I miss those talks we used to have. They seemed a part of me, and they have grown into a habit. For often now when I have a decision to make, I just try to imagine I'm talking it out with Dad. And I can almost always see what he would be likely to say. It is like getting advice from him. At least it makes me see all sides of a question."

Cameron was astonished to find a girl like this. Most of the girls he knew were taken up with wanting their own way; they formed their own opinions, and thought it smart. This girl seemed to have grown up so sensibly and sweetly with a wise father, that she had come to recognize that experience counted for at least half, in making wise judgments, while the modern girls dismissed the experience of their parents with a shrug as being behind the times, and let it go at that. Cameron found himself admiring this quiet girl with the strong lovely face and the manner of a young princess.

Then suddenly the lawyer arrived and they were plunged at once into business.

The lawyer was keen, with sharp eyes that read character, and he studied the two who waited upon him with interest. He asked a leading question now and then, looking from one to the other, and soon had the whole story before him, as if it had been a moving picture at which he was looking, registering every little detail.

It developed that the lawyer knew all about the property that had been purchased, and had had instructions from Mr. Faber what to do in case he was able to get it. It appeared that Mr. Faber must have had some idea that his death might occur at any time, must have known he was in a critical condition when he started on his journey. The lawyer also knew the son, had arranged several business matters in his behalf before, and understood the situation thoroughly. There would be no difficulty in making him believe all that had happened and the two soon discovered that their job was not to be half so difficult as they had feared.

"Now," said the lawyer gathering up the papers they had given him, and arranging them in two piles, "can you two hold yourselves in readiness to appear in court any time in the next two days? Perhaps three? I'll do my best to arrange it sooner if possible, and let you know by phone. And that doctor, and the nurse. Are they available? It will be necessary to have testimony from the doctor and nurse as to the man's condition."

"I have a signed written statement from

both of them," said Cameron, handing out an envelope.

"That's good," said the lawyer opening the envelope and glancing over the papers. "I see you have a legal mind."

Cameron smiled.

"The doctor suggested it," he said, "when I asked him if he would be available for testimony. He was on his way to New York for an operation and wasn't sure he could get back tomorrow, though he's going to try. He will let me know and be here as soon as possible. The nurse goes with him, and they will stop over to make an affidavit if you can arrange for that."

"You have his New York address?"

"Yes, it's on the envelope."

"Oh, yes, I see. Well, I'll see what I can do. I may want to talk with this doctor by telephone, in case I find it difficult to arrange. All right. Now can you give me two more copies of these papers, and one more copy of these?" He handed the two piles of papers over, and they rose. "You know it is best to keep this thing between ourselves."

"Of course," said Cameron. "Miss Everson says she is willing to do any typing connected with the matter."

"That's very nice then," said the lawyer. "I'll see what I can do with the judge this morning, and will try and telephone your office, Mr. Cameron, around two o'clock. Will you be there then? Or perhaps half past one. And you can send those papers over to me as soon as they are copied."

"Now," said Cameron when they were down in the street again, "shall we go and snatch a bite, or would you rather wait until the copying is done?"

"Oh, I would rather get the copying ready first. We can eat any time, and it might make a difference somehow if he had it soon," said Astra.

"That's true, I suppose. Well, then, I'll take you over to my office. We have an extra machine there, and you will be undisturbed."

He signaled a taxi, and they were soon at Cameron's office.

The rooms looked as she would have expected Cameron's office to look, pleasant, uncluttered, furnished with dignity, simplicity and good taste. The secretary to whom she was introduced was a plain sensible girl, brisk, cordial and capable looking. She at once put Astra at her ease, gave her a desk, uncovered the typewriter she was to use, indicated where to find paper, carbon and erasers, and then left her. There was no evidence of curiosity concerning a strange typist brought in. She gathered that the feeling in the office was one of great respect and confidence in their employer, and an interest a little more than the mere business relation between employer and employee. Her brief stay with her cousins in the west had stressed the questioning of all these matters, the formal things of the world, and made her wonder if perhaps she was wise in going with a stranger to his office. She knew that would be the first question her cousin Miriam would ask if she were here. "What do you know about this stranger? How do you know he is respectable?"

So Astra was pleasantly relieved to find everything so altogether beyond question.

An hour later when Astra went to Cameron's private office with the completed papers she noticed a silver framed photograph standing on Cameron's desk, a lovely elderly woman with wavy white hair, and gentle lines about her mouth that showed she had met suffering and pain and come through unbroken; it was a strong face with beautiful triumphant eyes that reminded her of the young man. She was studying the picture while he looked over the papers she had brought. Suddenly he looked up and saw her.

"That's my mother," he said gently as if he

were introducing her to royalty, and there was a hungry sound to his voice.

"She is lovely," said Astra.

"Yes," said Cameron. "And she was wonderful!" Then he added in a quiet voice that sounded as if it came from the tolling of a sweet bell down in his soul:

"She went away to Heaven when I was twelve years old."

"Oh!" said Astra, in a tone like a cool comforting hand on a fevered brow. The two stood for a moment more looking at the picture, as one looks down at a sweet face in a casket with a background of gentleness, and self-sacrifice and love, and hard work, bordered by a wealth of pleasant flowers. Wistfully, with no regrets, and only a hopeful looking forward to another life, and something precious that will never fade.

Then Cameron drew a quick deep breath, and turned to her with a hover of a smile on his lips.

"Well, now, shall we go to lunch? Perhaps we had better take these papers with us and make sure they get to the lawyer at once and without intervening hands. Is that all right with you?"

So Astra walked out with him, carrying in her mind the sweet expression of the pictured face on the son's desk.

 **6** The Cameron family got a place for Charles in the town bank as soon as he was out of college. He was the youngest of the flock, and their father was old, near to the end. They considered themselves somewhat responsible for him, at least responsible that he should be a credit to the family.

They ignored their stepmother. In fact they had always ignored her since she came among them, although she was a quiet, respectable, dignified woman with a modest fortune of her own, who did not need to be considered financially. There was nothing wrong with her except that they resented anybody taking the place their own mother had occupied. It was a pose they encouraged in themselves.

They considered that they had done very well for Charles in getting him this position in the bank, where there was great possibility of his rising. He might even get to be president some day. He was bright and smart, and the Camerons never did anything half-way. They gave him to understand that they were expecting great things of him.

Charles himself had been docile enough at first. He had taken his collegiate course seriously, and had scarcely come out of its atmosphere as yet to realize that it was over and a new era had begun. His immediate thoughts were for his father who had always been a strong, steady, dependable background in his life, the one to whom he was accountable, and for whose sake he was doing his best. It had never seemed as if his father would die. Of course all men die, but his father had been like a rock that never aged, and was always there, wise, ordering, approving, almost never disapproving. And now that Charles was at home again he suddenly realized that his father was soon going to leave them. There was a gray look beginning to shadow the beloved face, the same kind of shadow he remembered on his loved mother's face before she left them. He had been a small boy when his mother was taken sick. He had hovered around her during her last illness, and had watched the shadows gather. Now he recognized that they were gathering again, and his heart was grieved.

They had never been an outspoken family, always reserved, saying little of their personal affections. So Charles entered upon his new duties in the bank with quiet gravity, a youthful dignity that made a fine impression among his fellow workmen.

"Now, Charles," said his sister Rosamond

who had lived for a time in New York and had sophisticated ideas, "don't forget that great things are expected of you. You are on your own now, but don't relax your vigilance upon yourself just because father is too sick to keep watch over you. Remember the Camerons are a fine family, and have always stood at the top. Remember you've your fortune to make, and it wants to be a big one, too. You will of course get your share from the estate, but naturally when it is divided among us all it won't be so great, and you will need to understand that from the first and be on the watch to increase it. We want our youngest brother to be as wealthy and influential as any of us. We want to be proud of you, you know. And in your position in the bank you will of course have opportunities to know of good investments. So, I say, be on the watch from the beginning to build up your fortune. Of course you will save a little from your salary every month, and even a little can be the nucleus of a fortune if you are constantly on the alert. You are a young man and will want to go out socially, but settle it in your mind how much you are going to spend that way, and don't let yourself be tempted beyond that, else you will have nothing ahead when you want to marry."

Charles looked at Rosamond with a mild perplexity as she delivered this worldly advice. Rosamond had always been the worldly-wise one, not at all as he remembered his mother, nor like the father he knew. He and Rosamond had never had much in common.

"I shall of course," went on Rosamond, "do as much as possible to get you into the best circles. Fortunately I am well acquainted with a number of girls and young men who will be excellent companions for you, and serve to take the place of your college friends, whom of course you must miss greatly. You will be invited, and be able to have some gay times. If you would like to come to the city and visit me next week I could begin to introduce you to some of them. I could give a little dinner Saturday evening. Would you like that? There is an especially nice girl I'd like to have you know. She is wealthy and sophisticated and will help to put a polish on you that you really need, Charlie."

Charles looked at his sister with a quiet aloofness in his face.

"That's kind of you, Roz, to plan for me, and I thank you," he said, "but just at present while father is so ill I would rather stay right here, and be with him as much as I can."

"Well, that's sweet of you of course, Charlie, but I don't think that's a bit wise. You need to get out among people and brush off that solemnity of yours. It isn't good for a young man to be around old sick people much. It will break down all your gaiety. And a little gaiety is what you need. It will help you on in the world! It will help you in your business, it will help you socially and it will help you later in life to get on with other men. You'd better come with me this week-end, Charlie."

But Charles' lips set in a pleasant firmness.

"Not now, Roz," he said pleasantly. "I'm staying with Father. He said he liked to have me. I read to him now and then, sometimes I tell him about college, and sometimes he likes me to talk about politics."

"Nonsense, Charlie," said the sister. "Father won't miss you. I doubt if he knows the difference between us half the time. He scarcely looks at me when I go in, and he never opens his lips to speak on any subject."

"Nevertheless," said Charles firmly, "I'm staying with Father as long as possible. Afterwards we will see."

"Well, you'd better not put it off too long, brother. This perfectly wonderful girl may

98

not be on the market forever, and if you have her for a friend you'll have something worth while working for."

Charles smiled.

"I'm not in a hurry for a girl," he said. "That will keep. At present I'm not in a position to waste my time going around with girls. And if I were there are plenty of girls in our home town."

"Oh, mercy! Charlie! You don't want to get a girl from around here. You are going to rise, you know, and become rich. You'll want to go to New York eventually and get into something big in a money way. There's more opportunity in a big city. And if you amass a fortune you will want to find a girl who will know how to preside in a wealthy home, and to guide your fortunes. You couldn't marry a girl from a little country town and hope to rise anywhere."

"Couldn't I?" said Charles with a comical smile. "Then why rise?"

"Oh, Charlie! You're simply impossible!" said Rosamond.

Rosamond was called away to meet a guest, and presently came Janet. Now Janet was a sweet sister and had married a doctor. She also lived in the city.

"Charles," she said, "you know we think a lot of you, and we'd like to have you run in and see us as often as you can. Before they got this bank position for you I had sort of hoped you'd get something in the city and come and live with us awhile. I know Milan would like to have you. He said once if you didn't get anything right away he'd offer you a place as office boy. You know he really needs someone to be there especially evenings when he has to go out sometimes. Of course, though, he couldn't pay much. But you may be glad to know of it sometime if things don't work out here."

"Perhaps, Janet," said Charles. "That's good of you. You know I'd enjoy being with you, if you'd just promise not to fling a lot of girls, or even a special girl at my head, the way Roz did!"

"Did Roz do that?" laughed Janet. "Well, I promise. But I certainly wouldn't want you to bring any girl of Roz' choosing into our family."

It was the sister Marietta who came to Charles to complain about the stepmother.

"Charles, I've been worrying a lot about this house and what is going to become of it if anything happens to father. Can't you talk to him a little about it? It doesn't seem as if our mother's house, the house he built to please her when she was a bride, should go to that interloper!"

"Marietta, that isn't a right way to talk. Our stepmother is no interloper. She's our father's honorable wife, and she has made a home for him during these years when his children have been away from him and he would have been lonely without her. She's made a good stepmother to me, too, Marietta. I have no fault to find with her. She has always been kindness itself."

"Yes, I suppose you would say that, Charles! You've always been a perfect saint the way you put up with her, and it's been hardest of all on you. But you know perfectly well, Charlie, that kindness is no substitute for love. And besides, any one of us children would have been glad to come home and live and keep house for father if he had asked us. John and I would have come or Harold and Rosamond, or Elizabeth and Reamer and their horde of children. Especially Elizabeth. It would have been a real godsend to her. She hasn't had any too easy a time, Charlie. And Mary would have come of course; she and Joe would have been delighted and have made father a good home, much more like it was when mother was here. Though Elizabeth cooks more like mother, and father would have liked that. And of course any of the boys would gladly have come. They always liked the old home and their wives would have been tickled to death."

"You forget, Marietta, that father and I went on here three years together, without anyone of them suggesting such a thing! And besides, Marietta, it was father's right to do what he pleased. And our stepmother is really a fine woman."

"Well, she's no right to take the old home from us. She ought to get out and give it to us if anything happens to father, and I think it's your place to suggest it to him, or to her, if you prefer that. You have always been closer to her than any of the rest of us, and I think you should take it upon yourself to see that that is all arranged. Suppose you talk it over with father when he seems to have a good day and make him see how we feel about it. It would be a great deal better of course if *he* would arrange it, not so awkward you know, and I'm sure he could say something to his wife that would make her feel right about it. It isn't as if she didn't have property of her own, and another house that belonged to her first husband. If she has any delicacy at all she'll think of it herself. Though I doubt it, unless father arranges it, and the law can come in and make it easy for us all. Will you attend to that, Charlie?"

"No, Marietta, I don't think that would be right. That would be entirely a matter for father and our stepmother to arrange for themselves, and I should certainly not like even to suggest such a thing. I don't think it would be in the least fair to her. She has had enough to bear already with the foibles of my sisters, and the cold looks and sarcasm."

"Yes, that's you all over, Charles, always taking the part of the down dog. You never think how much *we* have to suffer, and what a sacrifice it will be to have our old home taken away from us."

Charles suddenly got up and looked at his elder sister almost sternly.

"I wish you would stop, Marietta," he said sadly. "Our father is still living, and quite alert and able to attend to his own business at times, and I certainly shall not meddle with his affairs. It has been enough he has had to suffer with having his own children turn against the woman he married, and treat her as if she were an interloper, without having us torment him in his last hours about a paltry house. I should be ashamed to mention the matter to him, and I sincerely hope that none of the rest of you will. As far as I am concerned I feel that it would be perfectly right for mother to have the house, and I am sure that all rightminded people will feel so."

"That's because you were so young when our mother died that you don't remember her," sobbed Marietta, suddenly wiping away hastily summoned tears. "Of course I should have remembered that. You wouldn't remember the dear old dishes that were mother's. We girls can remember spending hours washing and drying them so tenderly and putting them away in mother's corner cupboard. I just know *she*'ll claim them all. I've heard her admire them many times."

"Oh, be still, Marietta. You're disgusting. Do you think our mother would ever have such hateful thoughts? This woman has been wonderful to dad. She helped him back to normal living after his heart had been broken by our mother's death. Don't talk any more about it. You must know that death is drawing nearer to our father each day, yet you can turn your thoughts to such selfish trivial matters. Let me get out of here. I want to forget what you have said. I am sure when you think it over later you will be ashamed yourself to harbor such notions."

Charles arose and went quickly outside, down the wide steps and out into the open, his eyes full of sadness and disgust. Oh, why would his sisters keep up this contemptible little jealousy? Why would they not see what a distress it was to their father?

He walked down the path to the front gate, looked down the road a moment, then skirted the fence around to the side meadow and walked out across to the little slope that went gently down to the stream and wound with silver thread through the meadow, disappearing into the woodland. He walked slowly along by the stream to the fishing hole where so often as a boy he had been sent down to get trout for supper. How he loved it all, the wide meadows, the rippling stream, and the quiet fishing place where he had spent many happy hours with his father when he was a little boy, just after his mother died. Before there was any thought of a stepmother. He had been used to sit for hours quietly watching the speckled trout stealing toward the bait, casting shy glances at the stern face of his father. The father who seemed to pay so little attention to him, yet always wanted him to go along. It was so he had got to know how lonely his father was after the mother was gone. Sometimes his father would sigh, deeply, and little more than a child though he was, Charles had seemed to sense the deep sorrow that was behind that sigh.

Then the rest of the children who were

still at home would troop noisily back from school, and down to the quiet shadowed woodland where light and shade flickered among the leaves of the trees. They would come with their noisy outcries, and his father would sigh again, haul in the last fish, and gather up his things preparing to go back to the house. And Charles, being the youngest, and always the butt of all their pranks because he was known to be a good sport and would not tell on them, trudged wisely behind his father, carrying his own string of fish. So, early he had learned to be a good fisherman, and incidentally to have patience and self-control, and wisdom to hold his tongue. And his sisters were learning that they could not mold this young brother as they had hoped to do. For just when they were thinking that they had won him over to their wishes, he would suddenly walk firmly out in a new path, diametrically opposed to the one they had suggested. Often there was nothing for them to do but lay it all to the baleful influence of the pestilential stepmother, as they called her.

But it was not alone in the line of business that his family tried to control Charles. As the days went on and he became apparently well established in the bank, they produced a definite girl for him, and demanded that he give her his exclusive attention. But Charles only smiled and went on his quiet way, doing as he pleased and letting the girl go her way.

Mortified, the sisters tried other girls, each one doing her best to interest him in some girl of wealth and prominence. They planned ways to inveigle him to meet them under pleasant auspices, but almost always he slipped out of the meeting, especially if he found out beforehand that a girl was to be presented to his attention. It annoyed him beyond measure to have this going on. Whenever he went to see any one of his sisters some girl would be more or less flung in his face. If she wasn't actually present, the conversation would immediately turn to her virtues, and likes and dislikes, until he dreaded to visit his sisters.

Finally failing in getting any reaction other than definitely negative, the sisters formed a sort of directorate to concentrate on one girl with pleasant insistence until they made some impression.

After much discussion, and bitter disagreement, they finally compromised on a girl who lived officially in Philadelphia, though she spent her winters in Florida or California, and her summers in the mountains or at the shore, when she was not traveling to some strange place around the world. And she was the lady of the mink coat whom Astra had seen with Cameron in the station. Her name was Camilla Blair, her father president of the Blair and Blair Company, of national repute and fabulous wealth.

There had been much maneuvering to effect the first meeting of Charles with this lady, and great annoyance that he was not at once intrigued by her.

But Charles about that time was planning other things for himself, and was absorbed in arranging his life after a new pattern. He did not seem to take much notice of this undeniably attractive girl who was so constantly and obviously flung at him on all occasions.

"It's a queer thing," said Marietta discontentedly to Rosamond whom she was visiting for the week-end, "but Charlie just doesn't seem to see Camilla at all. He looks right at her with his most gracious smile, and he might as well be staring at a blank wall. His thoughts aren't there. I wonder if it could be that he got interested in some girl while he was at college? Surely there wouldn't have been any worthwhile girl in that little hick town."

"You can't tell," sighed Rosamond. "Charlie is definitely queer, and it might just be that he has involved himself with some little common country girl he was sorry for, and thinks it would be disloyal to have anything to do with anyone else. He is so uncomfortably conscientious. It's queer he doesn't understand that he has some duty toward his family, and the old family name, as well as toward some poor forsaken creature he feels sorry for."

"Yes," sighed Marietta. "He's very much like father, don't you think? So silent and grave, and frightfully virtuous."

"Yes, but it's our duty to rouse him to his privileges. Somehow he's got to be made to see that he must bring this Blair fortune into the family." This from Rosamond with a deeply troubled look. "I don't understand why he doesn't see it himself. Such a lovely girl, and so gorgeously dressed! Did you notice the material she was wearing last night? It was one of those exclusive weaves. I declare I nearly died of envy. And the way she wears her clothes is something wonderful. They just seem a part of herself, so supple and graceful in their hang. I certainly envy her her figure. It is not always that a really wealthy girl has such looks. Charlie doesn't know what he's missing. And I just know she's crazy about him. She said the other day that she thought my brother was rare. That was a good deal from her," said Rosamond.

"What a pity it is that Charlie never took up skiing. They could go up to some of those mountain places and have a wonderful time. I think it would be easy to persuade him for that. We could say that she wanted awfully to go and there weren't any of her friends free to take her this week-end, or something like that," said Marietta.

"Well, he never did take up skiing, so that's that!" said Janet. "Besides I see you trying to make him ask her! He would have forty thousand things he had to do instead."

"Well, if he really felt that she was troubled because she couldn't go, he might," Marietta put in. "He's great on helping people out when they're disappointed."

"Yes?" said Rosamond in a tone of discouragement. "Just try and do it, that's all I've got to say. You can't catch birds by putting salt on their tails, no matter how hard you try, and Charlie's the worst kind of a bird when it comes to getting him to go off with a girl."

"The only way you can ever do it," said Mary who had just come in and was listening, "is to get some unpleasant duty that nobody else can do, and ask him as a special favor to do it, and then rope your girl in on it unawares. Why can't you go off to a funeral or something, Roz, and ask him to take care of the children? And then send Camilla over to the house to call while you're absent. Couldn't Junior be counted on to upset the honeypot on the stairs or something, so Charlie would have to ask her to come in and help him clean up? Give your maids the afternoon off, you know, and leave Charles helpless."

"Helpless!" sniffed Rosamond. "Not he! Sure, you could count on Junior to do his part nobly, but not Charles. He would rather clean honey off ten flights of stairs than ask that perfect piece of maidenhood to come in and help him. Besides, I doubt if Camilla *could* do it, and the result wouldn't be so good. Charles still thinks that all good women ought to be just such efficient house-keepers as our mother was. However, I'll keep the idea in mind. There may be something in it. I'll see if I can work it out. For the certain something has got to be done about Charles. We can't let this wonderful opportunity be lost."

So they plotted, and Charles went quietly on his way.

And then the father died, and Charles was sadder and graver. And while the sisters, and some of the brothers congratulated themselves that they had Charles safely located in the town bank, where he was likely to rise and stay put, and develop in spite of himself, Charles was quietly planning other things.

Suddenly one day he sprung it on them that he had taken over a business in Philadelphia on his own, and intended removing there at once, and the poor harassed sisters rose up in rebellion. After a hopeless clamor they subsided, to get into another huddle and plan where in Philadelphia he should live, and how he should be placed in proper social relations. But they discovered too late that Charles had already located himself, and was not open to suggestions.

"You run your lives and I'll run mine," he smilingly told his sisters. "And no, I didn't ask father anything about the house, nor I haven't said anything to our stepmother about it. I don't intend to and I sincerely hope you won't. You don't want the old house, anyway, you know you don't! You wouldn't one of you go there to live if you had it. You'd sell it and never go near it again, so why should you try to make unpleasantness? And all this fuss about furniture! You never cared for the old things when you lived here, why should you make dissension now that those who bought it, and loved it are gone? No, I tell you I can't make trouble for our stepmother. She's been good to me, and I honor and love her for it. Now, is there anything else?"

"Charles, I'll bet you've gone and invited the stepmother to come and live with you! I'll bet you feel sorry for her and you've told her to make her headquarters with you the rest of her life!"

Charles turned on a pleasant grin and looked from one sister to another.

"Well, and what if?" he asked.

"Charles, you *didn't!*"

"But you just said I did!" He grinned with a twinkle in his eyes that reminded them of the look in their father's eyes on the rare intervals when he relaxed and grew a little merry with his children.

"Charles, what have you done? I *insist* on knowing," said Marietta, snapping her eyes and putting on the older-sister air.

"Yes?" said Charles. "Well I did invite her to come to see me when I got settled. Told her my home was always hers if she needed it."

"Oh, Charlie!" moaned Rosamond. "That's just like you!"

"And what did she say?" snapped Marietta.

"Why, she thanked me very tenderly, and said she thought she would stay right here in the house father had left to her, for the present."

The girls looked at one another with angry resentment.

"Yes, I thought that would be it. That means the dishes too, and all the lovely old ancestral furniture!"

Then suddenly they saw Charles' train coming round the curve, and he picked up his baggage, called a smiling good-by, and was off, out of their clutches without warning. There was nothing for them to do but to go into another huddle to see what they would do next about Camilla Blair.

 7

When Astra got back to her room later that afternoon she realized that she was very tired. After all, she had been steadily on the move since she started on her journey, in fact, for two days beforehand. And there had been no time to sit down and think things over. Already she felt as if she had been away from the Lester house for several weeks, and had entered into a new world that was different from all her other experiences, rushing breathlessly from one environment to another.

When she came out of the office building with Charles Cameron they passed a great building that bore a modest brass sign at the central doorway on which she caught the name of Faber.

Cameron saw her glance at it, and nodded in assent.

"Yes, that's Mr. Faber's building," he said. "And now that he's gone, what will become of that great successful business?"

"Yes," said Astra with awe in her voice. "And where he has gone it doesn't make any difference how successful he was down here. Isn't life strange, and wonderful — and *awful?* How little we think of it in that way. I mean how little we think about the end of it all! And it sometimes comes so soon for some!"

Cameron bowed.

"That's true," he said thoughtfully. "I wonder what effect it would have upon business generally if all successful business men would spend a little time occasionally, thinking that over."

"I wonder!" said Astra. "But of course they don't, not many of them anyway."

They went to the lawyer's and found a message that they were to be ready for a telephone call at three o'clock when he hoped to have a definite word about their appearance at court.

"Now," said Cameron pleasantly, "I think we have earned a good meal, don't you?"

Astra smiled reservedly.

"Yes, but please don't feel that you have to be responsible for me. I can get something to eat, and be waiting in my room for a telephone call."

Cameron looked at her meditatively.

"Yes," he said pleasantly, "I know you can, but I sort of fancy we'd stick together till we know just how this thing is going to turn out. Don't you?"

"Are you afraid I'll run away?" laughed Astra. "After all everything is copied now, and we have signed before the lawyer. It wouldn't make so very much difference if I did disappear at this stage of the performance, would it? Of course I wouldn't, but I don't see that you need to worry. I'm not so important as all that."

He eyed her gravely.

"Yes, I think you are quite important," he said, "but I wouldn't ever think of you as one who would desert a cause. That's the reason I have perfect confidence in you. And I may as well tell you that I have reason to believe that we are up against a rather stiff proposition if that old lady finds out just what went on at her husband's death bed. She won't leave any stone unturned to frustrate any of his plans that have to do with that stepson of hers. And I for one am sufficiently interested in carrying out Mr. Faber's wishes to the extent that I mean to do all I possibly can to help this thing go through without a hitch anywhere."

"And so am I," said Astra earnestly. "It seems somehow a heaven-sent duty."

"Yes, doesn't it?" said Cameron with a sudden lighting of his eyes as his glance met hers.

He took her to a pleasant quiet restaurant where they had a comfortable meal, and then they went out and called up the lawyer's office again. Astra waited in a reception room, in a great easy chair, realizing that she was all keyed up and it was good to relax and rest for a few minutes.

Cameron was not long gone and came back with a look of satisfaction on his nice tired face.

"Well, that man Faber knew how to select a good lawyer," he said as he took his place beside her. "He's a busy man but he has managed to cover a good deal of ground in a short time. The judge has given us a tentative hearing for tomorrow morning. The lawyer got in touch with the doctor in New York. He's game to do all he can. He seems to understand the situation pretty well, and advises getting the matter settled according to law in a hurry. Mr. Faber must have dropped a word to him of the importance of the situation before we came on the scene. Anyway he's coming as soon as he can. And now, lady, it's time for you to go to your room and rest. You want to be fresh as a daisy tomorrow morning. Excuse my demand. I feel it is important. And by the way, is there anything of your own that should be attended to? I'll be glad to help out in any way I can if you will just tell me. Are there messages to send, or people to see?"

"Oh, no," said Astra smiling. "Nothing at all important. Nothing but what I can do with a phone call or two if I decide it should be done tonight."

"Couldn't I help in that?"

"Oh, no thank you. It's just an old friend of father's I may decide to give a greeting to. But probably it can wait until tomorrow."

"That would be better, I should think. You look decidedly weary."

"Oh, thank you, I'm all right. You're judging me by yourself perhaps. I think you are tired yourself."

"I am," he said wearily. "There wasn't even time for a very sketchy doze last night. I think I'll turn in early tonight."

"I will too," smiled Astra. "Good night. Don't hesitate to call me up no matter how late if I am needed. I don't suppose I will be."

"No," said Cameron, "I think not. But you certainly are faithful and willing. You somehow seem like an old friend of the Faber family. Well, good night!"

His handclasp was warm and hearty, and his smile was pleasant to remember as she took her way in the elevator to her room, until somehow that mink-coated girl managed to stand in the hallway above to meet her as she got out at her floor and went along the hall to her room.

"Now the very idea!" said Astra to herself.

119

"Don't bring that up again! What difference does it make anyway? He's very nice, but he can have all the mink-coated girls he wants for all me."

She went into her room, got into a comfortable negligee and lay down, with two pleasant magazines beside her that she meant to read after she got a little rested. And then the very first page she opened, behold there was a woman in a mink coat with a lovely rose in her hand, and a charming smile on her piquant red lips. She promptly closed the magazine and flung it from her in disgust, turning over and closing her eyes. She wouldn't have anything more to do with that magazine until she was thoroughly rested and could look on a mink coat and smile without any silly ideas.

When Astra awoke it was half past five and dark in her room. She awoke with a definite feeling that she must do something at once about her immediate future. This Faber business would soon be over and she must know what her next move should be.

She glanced toward her window that looked out on a park and showed the lights across on the next street. It was a pleasant room with a nice outlook. Cameron had selected it, and likely felt that as long as she was doing this work for the Faber family he wanted her to be comfortable. She had a flash of gratitude as she got up and went to look out.

Over in the park lights were flashing. Red and green. Across on the next corner she could see an enormous Christmas tree done in blue and white lights; another farther down the street had a color scheme of red, white and blue, with a tiny perfect flag at the top. It was a lovely sight; it was fascinating to watch more and more lights flash out as she stood there. Over across the square was a great building, an old mansion, probably, being used as a club house of some sort, and there was a Santa Claus smiling and about to descend the great stone chimney, waving one hand in farewell to the street below. It was all very gay and festive. Up the street was another tree, all green, with a great white star at its summit, across from it were letters: UNTO YOU IS BORN A SAVIOUR —. She couldn't see the rest of the legend, but she finished it out in her mind "WHICH IS CHRIST THE LORD." Was that true? Did all the people who read believe that? No, of course not. Only a comparative few. But it was good to believe. To know that that Saviour was hers. She might be desolate and alone in the world, but He was *her* Saviour. She was glad she believed!

There came a little thrill to her heart as she used to feel it sometimes when her father said such things to her. It was as if a definite message had come down from her own dear earthly father, that she wasn't alone. As if that white star up the street had a distinct message, just for her.

She turned on her light, gave a dash of cold water to her face, smoothed her hair, and put on her hat and coat. She would go to the telephone and try to get Mr. Sargent at once. Then, if he was at leisure she would perhaps go and see him a few minutes this evening and find out if it was possible to get an advance on her next month's allowance. That was what she ought to have done before she lay down to rest.

Also she should count over her money and be sure just what she had left. It certainly was very little on which to depend for two whole weeks till the holidays were over and she could venture to call up a few friends and offer them a brief visit. She was on her own, and she must live as frugally as possible. A glass of milk and a few crackers would do for supper tonight. She had lunched royally this noon. But she would bring a bottle of milk and a box of crackers back with her when she returned from her walk.

So she went to the telephone and called up the Sargent home.

But the voice that answered was not familiar and turned out to belong to a new servant who did not know Astra.

"No, Mr. Sargent isn't here. He's in Florida. He's been very ill with pneumonia, and he may be there some weeks. They won't dare bring him home till spring now I guess, coming out of that warm climate, you know."

"Oh!" said Astra in dismay, her heart sinking. "I didn't know he was sick."

"Who is it?" asked the woman. "Is there any message? Did you want to speak to anyone else?"

"Oh, why, I don't know. I'm Miss Everson. Mr. Sargent is an old friend of my father's, and he has charge of my financial affairs. I wanted to talk to him on business as well as because he is our friend. But isn't anybody else there? Is Mrs. Sargent there?"

"No, she went with her husband."

"Well, is anybody else of the family there?"

"Only his nephew Mr. Will. He's looking after the office while his uncle's gone. Perhaps you'd like to speak to his secretary. Mr. Will Sargent isn't here tonight. He went up to New York, but he left one of his secretaries here. Maybe you'd like to speak to her. Here she comes now. She's just come in from the office."

So Astra had a brief talk with the secretary. But she was a new acquisition, and had no knowledge of affairs at the office yet.

"I think Mr. Will would know about your affairs," she said. "He'll be back day after tomorrow I think, although he might not come till after Christmas. He had an invitation to go to some ranch house, or club or something in the mountains, and he said he might go. He said there wouldn't be anything much doing in the office now anyway till after the holidays. I can't even give you that address because he hasn't sent it to me yet."

"Well, I wonder if you would have any way of finding out a few things about my account," said Astra in desperation. "My money came last week while I was out west, and most of it was stolen from me before I started east. I had a time getting enough together to come, and I wanted to know if I could have a part of next month's allowance in advance."

"Oh, I wouldn't know anything about that," said the secretary coldly. "You'd have to wait till Mr. Will gets back."

"Oh!" said Astra, dismay filling her lonely

soul. "Well, couldn't you give me Mr. Sargent's address and then I could wire his wife. She could surely ask Mr. Sargent a question or two."

"We're not allowed to worry Mr. Sargent with anything. The doctor said anything we couldn't settle ourselves let go till he gets back."

Astra turned at last from the telephone with unbidden tears welling into her eyes. There just wasn't anything to do but wait until that Will Sargent got back from his holiday. The strange young secretary had declined to give her his address. Had probably been told not to give it to anyone, and was evidently suspicious of the young woman who wanted advance money on a cock-and-bull story of having had her money stolen from her. Astra had at last persuaded her to take down her own name and address and promise to call her up when the young Mr. Sargent should arrive, but that was all. Well, that was that. She was very much on her own again!

She went out and got her bottle of milk and her box of crackers, and went back to her cheerless little room. There were still Christmas lights out the window, across the park, and down the street, and the great white star still shone with its personal insistent message burning bright against the tree, "FOR UNTO YOU IS BORN —" but Astra's heart was very heavy, and she sat there at her window nibbling a cracker with troubled eyes for some minutes before the old thrill came with the bright words: "UNTO *YOU* — A SAVIOUR!"

Well, then, she would test out her faith. If He was her Saviour — and she had no doubt about that — she would just trust Him. He would look out for her! He had always taken care of her. He *would!*

So she drank her milk and finished her cracker, knelt and laid her affairs in God's hands, and then went to bed and to sleep.

When she woke in the morning she resolutely refused an entrance to worry though it tried to get into her soul and distract her. Her job today was to stay in her room, ready for a summons if one should come. She had done her best to get in touch with Will Sargent once more, and if no word came from him she would just forget it until she was through with this work for Mr. Cameron.

She went down to the Association restaurant and got a simple cheap breakfast. She mustn't waste a cent, for there was no telling how long it would be before she could replenish her fortunes. Then she went back to her room, leaving careful directions at the desk to be called if anybody came for her.

A call to the Sargent home elicited only the information that the other secretary had telephoned that Mr. Will would not return for a couple of days yet, and that she had left word with her assistant that all she knew about the Everson account was that the usual amount had been forwarded to her western address at the usual time. She had no authority to advance any on next quarter's installment. She had made a note of it and would consult Mr. Will as soon as he returned.

So Astra settled down to read and tried to forget finances.

About ten o'clock came a message from Cameron's secretary that he would call for her at two o'clock on his way to the lawyer's office, whence they would proceed to court if the doctor and nurse arrived as hoped.

They went to court as scheduled, and the doctor and nurse walked in soon after them.

The proceedings at court were very brief and simple. The lawyer had everything arranged. There were no hitches and no interruptions. No unwelcome stepson appeared, and no irate widow with another lawyer. It was all carried off in a quiet quick manner. The doctor and the nurse took the next plane returning to New York, Cameron and Astra went down to the street together.

"And that finishes it, doesn't it?" she said as they reached the street door. She had a feeling that now she would be seeing Cameron no more, and it seemed as if she ought to ask him a question or two about getting a job if she needed one. She felt strangely desolate at the thought that there would be no one now, when he was gone, even to greet her with just a business-like good morning.

"Well, not quite," said Cameron. "I have a little business to settle up with you for the Faber estate. Yes, those were my orders. Mr. Faber spoke a few words with me after you left us. He rallied. It seemed as if there were things he felt he must say before he left this world, and one of those things was to ask me to thank you and see that you were repaid. He told me what to give you."

"But I don't think I should be repaid for a little favor to a dying man. It doesn't seem ethical to me."

Cameron smiled appreciatively.

"I understand of course. You can call it a gift of gratitude if you want to, but I think you'd better take it. You surely can make better use of it than that virago of a widow of his would. Don't you think so? And then there's another thing, it wasn't just the matter of a little stenography and typing, and the trouble you've had to take to go to the lawyer and to court. That he would pay for of course. But he was most grateful to you for that prayer. Remember if it had been his minister, or any passing minister who had prayed for him in his dying moment, he would want a substantial gift of money presented to him. And he spoke of the prayer especially. Of course his breath was almost gone, and he could only gasp detached words, but evidently your prayer made a great impression upon him. It seemed as if it had taught him the way to expect entrance at the Heavenly gate."

"Oh!" said Astra, her eyes suddenly brimming with quick unbidden tears. "That is pay enough for what I did. I don't want anything else!"

Some men coming out of the court house just then turned and looked curiously at her and Cameron drew her away toward the edge of the pavement and summoned a taxi.

"I understand," he said comfortably, "but would you mind coming over to my office a few minutes till I tell you a few things? And there'll be some papers for you to read and sign."

She let him put her in the taxi, and when

they were on their way again she looked up, a resolute expression on her face.

"Please," she said wistfully, "I'd rather not sign any more papers. I wouldn't like Mrs. Faber to know even my name, or find out where I am."

"Of course not!" said Cameron. "I wouldn't think of suggesting anything that would give her a clue to you. But I would like to hand young Mr. Faber papers showing what his father asked us to do. Of course the lawyer will deal with that too, in his statement, but I felt that Paul Faber merited a little more personal statement from us who came closest to his father in his last hours. If you object, after reading what I have dictated, you need not sign."

"Oh, of course I'm willing to sign anything you think ought to be sent to him. I thought maybe it was something for the family. I really wouldn't like to meet that woman again. She was insulting. You don't think I should go to the funeral, do you?"

"Why no, of course not. Now we'll get this business over as quickly as possible, and then I suppose you'll be very glad to be seeing the last of me. I hope I shall not have to be troubling you any more with annoying requests."

"Oh, I'm sorry I objected!" said Astra.

"You haven't been in the least annoying. It has been very interesting, the whole affair, and you have been most kind. I'm afraid I am going to feel quite stranded after you are gone. You have made me feel as if you were an old friend. And I have discovered that the friends with whom I expected to spend Christmas are sick and gone to Florida, so I'm quite on my own for a few days until I hunt up some of my other friends. You see the business you have provided has really helped to fill rather lonely days. You mustn't feel you have annoyed me, please."

"Well, that's nice," said Cameron smiling genially. "That's better than I had counted on. Now, here we are at the office. Shall we go up?"

Astra found the statements she was asked to sign were very simple indeed, just the story of how she was called to take dictation. When she had signed them Cameron handed her an envelope.

"Just take that home with you. It's nothing I am responsible for, so you don't need to open it now. It's what I was told to give you, and there's no one alive now to argue it out with except the old man's wife, so I advise you to accept it and not worry any more about it. Now, my secretary thinks she found a handkerchief or glove or something you must have left when you were here typing. If you'll just step into the outer room she'll give it to you. Sorry I can't see you back to your abiding place, but I have a man waiting for me who is in a hurry to get back to New York. I guess you won't have any trouble in finding your way. I told Miss Harmer to order a taxi for you. I hope you won't have too desolate a Christmas. Sorry I can't do something to make it a pleasant one, but I promised my stepmother I'd spend the day with her. This will be rather a lonely time for her, the first Christmas since my father's death. But I'll be calling you up before I leave, just to wish you Merry Christmas, anyway. You are going to stay in the same place until after the holidays?"

"I think so," said Astra putting on a brave little smile. Then Cameron's secretary appeared at the door with a tall gentleman behind her carrying a brief case, and Astra followed her back to her desk and retrieved the lost glove. She thanked the secretary and turned to go out, with the other girl's pleasant formal little Christmas wishes ringing in her ears. Suddenly a great loneliness enveloped her, and she had to swallow hard to keep down the tears which were imminent. What was the matter with her? She wasn't a crying girl, and she had been through a lot of utter loneliness since her father died. Why should just going out away from a stranger with whom she had been working for a few brief days knock her out so? This feeling of having left her only friend, whom she would probably not see again, and the holidays upon her. Long, lonely holidays without a soul to speak to! Oh, but this was foolish!

She dashed the tears away and went out to her taxi which drove up just then, gave her address and set herself firmly to get her emotions under control before she had to get out and go into the brightly lighted hallway.

When she got out of the taxi she was met at the door by a telegraph boy with a yellow envelope for her, and her hand was trembling so that she could scarcely sign for it. But she managed to get quietly to the elevator and up to her room. When she sank down into a chair by the window to read it, she found she was trembling from head to foot. Then she read her telegram. It was from her cousin Duke Lester in California.

I insist that you return to our house at once. You had no right to leave in this way. We trusted you to look after house and servants. Miriam left work for you to do. We always supposed you to be conscientious and trustworthy. Can scarcely believe that you have suddenly deserted, sulky because we didn't take you with us. Lose no time in returning. Miriam greatly worried. You are doing your best to spoil our holiday. Start home at once! Wire what train you are taking, or I shall call on the police to search for you. See that you obey orders! Remember we are your guardians.

Duke

Suddenly Astra's tears were turned into merriment and she put her head back against the chair and laughed aloud. How very like Duke that telegram sounded! But how in the world did he find out she was gone yet, and how did he know where to reach her?

Then she remembered. Those maids must have telegraphed him at once as soon as she was away. And he had sent his message in care of Mr. Sargent. The Sargent secretary had sent it on to her. Careful examination of the telegram confirmed her conclusions.

Yes, the telegram had been sent in Mr. Sargent's care. Well what should she do next? She could not reach either of the

Sargents now to ask advice, and if she did not reply to this telegram at once it would be just like Duke to carry out his threat and send the police after her. Then where would she be? In disgrace! Steady, *steady!* She must think what to do. She must pray for guidance. One wrong move now could make all sorts of trouble for her. And she certainly did not intend ever to go back to the Lester home again! But the answer to that telegram must be both dignified and convincing. Of course if Mr. Sargent were at home and well enough to talk with her it would be all right. Or if Will Sargent were there. But she couldn't let this go long enough to get to either one. Not only the police, but Cousin Duke himself would come on and deal with her. When Cousin Duke was roused he could be quite unpleasant and most unreasonable. No, there must be someone whose name would represent authority. Someone Duke would recognize as one who had a right to speak for her.

Stay! Wasn't there a lawyer? Mr. Sargent's lawyer? Wouldn't he know definitely about this business of guardian? She was sure her father would never have made Duke her guardian, not the way he felt about him. She had always thought of Mr. Sargent as her guardian. He must be of course! What in the world did Duke mean? If she could only remember the name of Mr. Sargent's lawyer!

Then she remembered the little book her father had told her to read often. Of course she had read it many times in a casual way, although not all the way through. She understood pretty well how much money she was to receive each quarter, and the general formula of the coupons and so on that she had to sign at set times, but there was a great deal in that little book that she seldom looked at, and then only to glance over as she hunted out some particular item. Perhaps there was some note about a guardian that she had never taken into her consciousness.

So she got up quickly, took off her hat and coat and went to her suitcase to find the little book.

 **8** When Cameron bowed his New York visitor out of his office with just time to catch his train, he turned back to his desk with a sense of having left something unfinished there. But when he looked about him he realized that it was only Astra he had left unfinished. And Astra was gone! Perhaps he would never see her again, and he had a feeling that he had said good-by to her in a most casual way. She had worked hard and helped him through a trying place, and he wanted her to feel that he was grateful, yet he had let her go with a common little wish for a pleasant holiday! It wasn't the way he wanted to leave her. He wanted to make her feel that he was her friend, to offer to help her somehow. She had been so willing and of such good understanding. Well, he couldn't help it that this particularly important man should turn up just when he was trying to tell her what Mr. Faber had said. How much did he tell her anyway? Not much, he was sure. He thought she had a right to know about that last brief scene when he was summoned to the death bed. Well, he must call her up and make an appointment. Perhaps take her to dinner somewhere and have opportunity for a good long talk. Somehow he felt that she

was a girl worth knowing. She must be with a father like hers. He remembered articles he had read by the eminent Mr. Everson. It must be the same one for the girl was different from most modern girls. She had a real background, and a girl couldn't have that and come out just like every other girl of course. Well, he must keep in touch with her, get to know her better.

Then his secretary came in with a pile of important letters from the afternoon mail, and there was no further time for thought. But he went on to his end-of-the-day work with still that feeling of having left something important unfinished.

Presently the telephone interrupted. It was the smooth silken voice of Camilla Blair.

"Is that you, Charlie? Oh, I'm glad I caught you. I was afraid you might have left the office, and then I would have a lot of trouble to find you. Why, you see, I'm in town for overnight with not a thing in the world to do, and I wondered if you wouldn't take me to dinner somewhere and then we could go dancing around here and there. You'll know the best places, and I'm bored to death. I do want to have a little fun. All my best friends around here are off to Florida. I thought you wouldn't mind if I called you up."

Cameron had a passing wonder what it was about that girl's cultured voice that could be so irritating to him, and then he set his mind to work for an answer when she should have finished her request.

So he caught at one of her questions as an opening.

"Why, no, I'm afraid I don't know the best places, Camilla. You know I haven't time for running around dancing. I'd be glad to try to amuse you somehow if things were so that I could, but it couldn't be by dancing for I never learned to dance."

"Charlie! You can't mean it! Why, how simply unbelievable! I can't understand how your sisters let you come up with that deficiency. But that's all right, Charles. I'll be glad to remedy that lack. I can teach you to dance. I've taught a lot of friends and I just know you'll learn quickly, you are so graceful. There are places where we can go and let you try out the different steps a few minutes, where we shan't be noticeable. I just know you'll do beautifully."

"Well, you're very kind, Camilla, and far more sanguine than I would be if I were to allow you to attempt it, but you see, even if all that were true, the fact remains that I do not care to learn to dance. It isn't in my line at all, and I would have no use for the knowledge after I had learned."

"Now Charlie, what a way to talk. That isn't very nice of you when I'm offering to teach you. And besides, when you've learned, you'll change your mind. You honestly will, I'm *positive!* And you don't have any idea what joy you're missing until you've tried, and once got the rhythm of dancing into your soul. Now come on, Charlie, be a good sport, and come over and get me. We'll talk about it while we're eating dinner, and I just know you'll change your mind."

Cameron was making up his mind very firmly while she talked. He was not going to take this girl out to dinner, and he was not going to let her teach him to dance!

"Sorry to disappoint you, Camilla, but you'll have to excuse me from anything tonight. I have some important unfinished business which cannot be put off. I can send you over some tickets for a good symphony concert tonight, if that will help out, and you may find some friend of yours still in the city who can enjoy it with you."

"Symphony concert! Oh, mercy! I'm not in the least musical and I get fed up with those over in New York. I told you I wanted to go somewhere and dance tonight."

"Well, I'm sorry, Camilla, but you'll have

to find somebody else to accompany you, for my evening is full."

"Oh, but *Charlie!* Couldn't you possibly put off your business?" pleaded Camilla.

"Sorry, not possibly."

"Well, what time will you be back at your hotel?"

"That would be hard to tell, Camilla. My engagement this evening depends on other people and the outcome of my arrangements."

"Well, then, Charles, suppose I call you up late. Quite late, you know, after most places are closed, and only a few night clubs open. Would you take me out for a late supper? You see, I'm quite anxious to see you. We've some plans, your sister Rosamond and I, and I was to talk them over with you before we go on to work them out. We need your help and I told Rosamond I would make it a point to get a good talk with you while I was here, and see what times would be convenient for you."

"Sorry," said Cameron firmly. "You would do better to leave me out of any plans. I'm going to be exceedingly busy the rest of the winter, and I wouldn't have any time this week even to do any talking. Just go ahead without me. That would be best."

"Now Charlie, I think you're horrid! Just

141

turning me down at every suggestion. How do you expect to get on in this world if you don't cultivate your friends, and have a few minutes now and then for relaxation?"

"Well, I'm not so sure I'm trying to get on in this world," laughed Cameron. "I have my work to do, and I'm doing it to the best of my ability. Sorry you don't approve of my way of life, but I guess it will have to stand."

"And you won't even take me out to dinner? Not even briefly?"

"Not possibly, Camilla, I'm leaving the office right away for a long evening, and perhaps a hard one. I do hope you'll find a way to have a pleasant time without me. And, if I don't see you before, I wish you a Merry Christmas."

As soon as he could get rid of Camilla, Cameron signed the finished letters his secretary had just brought in, handed them to her to mail, said good night to her and went. It was fairly possible that Camilla might even pursue him to his office and further try to inveigle him into doing something to amuse her yet. She was a girl of many resources, and was not one who was shy about proposing them. Moreover, now that he knew Rosamond was in on this thing he was most suspicious. Away from his office now, and free, he allowed that sense of unfinished business to become acute. He *had* some important unfinished business. It was Astra. He couldn't leave her high and dry that way with such a casual farewell, and perhaps no chance of ever seeing her again. Every step he took to the elevator, and down on the street, made it seem more and more important that he find her and satisfy his feeling about this, else he would go on being troubled by it.

Cameron had made it a rule of his life to finish up a thing at once, after it had become important, else he found it would go on obtruding itself into items of business and confusing his mind. So now Astra had taken that position, and he must make himself satisfied about her. Oh, he didn't expect to see her much, but he didn't want to have that feeling of self-accusation toward her, she had been so exceedingly kind in the strange circumstances of the brief time he had known her.

So Cameron went around the corner to a little obscure drug store where he knew there was a telephone booth that was fairly secluded, and called up Astra.

He called and called, and grew almost annoyed at the operator but still the answer came back from the office boy that Miss Everson's phone did not answer.

At last the boy in the office recalled that he had seen Miss Everson go out a little while ago, and he was sure she had not yet returned.

Well, that was that. What should he do now? He had told Camilla that he had important business, and now there was no way in which he could complete it. But Cameron had a sense of honesty that held him to his purpose. Having made that business an excuse he must stick to it until he could find Astra, and somehow get rid of this feeling that he hadn't been quite fair to her. So he left a message for her when she should return, that he wished to see her, and would she kindly leave a telephone number where he could reach her if she had to go out again before he could call her.

He went to a small cheap restaurant where he could not possibly come into contact with Camilla and took a cup of coffee and a sandwich, read the evening paper with all the while an undertone of uneasiness about Astra. Yet there was no real reason for that feeling, of course. He was under no obligation to her. Yet try as he would he could not get away from a desire to make a pleasant time for her, at least until she could get into touch with her old friends. She was too friendly a soul to have to spend her holidays absolutely alone, as she had suggested she would be likely to do.

Well, since he was booked to spend Christmas Day with his stepmother, what could he do beforehand to make her have a pleasant time? Music? Yes, he had the symphony concert tickets of course. She could likely find an acquaintance to share them with her. He wasn't sure she liked music, but it seemed fairly probable. She was cultured in other ways, and must have had a well-rounded education. Music would have been a part of it of course. Well, he would try her on that. Should he offer her both tickets, suggesting that she might have a friend who would like to accompany her? Or should he just ask her to go with him? Would that lead her to think that he was trying to get in with her? Was there any possibility she might misunderstand? No, of course not. She was not a girl who was expecting every young man to fall for her. And after all he was an utter stranger to her.

Well, whatever he did he meant to see her tonight if she was seeable. He would go back to the place where she was stopping and sit in that reception room till she arrived. For surely she would be returning before very late. That is, if she were the kind of girl he judged her to be. Then he would judge by her welcome just how much farther he should go, whether he would offer the tickets, or ask her to go with him. Or perhaps he wouldn't do anything except to say that he just wanted to ask if there was anything he could do to help make the next few days less dreary till her friends were back at home. Well, he would see. And then afterwards he wouldn't be haunted with that nagging worry that he had turned her off abruptly.

Cameron waited until nine o'clock, too late, really, to go to the concert, and then went back to Astra's stopping place, but they said she had not as yet come in. So he settled down to wait, growing more and more uneasy about her as the minutes lengthened into an hour and then went on. Of course he kept wondering where she was, what might have befallen her perhaps, and he found that he was almost as worried lest she had gone into a world that did not seem to belong to her, as he was lest some harm had come to her. He did not want to be disappointed in her.

It was almost half past eleven when he saw her come wearily in at the street door. There was a gray look in her face as if she was about worn out, tired beyond expression. In his own brief experience with her, working on Mr. Faber's business, he had never seen her look like that. It seemed as if there was utter discouragement in her whole bearing. Had something happened to her? It couldn't be just loneliness that had made her look like that. It was almost as if there were fear in her big troubled eyes. Yet she wasn't a girl one would expect to be afraid of any ordinary thing. That was his first impression as she came toward him. He felt his duty toward her was all the more binding. She was a girl alone, at least temporarily, and he was a gentleman who knew her just enough to feel interested in her welfare. Perhaps there was something more practical even than escorting her to a symphony concert that he could do for her, and he simply had to find out what it was before he left. Was that going to be a task?

And then she saw him, and instantly her face changed. A kind of glad light came into her eyes, and a relief brightened the gray look over her countenance. She was really glad to see him! He knew that instantly, and the anxiety in his own eyes answered the welcome in hers. Well, at least he had his answer about a concert sometime. She would not resent his asking her to go with him.

With a sudden lightness of heart he got up and came to meet her, putting out his hand

and taking hers into a warm clasp. And with her small young hand in his he was instantly touched at its smallness and helplessness. She hadn't struck him as being helpless before. She had been a quiet, self-contained young woman who was fully able to direct her own life in a self-respecting manner. Yet now, as he held that small hand for that one briefly prolonged clasp, something appealing was there. The light in her eyes had called forth an answering light in his own he knew, and there was a surprising thrill in that hand-clasp which he had not been expecting. Yes, definitely, something electric and soulstirring had passed from one to the other.

It wasn't anything they could recognize except by the flash of a smile, that seemed to go on like treasured words into their startled senses, and make them understand that it was good for them to be there together. Good for both of them. They were not stopping to think about it, it was just a gladness pouring from one hand to the other, with a lingering dread to break it, that kept them standing there that extra prolonged second, and looking deep into each other's eyes, not aware that there was anything but just plain gladness in their gaze.

Then suddenly there were other people

coming in the door, staring wonderingly at the stranger who was there with that quiet girl by the hand. Who was he? Her brother? Husband? Or just a friend?

Cameron roused first.

Very quietly he let go of her hand, and turning led her to the couch in the far corner, away from the main hallway.

"I've been waiting here a long time for you," he said in a low tone, his eyes upon her face. "I wanted to see you a minute or two and make sure you are all right before I go away. And then afterward when you didn't come I got worried about you. I know you are acquainted with the city, but a city is such a desolate place at night for a woman alone, and there are so many things that can happen. I thought I'd just stick around and see if you were all right."

"Oh," she said with a little faint color tinging her pale cheeks. "That's very kind of you. And I'm sorry I kept you here so late. It was really carelessness on my part. You see I got a rather disturbing telegram, and it seemed necessary for me to hunt up the lawyer who had looked after my father's affairs. But he had moved to a new suburb that I didn't know very well, and when I finally reached him he was just going out to a banquet, and could give me but a very few minutes. That would have been all right. He told me what I needed to know, and how to get in touch with the people I needed to reach, but I hadn't realized that the suburban station would be closed, and there seemed no one at hand to ask where I would find a bus line. So I missed my way and had to do a good deal of walking. That is what makes me so late."

"And you were walking through strange country lanes alone as late as this!"

Cameron's face was deeply disturbed.

"How I wish I had known and might have gone with you! How gladly I would have driven you wherever you needed to go!"

"Well, I certainly thank you!" said Astra, the color coming sweetly into her cheeks now. For the look in Cameron's eyes stirred her more than she dared to believe. It was out of all proportion to the danger she might have been in. It gave her a sense of belonging to him, at least as a friend who was highly valued.

She struggled to get above the embarrassment that the situation brought upon her. She must not act as if it was anything unusual for a young man to express concern about her. Probably her own weariness and anxiety were making more of it than was really there. Yet she could not rise above her embarrassment. She was so tired that she wanted to sit down and cry, and she must get over this. Cameron was only being kind, and she mustn't be silly.

He sat there watching her for an instant, and then seeming to sense what was the trouble, said in a matter-of-fact tone:

"When did you have your dinner?"

Confusion came into her eyes at once as she glanced at the clock across the room.

"Why — I — don't just remember the hour," she evaded.

"Did you have any dinner at all?" he asked again, his eyes keenly upon her. The color came guiltily into her cheeks.

"Why — I — don't — *know!*" she said and broke down laughing. "I guess I didn't. I was so worried and so busy that I didn't think of it till you mentioned it."

"Exactly!" said Cameron reaching for his brief case and hat. "That settles it. We're going out for a good supper. I need a meal too. I had nothing but a sandwich and some coffee about five o'clock, and I've been waiting for you ever since. You'll have to take pity on me and eat some dinner! Come!"

He arose and took her hand, lifting her to her feet.

"Oh — no — I *couldn't,*" she said with distress in her voice. "Do you know how many times you have had to feed me? I'm just ashamed. Please let me go. I have some milk and crackers up in my room. I really shall be all right. You go and get something to eat. Find some of your friends, and don't bother any more about me."

"Well, I'm sorry you don't count yourself one of my own friends, for I was hoping you did. But friend or no friend, I'm going to make it my business once again to see that you eat a proper meal, and that before I take time out for conversation. And I really wanted to talk with you for a few minutes. Come on! I won't take no for an answer."

Almost on the verge of tears, she lifted a sudden grateful smile to him and went.

He put her into a taxi and took her to a very quiet little restaurant which he was sure Camilla would never have heard of, and he ordered a few delicious dishes for which he knew this special place was famous.

"Now," he said. "Do you like music? Maybe you'll think that question is irrelevant, because there won't be any music here. They never have it. I came here because I knew it would be quiet at this time of night, without a lot of blathering idiots screaming around and carrying on. But I really want to know if you like music."

She recognized that he was trying to put her at her ease, and she rallied quickly to be her normal self.

"Why, yes, of course, I love it. I was going to try to hunt some up tonight, if it hadn't been for that disturbing telegram that sent me off on a wild goose chase. Of course I love music. I wondered if this wasn't the night for your great orchestra concert."

He smiled.

"Yes, it was, but tomorrow night it's the orchestra and Choral Society together. *The Messiah*, you know. I was wondering if you count me enough of a friend to go with me?"

Then for an instant there came again that glad light into her eyes, and shot down into his soul doing definite things to their relation, the same light he had seen in her eyes when she came into the door and caught sight of him. His own heart bounded suddenly with a deep solemn throb of definite joy.

"Oh, I do," said Astra. "I don't feel that I really have a right to call you that because I'm just an utter stranger you picked up in an emergency, and I shouldn't have any respect for myself if I presumed on that acquaintance, but you certainly have been very kind to me, and it is nice to have you willing to go on being kind. Of course, I'll be glad to go to the concert with you. I'm not only hungry for food, but I'm really hungry for music. Father loved music and we always had season tickets for the symphony concerts and a number of other wonderful things. But since father is gone I've scarcely heard any. You see my cousins are not at all musical, and that rather barred me from even the radio concerts. If she heard a symphony or something really fine going on the radio my young cousin would come and turn it off. She had no patience with what she called 'stuffy music.' So I've been really starving for a little real music!"

"Well, now, that's nice! I've had all kinds of a time finding a companion who sincerely enjoyed good music. Most of them want to talk and laugh while it is going on. I'm fed up with that kind of a companion. But I sort of divined that you would be different."

"Well, thank you. At least I can promise you I won't do that. And I certainly am delighted to have a real concert to look forward to, after all the jazz I have had to endure the last two years."

That was the beginning, and soon they were launched on a subject that was of deep interest to both, and they forgot their momentary embarrassment, and enjoyed their meal as they ate slowly and talked, delighted to find how their opinions coincided.

Sitting there in the soft candlelight of the quiet pleasant shelter, they felt a oneness of spirit that brought a deep content. Even though both knew that it might be but a passing thing, still there was a great sweetness about it. And now and again their glances would meet and once more they would feel that flash pass between them. Sometimes Astra would remind herself that she ought not to have come here. This young man was a stranger, and there was the girl of the mink coat! She was probably a close friend. Didn't a girl with a mink coat love real music? It scarcely seemed possible she did not. Besides, Astra was going to miss this after it was over, if she let it go on. She was going to long to have a friend like this one. Decidedly she ought not to have come! The food was excellent, and the talk was exceedingly pleasant, but she should not have encouraged herself to enjoy things that could not be hers, for there would only be loneliness and heartache afterward if she got accustomed to delights like these.

And Cameron, wondering at himself, because he had not been a man to interest himself in girls, or to feel that they cared to talk intelligently about real things in these days, adjured himself not to watch Astra's beautiful eyes as they lifted with smiles that somehow went to his heart.

And when the dinner ended with a delicate ice and little enticing cakes, they sat slowly enjoying them, and Cameron suddenly spoke in a low intimate tone, as if he had a right to speak:

"Now, aren't you going to tell me about that disturbing telegram? I know I have no right to ask, but it does seem since you have come to my aid in a trying time, that I might presume to help a little in yours. I'll promise not to go any farther in my probing than you are willing I should, and I'll try not to be offensive in any advice, but I can't be quite happy about you until I know at least the nature of the thing that is worrying you."

For all the time they had been talking Cameron had been trying to figure out just what he ought to do. Dared he try to force her confidence? And would that precipitate an intimacy that would be unwise, or hasty, or one to which the girl could object? These thoughts were only in an undertone in the back of his mind, and at no time did his inclination or common sense yield to them in any way. His voice was uniformly kind and considerate, not in the least presuming, and neither did it seem so to Astra.

She hesitated a moment, looking down, a deeply troubled cloud suddenly overshadowing her face. Then she looked up smiling, taking a deep breath and trying to speak naturally.

"Oh, it wasn't such a terrible thing," she said. "It just upset me a little. I suppose there is no reason why I can't tell you, if you are interested to know. You might think it is worse than it really is. You know I told you that I had been making my home with some cousins since the death of my father."

Cameron nodded.

"Well, for some time I have been feeling that I would like to get away. They are rather worldly people, and were insistent upon my going their way into fashionable society where I did not feel happy, nor find congenial friends. Also there is a younger cousin who resents my presence in many ways, and manages often to put me into false situations. I thought it was time for me to return to the place where all my old friends were, and manage my own life in the way my father and mother would have wanted me to do. So while they were away on a trip to California I decided suddenly to leave. I wrote them a letter, thanking them for all they had done for me — although at my father's wish I had always paid my board while with them

— and I told them I felt it was time I should go. They were not expecting to return for a couple of weeks, and I merely left the note with the servants in the house and started. I did not want a big argument about it for I felt sure they would all be relieved to have the matter so amicably and quietly settled. But when I came back to my room this afternoon I found a telegram from my cousin ordering me to take the next train back to the house, and to wire him at once what train I was taking, or he would proceed to send the police after me. He said that he was my guardian and I must obey him at once! Naturally I was a good deal disturbed. Cousin Duke is not my guardian at all. He isn't even a real cousin. His wife was a second cousin of my mother's. My father didn't altogether trust him. He would never have put me in his care. I knew that Mr. John Sargent of this city was my legal guardian. I was sure there could not be a second guardian. But Mr. Sargent is sick in Florida. His son is away somewhere for over Christmas. Then I remembered there was a lawyer who looked after things, and I found his name in the book of instructions my father left for me, and started out to find him."

"You poor child!" said Cameron. "I should think you did need a friend. I wish you had counted me enough of a friend to have called me up and asked my advice. I would have been so glad to have helped."

"Well, I didn't think you ought to be troubled with the family affairs of a perfect stranger."

"Please, you're not a stranger any longer, you know. But tell me, did you get real help from your lawyer? Did he remember who you are?"

"Oh, yes, he has known me since I was a child and he told me definitely that Cousin Duke has absolutely no authority to give me orders. Mr. Sargent is my guardian. He advised me to send a telegram at once saying so, and letting him know I was among friends."

"Have you sent it?"

"No," said Astra. "I was just going to my room to write it when I saw you. I ought to do it right away."

"Yes, surely," said Cameron. "Have you planned what to say?"

"Not altogether," said Astra with trouble in her eyes again. "It would have to be a pleasant message for Duke has a terrible temper and if he gets angry he can certainly make a lot of trouble, even at a distance."

Cameron got out his pen and a pad from his pocket, and together they worked out

159

the message, which was finally sent.

Impossible to return now. Am among friends. Quite safe. You are mistaken about guardianship. Mr. Sargent is legal guardian. His lawyer advises staying as I come of age soon. There will be business to transact. Please forgive my hasty action. Sorry Miriam was disturbed. Letter follows by airmail.

Lovingly,
Astra.

Astra felt much better when this epistle was composed and started on its way. She bade Cameron good night with a brave smile, and a comforting memory of his close handclasp. Oh it was good to have a friend like this one, to whom she could tell her troubles, and not be afraid. A friend in whom she could trust. Suppose he did have a friend with a mink coat? He had a right to other friends of course, and just because she hadn't known him long didn't make any difference, did it? She could see from the way he was accepted everywhere, from their contacts with the Faber lawyer, from all that he did, his judgments, his wise ways, and carefulness of her and her reputation, that there was nothing to fear from him. And suppose he was attractive? She had to live and move in a world where there might be many attractive people. She had to run the risk of falling in love with every attractive man that came along. She simply mustn't allow herself to be silly or lonely.

Yet as she fell asleep, quieted and comforted, that last look from Cameron's eyes, that good night handclasp lingered in her heart with a glad little leap, and sent her off into a world of dreams where arrogant cousins could not follow.

 9 Camilla Blair had been calling up Cameron all the evening, intermittently, and had finally settled down to a box of chocolates and a book that everybody said of course she ought to read, having left word for Cameron that he was to call her as soon as he came in. So there was the message in his box when he stopped at the desk.

"Say, Mr. Cameron, that party sure is anxious to speak to you. She's called every few minutes for some hours. She must be dead and buried by this time, or else all her family," announced the fresh young clerk. He knew Cameron was not the kind that would report him. They were on pretty good terms, and Cameron always had a smile for those who served him.

Cameron frowned as he looked at the name, and made a little grimace.

"That so, Jarvis? Sorry she made so much trouble for you. It's likely only her handkerchief she wants picked up, or her shoe is untied. All right, I'll call her when I get upstairs."

So when Cameron was just ready to turn out his light he called Camilla.

"What's the matter, Camilla?" he asked.

"The house isn't on fire or anything, is it, you calling up so late."

"Late? Oh, Charlie! Don't try to be funny! This isn't late! The evening's just begun. But I thought you never would return. What can have been keeping you?"

"Business, always business," he answered promptly. "I had to wait on someone else. But didn't I understand you to say it wasn't late? Why fret now that I have come? What can I do for you? Is your hotel on fire? Do you need rescuing?"

"Now, don't be absurd, Charlie. I want a little amusement. I'm nearly dead of ennui. I want to be taken somewhere, either a late show or a place to dance, I'm not particular which, but at least you can come over and give me a sample of your brilliant conversation."

"You're getting that now over the phone, aren't you? You know I can't work all day and then play all night. I'm dog weary and I'm just about to climb into my little bed and sleep the sleep of the just. You'll just have to find someone else to play with you. I've grown up!"

"But Charlie! Don't you ever take time off?"

"Well, not at this time of the night if I can help it. Call up your friend Parkinson, or that song-in-the-night you call Sorrel. I should think they'd be tickled to death to help you out."

"But Charlie! Please! I want to talk to *you*, seriously. Won't you come over to the hotel just for a few minutes?"

"Couldn't do it, Miss Blair. I'm a working man, and I have work to do in the morning."

"Oh, Charlie, how aggravating you are! Well, then, when can I see you? That was one of my chief reasons for coming to the city. I wanted to see you. I have a plan and I need you to help me carry it out."

"Well, now, that's too bad! But honestly, Camilla, I haven't even a fragment of time from now till after New Year's. It's all been mortgaged up. Besides, I've promised my stepmother that I'd get home just as soon as possible and help her to have a pleasant holiday season. Nobody else will, I'm sure of that!"

"Well, I should say not! How absurd you are! Such a stepmother! Why should you want to do that? She certainly hasn't made it pleasant for the rest of your family. But say, Charlie, if you really mean to do that I might even sacrifice myself and come over for a few days, and help you entertain your childish stepmother."

"Quite unnecessary, my lady. That step-

164

mother of mine is more than uncommonly canny. She would see right through you like a pane of glass and know you didn't like her. I don't think you'd feel at all comfortable, and I'm sure I shouldn't. I would be feeling almost sorry for you, for she has a dignity all her own that can show you up to yourself until you lose all your cocksureness, and you'd come out of it, if you stayed long enough for good results, wishing you hadn't. And moreover, you'd have great respect for her, and almost admiration for her in spite of not liking her. However, when I go home to entertain my stepmother, I prefer to go unaccompanied. We get along excellently together when we are alone. And now, Camilla, isn't that about all we have to say? Run along and hunt a playmate, for I'm sort of tired."

With a few more bitter words Camilla Blair hung up sharply. She just wasn't getting anywhere. She decided it must be another girl. Although all his sisters said there wasn't one, Camilla decided there must be. But Charles Cameron went about his preparations for rest with a genial grin on his face. He was wondering how much longer he was going to have to be hounded by this persistent Camilla. And as he drifted off to sleep, he was comparing her insistent demands to the quiet withdrawal of the girl he had found on the train. So far he hadn't seen anything yet in Astra that disappointed him. Tomorrow night would be a good test. He could tell whether a girl enjoyed real music or whether she was just putting up a cultured front.

Astra, when she woke in the morning was immediately aware that today was another day, and held great possibilities. True, there was a concert in the offing with a young man whose company she must own she enjoyed, but that was a long way off, and when evening came no telling what might have happened to prevent her going.

For by this time her telegram must have reached California, and it was quite thinkable that Duke might be angry enough even to waste money taking a plane to come over and visit vengeance on her head. He had been known to do things like that, even at a time when he was very hard up financially. So it was up to her to get some very definite immediate knowledge concerning her rights, and just where she stood according to law.

She dressed hurriedly, ate her meager breakfast of crackers and milk, and spent a few minutes studying her father's little book of directions. Then she wrote a kindly letter to her cousin Miriam.

Dear Miriam:

I am sorry to have to write this letter under these circumstances, I did not want to talk about anything disturbing while you were on a holiday. But since Duke's telegram came I felt I must explain more fully than I did in my note.

For a long time I have been thinking that I ought to leave the shelter of your home and strike out for myself, for I could see more and more that I was in many ways a hindrance and an annoyance to Clytie, although she has tried to be very nice about it. Also, I could see that I must be a disappointment to you in many ways. I am not fond of parties and operas and social affairs, and it brings a frequent difference of opinion between us, which does not make for happiness of course. So, as I thought it over after you left, I felt it would be a good thing for me to go now, while you are away, and there would be no chance for discussion. I'm sure, when you understand my reasons you will agree with me that it was just as well for me to get it settled and over with and not make you feel that you ought to urge my staying.

For you have been most kind, you know. But I am sure my father did not expect me to become a permanent burden on you, and he often talked with me about what I would do when I was entirely alone. So I am not without his advice in this matter either.

You see, father was anxious that I should do some revising and copying on some of his articles that he was not able to prepare for publication himself.

At first it did not seem to me that I could get out his beloved work and go at it by myself, but now, after the good rest I have had in your home, I find I am growing eager to get at it again. The more so that I received a letter a few days ago from his publisher, urging that I send them the manuscript he had promised them before he died.

Also, there was some writing that my father was very anxious for me to do on my own account. Writing that through all the years he has been preparing me for. And I feel as if the time had come for me to get started on it. Of course I can do that better here, where we had worked together. And that is why I felt I should make the break now, while you are away, and it would not be so hard.

You know, too, that it is only a little over a month now before I shall be coming of age, and therefore have a right to order my own life.

I am here where all my old friends are, the Sargents, our old lawyer, and doctor, a lot of my own schoolfriends, and I am hoping to be very pleasantly located after Christmas, in a place that I shall enjoy, because my father and I were there together.

So I hope that you will not feel badly about my going, and I feel sure you and Cousin Duke will soon come to feel it was for the best. Hoping you will continue to have a lovely trip.

With loving wishes for you all,
Astra.

Astra read over the letter carefully, hoping that she had not left in any of the rancor and hard feeling that the telegram had brought to her heart. Then after careful consideration she added a postscript.

I have left a few things behind because I thought they would be much more useful to Clytie than to me, in the life that I shall now be living. I'll be so glad if she will keep the fur coat. I thought it was so becoming to her when she wore it away, and my squirrel one is all that I

169

shall need this winter. If I have left anything she doesn't want, just throw it away or give it to someone who can use it.

Astra addressed the envelope quickly with a glance at her watch. She was to meet Mr. Lauderdale at his office at eleven o'clock and there was barely time for her to get there promptly.

The lawyer smiled as she entered his private office, and arose to greet her.

"You are like your honorable father, aren't you? Exactly on time. Sorry I had to hurry away so rudely last night, but it was important that I get there before the people sat down. Now, will you sit down, and we will go over your affairs. I have the papers ready. Mr. Sargent asked me before he went away to look after you. He was very anxious, although I don't think he expected you to come east."

"No," said Astra. "I decided suddenly, while my cousins were away. I felt it was time I came back and got to work in the way my father had hoped I would. I knew it would be easier to get away without argument if I left while they were gone. I sent the telegram last night as you suggested."

She laid down a paper containing a copy of the telegram.

170

The lawyer read it, and nodded. "Very good," he said, "I don't see how they can take offense at that. Besides if they make any further trouble just let me know. I have your father's papers with rather definite directions about your coming of age. And do I understand that you have been paying your board as your father provided for?"

"Oh yes. They objected to taking it at first, but soon got used to it when they understood father wanted it done."

"And they gave you receipts?"

"Why, father said the checks would be receipts. I have kept the checks of course."

"That's good. And I think it was a very wise thing to come away at this time. It is just as well not to have other people knowing all your private affairs. And by the way, you asked about guardianship. Here is the paper, written in your father's own hand, which arranged that Mr. Sargent should be your guardian. And in the event of his death, or incapacitation, his brother Lewis and I were to share in looking after you and your affairs until you took them over yourself. No mention was made of your cousin, Mr. Lester, and none of young Will Sargent in connection with your affairs. Your father felt that Will was too young. He is rather a gay irresponsible fellow just now of course, and

171

I wouldn't advise you to consult with him. He knows very little of his father's actual business. And now where are you staying, and what were your plans? Can I help in any way?"

"I am at the Christian Association apartments, but I intend as soon as I can get my bearings to hunt around and find some place where I can feel at home where it won't cost so much. The Association is more than I ought to pay, I guess."

"Not at all," said Mr. Lauderdale. "It was arranged by the will that if at any time before your majority it seemed wise for you to establish a place of your own, one of the houses owned by your father's estate, or an apartment, or even just rooms in some suitable place, you were to be properly financed. Suppose you look things over and decide what you would like to do, and we'll arrange the financial part. You know you will have enough to make you very comfortable, and I have the right to advance you money for your needs even before you are of age. My advice to you is to go slow however, until you are sure just what you want to do. And by the way, there are two of your houses available if you should want either. One is the little stone cottage out Willow Haven way. You probably remember it. The old lady who has been renting it, a former nurse or servant of some sort, of your mother, seems to think she has to leave it. She is living on a small pension, and I believe her son-in-law has persuaded her that it is more economical for her to come and live with them and pay her board instead of staying by herself."

"Why, that would be Tilly Dager, our old Tilly!" said Astra joyfully. "I was wondering where I could find her, or if she is still alive. I'll go out and see her and find out about it. But I don't believe I would care to go out there to live. It has no memories for me like the other. But I'd like to see Tilly."

"Well, suppose you sound her out, whether she wants to keep it. We'll need to know when her year is out, and that's pretty soon. Poor old soul, I think her son-in-law is calculating on getting a new car, and he wants her pension money."

"Well, I'll see what can be done about it. If Tilly wants it I'd be glad to help her stay there."

"And then there is your old home, about to be vacant," went on the lawyer. "Mr. Albans and his wife have been living there, you know. A good deal of your family furniture is still stored there, I think."

"Yes," said Astra eagerly, "I was going to

ask you about that. Father's notes and books and desk and everything are there, and it is with them I want to work pretty soon. Would I be able to go there now and look things over?"

"Why, I guess you could. I don't see any reason why not. Mr. Albans has had a nervous breakdown, and the doctor has told him that he and his wife both need to go to Florida, or California, and stay out in the sunshine. They called me up the other day and asked the possibilities. The doctor would like them to go very soon, but they do not feel they can afford to keep the house indefinitely, and they think they may stay and locate permanently wherever they go. They called me up to see if they had a right to sublet. Of course the fact that your goods are in the house made it a difficult problem to solve, so I told them I would consult with Mr. Sargent, and let them know as soon as possible. You know of course that the Albans were intimate friends of your father's, and they feel that they want to do the best for you. You might keep this in mind. It will not be an easy matter to rent the house again unless your goods are moved, and of course it could not be sold until they were out. I believe that your father's idea was that the house should not be sold until you are of age, lest you might want to keep it."

"Yes," said Astra with a wistful look, "I'd love to keep it. Suppose I go and look it over, and get some of my necessary papers, and then I can decide more intelligently."

"Yes, that's a good idea," said the lawyer. "Perhaps you'll call me up when you get back. I shall be in the office until five-thirty, and I'd like to know how you feel about it. Of course we would have to put your goods in storage somewhere else if we tried to get another tenant, for I wouldn't feel like putting a stranger there with your father's valuable things in the house, and you haven't ever looked them over yourself either, have you? Well, we had better attend to that at once. Suppose you find out from Mrs. Albans just what their plans are and how soon they would be wanting to leave. I'm sorry I can't offer you hospitality during the holidays, but my wife is out in Ohio visiting our daughter and our little new grand-daughter, and I'm scheduled to leave Monday night to join them till after Christmas. But we'll try and get you fixed up comfortably somewhere. How do you find it at that Association place? Is it very desolate?"

"Oh, no, it's quite comfortable," said Astra cheerfully. "I'm getting along beautifully."

"Well, you seem a lot like your cheerful father. But now, you spoke last night of having had some money stolen from you. Was it much?"

"All the last quarter's allowance! You see I had just cashed it, and paid my board out of it, having in mind the possibility of going away, perhaps coming here, and also getting some Christmas gifts for friends. But when I went back to my room after bidding my cousins goodby I found someone had been in my room and taken it."

"Do you suspect anyone?"

"Yes, but I would have no proof whatever, and I decided, since I was coming away, I would rather not do anything about it. It would embarrass my cousins very much if I should try to do anything about it, and it wasn't any of the servants, I am sure, for they are trusted servants, and wouldn't have to steal."

"But do you think it is right to let a thief go free?"

"No, but in this case it would be better for me not to be the one that told. It may come out without me. In any event I could not prove it."

"Well," said the lawyer, studying the girl's sweet face earnestly. "I suppose it must have been one of the family, probably that young cousin, whom I seem to feel is a hateful piece, and if that is the case I can see how you feel. I suppose I can understand why you are willing to let it go if that is it, though I'm not saying you are right. However, I can't see how you had money to come away lacking all that installment, unless you had saved a lot."

Astra's cheeks had crimsoned, and she lifted honest eyes to the lawyer's, but she did not deny what he had suggested, and in a minute more he asked amusedly:

"Just how did you manage your journey, my dear?"

Astra smiled grimly.

"Well, I had a few things I could sell, some bits of jewelry, old gold and silver. They didn't bring much, but every little counts. I had bought a few clothes that I really didn't need, and I found I could return them and get the money back. And for the rest I pawned some books that I didn't want to lose entirely. I can send for them as soon as more money comes in."

"Well, you certainly were resourceful. But now we'll end that matter once for all."

He swung around to his desk, wrote a check and handed it out to her.

"Will that see you through till we can have a settlement?"

She glanced at it, and her cheeks flushed.

"Oh yes, I don't need so much now. Just a little would help me out."

"That's all right. We'll fix it up when the time of settlement comes. And don't forget that if you need any help in any way just call on me till Mr. Sargent comes home. You'll be glad to know that I had word today that he is decidedly better, and I shall soon be able to tell him about your coming and get things straightened out. Now, are you anticipating any further trouble with that western cousin? Do you think you'll be entirely safe till I get back from Ohio?"

"Oh, I'm sure I will."

"Well, if you need me just call me on the telephone. I'll leave you my address and telephone number. And don't stop because you think it's expensive. Remember I'm responsible for you now till Mr. Sargent gets back. Now, don't forget to call me before five-thirty. Take that check down to the old bank and start an account. You remember where the bank is, don't you?"

"Oh yes," said Astra happily, and thanking him she hurried away. The air was clear and bright, the snow dazzling, a real before-Christmas day. God was in His Heaven, and smiling down upon her. Her own money in the bank, not borrowed. It almost seemed as if things were getting right in her world. Besides she was going to an orchestra concert tonight. The thought danced before her mind like a bright particular star.

After she put her check in the bank, she took a bus out to Willow Haven, thinking, trying to plan as she went. Suppose she took one of her own two houses. She couldn't live absolutely alone. Her father had been insistent about that. If she was older it might be all right, but a young girl had no business living alone in the world, he said. For one thing, although she might be in a perfectly safe place so far as harm that could come to her was concerned, it didn't look well. He didn't approve of girls going out into the world alone. They could always go to a reputable place where there were other respectable people. It looked much better.

But of course she would love to have her whole house, and Mr. Lauderdale had seemed to think she could afford it if she preferred that way of living. He had even spoken as if she could afford to pay for a sort of housekeeper who would be on the order of a companion. Would Tilly do for that? Was Tilly able to work and would she want to go back into service again? How old was Tilly anyway?

But these were things she would have to find out before she committed herself.

As the bus swung into town and drew up half a block from the little stone dwelling where Tilly lived she glanced at her watch to note how long it had taken her to get there. A little over an hour. No, that was too far away from town for her to live. She wanted to be near enough to go to concerts and meetings and to church evenings alone sometimes, and she wanted to be where there was taxi service, at least for the present. Sometime maybe she might have a car, but that was something she would not plan for. And a girl alone had no place in the country, unless she meant to stay at home the rest of her life.

The country was white with snow now. In some places along the road they had come there was no sidewalk, no place for the pedestrian except in the road, dodging among traffic, of which there seemed to be plenty, even so far from the city. There was a continual procession of great trucks, coal trucks and oil trucks and produce trucks of every kind and description. She saw herself making her way on foot along this highway alone at night, with snow underfoot and snow coming down from Heaven, and while she wasn't a coward in any sense, and was ready to do what had to be done, she knew her father would never have wanted her to locate herself where loneliness would be her continual lot. So the little stone house, pretty as it was, and attractive in many ways, was out of the question for a home for her. Neither was old Tilly likely to be the right companion for her days.

But she walked up to the door and knocked, and after quite a long minute the door was opened by an old woman with very red eyes who was tying on a clean apron, and trying to keep her face in shadow so her red eyes would not be noticed.

"Is this Tilly Dager?" cried Astra, her heart stirred by memories, as she recalled how often when a little girl she had seen Tilly hurrying to get her clean apron tied before opening the front door.

The old woman looked up keenly at the girl, and then her fumbling fingers dropped the strings of the apron and it fell to the floor between them while old Tilly put up her hands in startled recognition.

"Why, it's Miss Aster! It really is, isn't it? Oh, Miss Aster, wherever did you come from? Oh, come in, come in! Ef I'd only knowed you was coming I'd uv hed the house as fine as a new pin. But it's all upset, an' I'm that ashamed. Come in, come in, and set down, and please excuse."

"Don't worry about the house, Tilly. I've come to see you and find out how you are. But what's the matter? Tilly, you've been crying. Has something happened? Tell me all about it."

Astra stooped and picked up the crisp apron, and Tilly gathered it to her face and buried her tears in its clean folds.

"Oh, Miss Aster, I shouldn't be troublin' you with my worries." She lifted her tear-stained face in an attempt to stem the tide of sorrow, but the tears continued to drip from her lashes and the end of her plain little insignificant nose.

"There, Tilly, sit down in this chair and tell me all about it," said Astra, drawing up another chair beside the old woman. "Now, what is the trouble? Anything I can help about?"

"It's me son-in-law!" burst forth the woman, burying her face once more in the apron for another fall of tears, and then rousing and lifting her eyes again struggling for control. "He's that set on having a new car that he's determined ta get my poor little pension ta hep pay for it."

"Oh, but he can't do that!" said Astra.

"Yes, but he says he can. He says I'm ta come live with him and Matie, me daughter.

That it's extravagant fer us ta keep up two houses, and ef I'm with them I can hep worruk, and I ken stay with the childer when they goes out nights. That ud be all right ef he wasn't sa ugly in his home. He scolds my daughter when he isn't pleased, and he scolds the children something terrible, and he scolds me, and I can't abide it all. And me with me own little house he wants ta take away."

"But he can't do that, Tilly."

"Oh, but ya don't know! Just yester he went in town and he hunts up Mr. Lordedale the one I rents me house from, and he come back and tells me that Mr. Lordedale says I can't rent the cottage any longer for the price I can pay. He says the rent's raised ten dollars more a month and I've got ta get out next week, the end o' the month!" and Tilly went off in another paroxysm of weeping.

"But that's not so, Tilly!" exclaimed Astra eagerly. "I own this house, and Mr. Lauderdale didn't raise the rent at all. I was just talking with him a little while ago. He told me you sent him word you had to leave, that your daughter's family needed you."

But Tilly was weeping so hard she couldn't hear, and Astra had some ado to get the truth across to her. But at last after telling it over and over again, Tilly finally raised her bleared eyes, with a mingling of eagerness and unbelief.

"Do ya mean it's your house, Miss Aster? This house b'longs ta *you?* And you mean the rent ain't raised?"

"I certainly do, Tilly. And what's more I'm not going to let it be raised. Not to you. I'm going to lower it. From now on it's going to be five dollars less a month but don't you tell your son-in-law that or he'll try to get you to give it to him for his car. Let him buy his own car, and you keep your little house here. It's your right. It will be nice to have your grandchildren come and visit you. You can teach them a lot of good things the way you used to me."

Tilly wavered out a watery smile.

"Bless yer heart, Miss Aster. You was always such a dear little good girl! But my grandchilder, they ain't made ta mind. Their father won't let me teach 'em, and they are growing up sassy ta me. He makes 'em despise me. And ef I went ta live with them I'd havta sleep with Kitty, the oldest girl, and she's hateful. She takes the whole bed, and kicks me in the night till I'm that black and blue I can't rightly work next day."

"Well, Tilly, that's dreadful! Now Tilly,

you just tell your son-in-law you are going to stay in your home. Are you able to stay here alone, Tilly?"

"Oh, sure, I can stay here. Besides I got a teacher staying with me. She's young and alone, and she can't pay me much, but it's something."

"Well, then you just tell your son-in-law that you are not coming! He has no right over you!"

"But Miss Aster, he says he'll go to the pension people and tell them I have no right ta that pension, and they'll take it away."

"Well, there! Tilly! You needn't worry about that. Mr. Lauderdale is a lawyer, and he'll fix that all up for you. Now don't worry any more!"

At last she brought cheer to the worried old face, and went away promising to look after the rent and the pension and to come out and see her again soon when she got located herself, for she was probably coming back to the city to live.

As she sat down in the bus returning cityward she thought it all over and decided that definitely, no, Tilly was not the one to be her only companion. Tilly had her own mission to keep her little house and make a refuge for her daughter, and the wild little grandchildren. And she, Astra, would make it her business to see that Tilly had her house and that her pension should not be disturbed, nor get into the hands of her unscrupulous relatives.

It was twelve o'clock when she got back to the city, and now she was most anxious to get to the old house where she used to live when her father was with her, so she took another bus and went her way. Presently she was walking up the stone steps of the big old house where she had been born, and having a struggle to keep back the tears. Was Mrs. Albans at home, and what would the outcome here be?

10

Just about that time Rosamond Cameron and Camilla Blair were taking lunch together at the country club that was not too far from Rosamond's home, so that she could easily get a bus back home and change for her bridge club which met that afternoon.

"So you didn't get anywhere with my stubborn brother, you say, Cammie? I certainly am surprised, because he is usually so polite, *at least,* even if it's something he doesn't want to do."

"Well, I wouldn't say he was even polite," said the aggrieved Camilla. "I told him I had something very important to talk over with him, something you and I were planning, and —"

"Oh, that's a shame, Camilla! I ought to have told you not to mention my name. Just now I've been having several discussions with him, trying to get him to stay away from the stepmother, and he probably thinks this has something to do with it. I declare he is simply maddening. I hoped if you threw yourself on his mercy and told him how bored you were staying in a strange city he would do what you wanted. I believe you could wind him around your little finger, if

187

you only could get a start. He's really a darling, you know, if you just get on the right side of him."

Camilla lifted an offended chin.

"Well, I did everything I could, Roz, and he was just as oafish as he could be. I really don't think it's worth while for me to try any further. You know I'm not used to crawling on my hands and knees for attention, and after all I've got plenty of friends in the city if I only take the trouble to let them know I am here. But do you know what I think, Roz? I believe he's got another girl! Men don't act so positively indifferent that way unless there's another woman in the case."

"No, Camilla. It's not that. I'm sure! Positive! Charlie has never been much for going with girls. And then you know there's nothing like a bunch of sisters for finding out all there is to know about their brothers."

"Yes, but you girls have been away from home several years now. You don't know what's been going on."

"Indeed I do!" declared Rosamond. "We girls have had him on our mind, and we are determined he shall not spring some undesirable on us. You know he's pretty reserved, and not everyone can get near enough to him to find out just what he's aiming to do, but we girls understand him pretty well, and we've made it our business, one or the other of us, to get in touch with him once a week at least. We have a regular system for watching him. And so far he's fancy free. Of that I am definitely sure!"

"Well, I don't know. You may think you're sure of course, but I'd be willing to bet there's another girl somewhere in the offing!" and Camilla helped herself generously to more whipped cream over her Christmas strawberries.

"Well now, listen, Camilla, I've got a scheme. If you are just willing to co-operate I'm sure it will work out. How are you fixed for Christmas Day? Could you run down to my house and work in on a plan?"

"Yes, I suppose I could," drawled Camilla indifferently, "but you'll have your pains for your trouble. He told me positively that he had promised to spend Christmas Day with that pestiferous stepmother of his. You can rest assured the girl is some friend of hers, and that she has planned it all. He's probably going to meet her there. All right, what's your plan? I'm game. I'll try it."

"Well, you see," said Rosamond, "my husband has been trying for several years to get me to go on a trip with him for Christmas Day. He says the children are so young that one day is just as good as another to them,

189

and we can have our celebration with them when we get home. They won't know the difference. But I know they will know, they hear other children talk, you know, and my idea is to somehow prolong the celebration. I thought if I could get Charlie to come and stay with them they would think it was great. They just adore their Uncle Charlie, and he's always good fun with them. And if there's one thing that would make him beg off from the stepmother it would be because he pitied my kids who were to be left alone on Christmas Day of all days. So I would tell him I'd get some woman to come in and help out part of the day with them. And the maids would be there of course to get a festive little dinner, and look after the baby a little, and I thought if you would just drop in a little early perhaps, and happen to find Charles there, and offer to help him out or something, you could have a glorious day together, and it would be quite domestic. You would have a whole day to really get acquainted."

Camilla's large eyes grew speculative.

"Well, that might be a good idea, but I can see a hundred ways in which a plan like that might go haywire."

"Oh, yes," said Rosamond, "so can I, if you want to be disagreeable. I only suggested it because you seemed so anxious to see Charles. But I suppose it would bore you to be around with children a whole day."

"Indeed no, I'd love it. To tell you the truth I've never had much to do with children. However, if Charles was there he'd probably be the whole show. Surely, I'll cooperate! You'll have to give me the high sign, when to go, and what to say, and all that. How many children are there?"

"Three, a boy and two girls. And I'll write out some suggestions. Of course it may not work out. Charles is pretty stubborn. And then there is the old lady to deal with. She may hold him to his promise. I'll have to get in some work on her, make her see she's spoiling Charlie's chances. Mary can do that better than any of us. She hasn't got such a sharp tongue as I have. All right then, I'll be letting you know, be seeing you or calling you up, depending how soon I can make the thing work."

So the two ladies parted and went their separate ways. Camilla went into a toy shop as she passed and bought two dolls and a toy top that sang songs as it spun. The top was for the boy, assuming that he was the youngest and the baby. And of course all girls liked dolls, no matter what age they were.

That evening Rosamond called up her sister Mary, who thought the plan lovely, and eagerly accepted the office of attending to the stepmother and seeing that she did no damage to the scheme.

Sunday afternoon Mary in turn called the stepmother on the telephone, and incidentally let it be known that Rosamond was going on a trip with her husband for over Christmas, that is if Rosamond could prevail upon Charles to spend Christmas Day with the children. He was the only one she would trust to keep them happy and make them forget that she was away.

Sunday evening the stepmother sat down by her desk and wrote a letter to Cameron:

Dear Charles:

I have had a letter from my sister Nancy. She has fallen downstairs and broken her hip, and she is at home with two nurses, but she is very anxious to have me come and spend Christmas Day with her, so I guess I should go.

I have been looking forward to your coming of course, and am sorry not to be here, but I know you will not mind. You were always so reasonable, and since your father is not here for the holiday it cannot be so very pleasant for you, so perhaps this will leave you free for a little good time in your own way.

I knew of course that you were coming for my sake, because I am alone, and I appreciate your kindness, but I guess my duty lies with my sister this time, and perhaps you will come and see me on or after New Year's. And if you will like to bring somebody with you that will be very nice, just let me know.

Wishing you a very happy Christmas and a good New Year,

Your loving stepmother,
Margretta Ann Cameron.

But while she was writing this epistle Charles Cameron was preparing to take Astra out for the evening. He had a great deal of back work to catch up with for it had been a strenuous week, and he was far behind. But in between he kept wondering why he was so unreasonably happy. And now and again it would occur to him that it was Astra with whom he was going out, and he was sure that Astra would love the concert.

Meantime Astra was having experiences of her own.

She found Mrs. Albans down with a sick headache, yet getting up continually to wait upon her sick husband. She put Mrs. Albans to bed with tea and toast, and promised to stay a little while and talk to Mr. Albans, who seemed weak and desolate, but who cheered up wonderfully under Astra's ministrations and ate a better lunch than he had eaten since his illness.

And after a little they talked about the house, and about the possibility of Astra's taking it over, at least for a little while if the Albans ventured to take a trip to the south or west and investigate what would be best for the future.

Then Astra made Mr. Albans take a nap, while she went up to the third story where her father's goods were stored, and to the big safe built into the stone wall, where he had left his valued papers and notes of his writings.

Everything was just as she remembered it had been. Nothing seemed to have been touched, and she was relieved at that, for she had often got to thinking what if this or that happened, a fire or some repair to the house, that would necessitate disturbing the storage part.

Just touching, handling the beloved papers, reading a sentence here and there, brought such memories that the tears came often and blurred her eyes. But she managed to gather out a few papers that she felt she could get to work at very soon. Perhaps they would help her through Christmas Day. It would be like spending Christmas with her father.

When she came downstairs Mrs. Albans was up and feeling much better, and they had a nice talk. The Albans asked Astra if she wouldn't like to come in and stay with them, at least for a few days before they could get ready to leave, and longer if she chose, and Astra promised to think it over and let them know definitely soon. Then she went to the kitchen and prepared two trays for them. More tea and toast, and two bowls of soup, and she left them talking happily about the trip they were to take.

But Astra was almost out of breath with hurrying by the time she got back to her room. She wanted to be ready when Cameron came. She did not stop long over her supper. She was too eager for the evening. She put on one of her pleasant frocks that had been bought in accordance with her oven taste, not Miriam's. It was a simple little dress of soft heavenly blue that matched her eyes, and brought out gold tints in her hair, brought also a faint pink tinge to her cheeks. This with her gray squirrel coat made a lovely combination.

And there was a small hat with a band of squirrel curling about the crown like a feather. She looked very nice in it, and her cheeks were rosy with pleasant anticipation.

As she stepped from the elevator into the hall Cameron sat awaiting her, and he started with surprise and evident admiration at her changed appearance. He had never seen her except in the simple dark suit and hat she had worn on the train, and he was almost startled at her young beauty. He had admired her before, but he hadn't realized how lovely she could be in gala garb.

There was something deeper than just admiration in his eyes as he came forward to meet her, a spark of that flash that had passed between them twice before, yet touched with the tender kind of reverence a right-minded man gives to a lovely lady. Astra felt a warm glow about her heart. Oh, it was good to have a friend like this! There might be mink coats in the offing, but she felt she had as much right to a friendship as mink.

"You are looking very lovely," he said in a low tone, glancing down at her as he walked to the door beside her. "I certainly am going to be proud this evening, Beautiful Lady!"

Astra's cheeks went rosy red, making her all the more lovely.

"Oh, thank you!" she said, and then she added, "Not half as proud as I with you for an escort!"

"Keenly spoken," he laughed, looking down into her eyes, as he drew her arm within his own, and brought her close. Then again their glances went heart-deep and brought a thrill of joy.

But Astra was too well brought up not to be a little worried that she should feel so elated over this man's words, and tender looks. He was a stranger, she continually told herself, and there was that mink lady! And now his other hand was warmly upon hers that lay upon his arm, but it did not feel like a stranger's hand. It seemed like something well known and very precious. Was this surprising thought one that was going to make her trouble later on, perhaps when a mink coat appeared sometime? How silly she was! She simply must keep her thoughts in leash, and just enjoy the evening to its full, not making too much out of anything. That was the way. It was probably all the outcome of her being alone and lonely so much, this silly interest in a stranger.

Then he put her in the taxi his fingers lingering on her little gloved hand, as if he liked to touch it. Somehow he didn't seem like just the stranger who had called her out of the carful of unknown ones, to perform a service for another stranger. He seemed so like an old friend, and as if her father and mother knew him well and honored him. Why did she feel that way? She must put that question away to think over later when she had time to go into it.

The city was wide and bright with Christmas lights. Great stars looked quietly down from Heaven above on the tawdry super-lights of men, as if they were smiling at children's efforts to bring brightness to the world. And Cameron was there beside her, watching her, their shoulders touching in pleasant comradery. He seemed so strong and big as they sat there together, and in spite of herself she had that queer little natural feeling with him as if they rightly belonged together. What was the matter with her? Was the whole evening going to be spoiled for her by this silly interest in a strange young man, and must she go through the happy hours continually reproving herself? How altogether foolish! She hadn't done anything wrong or unmaidenly. Better forget it and have a good time.

They talked about the lovely lights along the way that came and went in reds and greens and blues. They admired the great

Santa Claus that stood like some sturdy giant at the cross roads. They heard distant chimes ringing in a far-off church, sounding above the traffic of the noisy street, telling of a living Christ above the effigy of a dead Santa Claus whom the world was half worshiping. They were halted by traffic again and again as they rode down the broad avenue toward the hall of music and they sat quietly studying the people who hurried by on the street, studying the faces of broad dowagers in cars, with sulky husband-escorts. It was all a motley crowd, and made them feel more and more apart to themselves, off to have a gala time. They did not talk a great deal. It seemed enough just to be there together, and say now and then a word or two.

And then they had arrived, and they started with the throng up the stairs in close-packed columns, a part of a great group of music's devotees. Or were they all, wondered Astra, as she studied the quiet peaceful faces of some of those who were of the company. Christians, maybe. They looked it. The music was definitely Christmas music. And people of the world generally were not particularly interested in definitely religious music. Of course at Christmas! And by old masters! That would make a difference.

When they were seated Cameron enjoyed watching the audience with her, pointing out certain celebrities that she might not recognize, certain well known men of the business and political world.

And then the music began. A solo voice, soprano, pure and sweet. "Comfort ye my people, saith your God," and there came a look into Astra's face of yearning, wistfulness, an eager receiving, as if she felt her need of comfort and was reaching out to take it.

Covertly Cameron watched the girl he had brought, and knew in his heart he had been right about her. She had rare appreciation not only of music, but of the great theme it was built upon.

And when the chorus burst forth in one grand prophetic strain, it seemed as though the girl's face reflected the great proclamation of the words: "And the glory of the Lord shall be revealed, and all flesh shall see it together; for the mouth of the Lord hath spoken it." As he watched her changing expression, it was as if she were standing on some high hilltop above the valleys that were to be exalted, were hearing the proclamation from the Lord Himself, and delight was breaking on her face, a great light in her eyes. As if she cared about this prophecy. As if it were something real that she felt was going to happen, and she might see it! Those words had never meant that to him. She must have something that he had never had. The Bible must be different to her. He had always taken it for granted that he believed it, but it had never seemed real to him. Never more than an uttering of a mere tradition. Undoubtedly it meant more to her than it did to him. How did she get that utter belief, that feeling of reality? Was it something he could have?

Then came the wonderful bass voice, speaking terrible words that if one really believed them must make the heart of the listener quail:

"But who may abide the day of His coming; and who shall stand when He appeareth? For He is like a refiner's fire."

The announcement was tremendous, and Cameron felt his own heart quiver with the thought. But looking quickly at Astra he saw no hint of fear in her quiet face. It was evident that the coming of the Refiner held no terror for her. How did she get that way? Was she born so, or had she learned this great peace that seemed so to belong to her? Sometime he would ask her, when they had opportunity to talk. He went on thinking about it as the music continued. How could anybody in the world be happy any more realizing what this meant, and truly believing it? Then like a pageant the world in its different classes and nations and peoples began to pass before him. People coming on and on through the ages to meet that time when the Refiner's Fire should come to them, and they would have to meet it. Could anybody be happy ever with the realization of such a Coming ahead?

The contralto had taken up the song now, but the change of voice did not arrest his attention. It might have been just another angel proclaiming the great plans of a great God. He seemed under a kind of spell. He heard none of the words of that solo except the closing, so soft and tender and sweet that it fell like a blessing, a benediction from the hushed roof. "Emmanuel, God with us." It left a tender touch in the air as it died away. There was gladness, too, almost too deep for utterance in the voice of the singer. And yet these words must mean the same God about whom the question had been asked: "Who shall stand when He appeareth?"

Ah! There were some, then, to whom the thought "God with us" brought nothing but wonderful joy. What a God was this? What joy to feel so sure one belonged to Him!

Cameron felt himself being carried away

by the thought, by the longing to share this marvelous joy that was evidently a possession of the girl who sat listening so intently beside him.

Then the joyous-voiced chorus took up the strain again, on to that great triumphant climax: "Arise, shine, for thy light has come, and the glory of the Lord is risen upon thee." Suddenly he felt that it had risen as he had never dreamed glory could rise. "The people that walked in darkness have seen a great light." That was himself! He drew a deep breath and tried to shake his mind out of this phantasm. It was all imagination of course, an emotion that came from the lure of the music and majestic words, whose effect he could vision in the face of this girl. Was that all it was with her, too?

Then softly as an angel might have sung above a sleeping baby, the music began again. The great company of sweet high voices had hushed their notes till they were far away in the clouds, but coming down, nearer, tenderly, exultantly, yet as if there might be tears in their voices, — tears of joy. And now the tremendous words:

"For unto us a Child is born!" and the deep voices of the men in that same faraway tone, as though it floated from an upper world: "Unto us a Son is given!" Then softer the altos, exquisitely the tenors. And what was it all about? A Child born! A Son given! They were all glad; and was his poor bound soul to have no part in the joy? Why should they all care about it, a Child born, a Son given? CHRISTMAS! Ah! Surely, *he* cared, too!

The answer to his why: "And the government shall be upon His shoulder; and His name — shall be call-ed!" Now the whole company were singing, each word like a polished precious stone of great brilliancy, which shone in the setting of this golden music as if placed there by a master workman. —

"Wonderful! Counselor! The mighty God! The everlasting Father! The Prince of Peace!"

Ah! What the world needed! What the world was longing for! What each soul, like himself, craved more than all else beside. He had never known his own heart to cry out for anything as it now cried out for all this.

And now the orchestra broke away into the pastoral symphony, and delicately the melody touched hidden suggestions of all that was left out of his own life — clear skies, sunny days, and the hushed sweet peace of green fields far away from toil and sorrow.

He could almost hear the murmur of night winds whispering among tall branches softly touching tired grass and sleeping flowers, humming a little tune with a tinkling brook. The birds were stirring in their sleep. He thought he heard one twitter. The world, the noisy world, was a long way off from this quiet place, where the meadows were all alone with the birds and the tinkling brook. And yet he was awfully conscious of his own presence in that holy place the music had brought into being, on that starlit hillside.

There were others waiting too. Indeed he was not sure if the whole world were not waiting with him to see what would happen. There were shepherds there, "abiding in the fields, keeping watch over their flocks by night, and lo — !" Now he could see the night sky, midnight blue, with its dotting of stars, and the glory that suddenly shone. Ah! He could see the light on the angel's face when he came, the frightened glory on the shepherds' faces, the wonder! It was there in his own heart, too. The story seemed all very new to him. Scarcely any inkling of it had ever reached his heart before. As with many others, Christmas had not heretofore brought its real revelation. His childish idea of the day had been measured by the amount of property acquired, in sticks of candy, toys and balls, in jewels cunningly set.

Now all softly came the music, "He shall feed His flock like a shepherd." He? Who? *Ah!* That same One of whom it had been said: "Who shall stand?" And yet this was a loving tender Shepherd!

And an invitation, "Come unto Him, all ye that labor and are heavy laden, and He will give you rest."

He found there were tears gathering in his eyes, but he had lost the sense of others looking at him. They were all under that spell of the music, the wonderful words.

And suddenly a great proclamation burst forth in melody: "Behold, the Lamb of God, that taketh away the sins of the world!"

So, this was what he was feeling. His own sins. He, a church member from his boyhood — yet *sins!* He had not thought of himself as a sinner. Quietly the chorus answered his thought: "All we like sheep have gone astray, we have turned everyone to his own way." Yes, he saw it now. It had been *his* way that he had gone, not God's way, and yet thought he was not a sinner!

"And the Lord hath laid on Him the iniquity of us all!" There was something almost terrible in the sweetness of this concluding sentence. What claim had he on the great Lord that his iniquity should be laid upon

Him? So this was the meaning of Christmas! Sins forgiven!

His soul was bowed with his humiliation. He heard them lifting up the gates, that the Lord of Glory might come in, and his own soul reached to swing the rusty hinges and lift up the gate of his soul that the Lord of Glory might come into his heart. He heard them shout their hallelujahs, and then the clear sweet song of highest assurance: "I know that my Redeemer liveth, and that at the latter day He shall stand upon the earth; and though worms destroy this body, yet in my flesh shall I see God. For now is Christ Risen from the Dead, and become the first fruits of them that slept!"

Charles and Astra went out when it was over, quietly, scarcely speaking. Almost wondering that people could chatter as they did.

"That program is too awfully long. I think they ought to cut out some, don't you?" one pretty girl said to her escort. "I was simply bored to extinction. But the orchestra leader was swell, wasn't he? So young looking, and so graceful."

"Yes," said the young man. "Rather stunning! I've always heard a lot about this oratorio, and never had a chance to hear it before, but I don't think I'd bother to go again, would you? It's much, much too long.

Yes, they certainly ought to cut it."

"I wonder," said Astra quietly, as they passed out ahead of the two, "which part they would cut out?"

"I'll tell you," said Cameron. "They would begin with 'All we like sheep have gone astray.' People like that don't want to known they are sinners and need a Saviour."

Astra looked at him astonished, and then a glad light came into her eyes.

"Yes," she said quickly. "You feel that way too? Most people don't take musical arrangements seriously, except from a musical standpoint."

"That's true," said Cameron. "But I feel tonight as if I had come a long way in understanding things that I've always taken for granted before, and never done anything about."

His words made Astra sure about several questions she had been turning over in her mind. He was a Christian then. Or in a fair way toward becoming one. That made her very happy.

As they arose from the pleasant midnight repast and started toward Astra's abiding place, Cameron said:

"How about our going to church somewhere tomorrow? Or had you some other plans?"

"Oh, no! I have no plans. Yes, that would be delightful. It's always rather desolate to go to church alone when one is almost a stranger in a city."

"Then we'll go. Have you some special church you like? To tell you the truth, I haven't located anywhere yet. I've been just sort of a religious tramp, dropping in here or there, and often not even dropping." He finished with a half-shamed grin.

"Well, of course I don't know how things are now, but there is a church not so far away from my place, where my father and I used to go when we lived here. Of course it may not be as fine as it used to be, but they were a humble sweet people and I can't think they have gone far astray in these few years. They seemed to have the spirit of truth among them."

"Then let's go there, by all means!" said Cameron with a smile. "It sounds good to me. I seem to feel for something real after tonight!"

Back in her room again Astra smiled to herself. He was going to be a real kind of friend, perhaps. And if he was that, what matter if he did have other friends? There would at least be someone who would be just comradely anyway, especially if he knew and loved her Lord.

11 The Marmaduke Lesters were in their hotel room resting a few minutes before it was time to get dressed for the wedding. Clytie was prinking in her room, which adjoined her parents' and the connecting door was standing open. Clytie always arranged to hear any family conversations if possible, lest she might miss something strategic.

There came a knock at the door and the bell boy presented a letter on a silver tray.

"Spec'ld'liv'ry!" he said under his breath.

Mr. Lester took the letter, gave the boy a tip, and shut the door.

"Well, her letter's come at last," he announced grimly as he tore open the envelope and unfolded the letter. "Airmail, too. I declare the service here isn't what it's cracked up to be. This has taken several hours longer than it should have done."

"Well, I'm certainly glad it's come before the wedding," sighed Miriam. "I shouldn't have been able to enjoy a minute of it, with all this anxiety on me. It isn't a bit like Astra not to have realized how she would upset me just before an important occasion."

"It seems to me you better save your rejoicing until you've read the letter," said her husband, frowning at the paper he held in his hand. "You can't tell what she'll do next. Not after this performance."

"At least it's better to know for a certainty."

"I'm not so sure of that either. This is certainly the smuggest letter I've ever read. It's almost as smug as that telegram. Listen to this:

"I am sorry to have to write this under these circumstances, for I did not want to talk about anything disturbing while you were on a holiday —"

He paused and looked up:

"You see she knows well enough that she's upsetting you. She's not half so holy as you try to make her out to be."

Then his eyes went down to the letter again:

"But since Duke's telegram —"

"'*Duke's* telegram!' Marmaduke Lester, is that *my* letter? Was it addressed to *me?*" asked his wife springing from the bed and going over to look at the letter. "Yes it is! And you're reading it! You have no right to do that, She's *my* cousin, not yours, and there might have been something quite private in it!"

"Private from me, your husband? Well, just for that I'll read it through first before you can see it. Lie down again and I'll read it out loud. We'd have had to talk it over anyway, and besides this is *my* affair. It was *I* who sent her that telegram, and this is evidently her answer to it. Miriam, if you want to hear this letter you better lie down and compose yourself, for I'll not read another word until you get quiet."

By this time Clytie with her hair brush in her hand had come and stood wide-eyed in the doorway. After a little more wrangling, Miriam, just because she knew her husband's stubborn nature, and because her eye was on the clock and it was high time they began to dress, subsided, growing anger in her eyes, and dropped upon the bed. Duke went on reading.

After he had read the letter Duke went and stood at the window staring out with a furious expression on his face.

"So!" he almost snorted, turning around at last to vent his anger upon his wife as if she had been the instigator of all this. "*So!* I'm *not* Astra's guardian! You've been telling me all this time that because I was her guardian we *had* to have her come and live with us. And now she says I'm *not* her guardian at all, and have no right to tell her to come back. I certainly will look into this! I'll go right away and hunt up that contemptible Sargent, and make them show those papers that they are boasting about having! Papers that Astra's father had made out! That was a contemptible thing to do, when he knew she would have to live off of us, and we would have to stand all her peculiarities, and tantrums —"

"Marmaduke! Stop!" cried his wife. "You know Astra hadn't any peculiarities, and never had tantrums! It's you that have a tantrum now, or you never would say that Astra was dependent on us. You know she paid her board, far more than ever it cost to keep the poor child!"

"Well, I'm going east on the evening plane. Telephone downstairs, Clytie, and find out what time it leaves. I'm going at once! You'll have to pack my suitcase while I get dressed. I won't have time to do both."

"Duke! You can't do that! You've *got* to go to that wedding! That's what we came all the way out here for, and left that poor child alone, just with servants in the house! And now you can't go off without attending it. Your people will never forgive you if you do that. Do get calm. One day more or less won't make any difference. Wait till after the wedding, anyway, if you must go and make a great mess of things. Astra isn't one to say a thing unless she knows, and she says she's seen the papers! You'll feel like two cents if you go roaring all that distance, and then find out you aren't her guardian at all!"

"Well, I *am* her guardian. Haven't I been in that place ever since she's been with us? Of *course* I am, and no Sargent nor anybody else is going to take it away. You see, Miriam, they're trying to get Astra's money away, that's what they are probably working this racket for, and it's important that I attend to it at once. When does she come of age?"

"I don't remember exactly. Very soon I think. Now, Marmaduke, get calm, and stop acting silly! You simply can't go away till after this wedding is over, and that's all there is to it!"

Then there was another sharp knock at the door, and another bell boy stood there with a silver plate and another special delivery letter.

This quite surprised Marmaduke out of his quarrel, and he came forward to receive the letter which his wife had taken, and was opening.

"Yes, it's for you," said his wife, "but you opened my letter so I'm opening yours. It's from a lawyer. His name is Lauderdale."

She scanned the lines quickly.

"Yes, he says you are *not* Astra's guardian,

and he is enclosing a copy of the papers about the guardianship. I guess, Duke, you better quiet down, and get dressed for that wedding, and after the wedding, if there's anything left to do you can do it. But really, from this letter, I don't believe you'll think it is very dignified to go running off to the east clamoring to be a guardian. They certainly will begin to think you've got some racket or other, just as you said about them."

Marmaduke made no reply. He slammed into the bathroom and began to shave, while his wife made the most of his absence to get her face and hair into proper shape. But Clytie stood uncomfortably in the doorway, first on one foot and then on the other, looking uneasily at her mother. At last Miriam, who knew the signs of her daughter's behaviour pretty well, asked her:

"Clytie, do you know how much money Astra had when we left home?"

Clytie promptly shook her head.

"No, I don't. Really, Mother. Astra was always very close-mouthed about her money and what she was going to do with it. I know she didn't have half enough for what she wanted."

"How do you know that?"

"Because I asked her to lend me a little

money, and she refused. She was practically always willing to lend me money when I asked her, but this time she said she couldn't do it. She said she had some things she wanted to do, and some things she wanted to buy, and she had just paid her board and she wouldn't have enough if she let me have any. She said I should go and ask my father if I wanted money."

"What did you want money for, Clytie? Your father had given you more than your usual allowance, I know, on account of your having to get a wedding present. Why did you want more?"

Clytie put on her most winsome smile.

"Because, mother dear, I wanted to get that darling pearl pin. It went so exquisitely with my blue and white dress."

"Well, but you have the pearl pin, Clytie. Where did you get the money for that? I know that pin cost about twenty dollars at least. It is a lovely thing, and I think you had very good taste to want it. But I don't understand where you got it. Did your father give you more money? Did he buy it for you?"

"No, Mother." Clytie hung her head prettily.

"Well, where did you get the money then?"

"Well, I got it from Astra after all. When I went back I got all she had."

"But Clytie, you must be mistaken. Where then would she get money to take this journey?"

"Well, I'm sure I don't know. That's her lookout, not mine. I suppose she has ways of getting more money out of that guardian, hasn't she? Or maybe she was holding out on me, and it wasn't all she had, but I got what I went after. Why do you worry, Mother? Astra will get along, and it's not your worry anyway."

"Now, Clytie, that's not a nice way to talk. You never knew how lovely Astra's mother was to me when I was a lonely orphan girl!"

"Oh, cut it out, Miriam! I'm fed up with Astra. Give us a change! Anyway she's gone and I'm glad. So let's let it rest there!" and Clytie turned and flung herself back into her own room.

Just then Marmaduke came breezing out of the bathroom, looking as fresh and clean as a babe new born, and found his wife patting away a few tears she had let escape her right onto her freshly powdered countenance.

"Now what's the matter with you?" glared Marmaduke. "Haven't you come out of your grouch yet?"

"Duke, did Astra pay her board before we left?" said his wife, lifting her dismal countenance.

Her husband turned and glared at her again.

"Yes, she did!" he barked.

"Paid it in advance?" asked his stricken wife.

"Yes, of course!" he barked again. "That's what she always does. It was none of my doings."

"Well, you oughtn't to have taken it!" wailed Miriam. "I don't see what in the world that child traveled on. It's dreadful to think that one of my own family was in actual straits like that! After the way her people took care of me when I had no one!"

"Oh, shut up!" said her kindly husband. "Look at the clock! Have you forgotten we came west to a wedding? You'll have to get in some repairs on your make-up, or your family will be ashamed to own you belong to them. As for Astra, she had money enough left. She always has. If we had been staying at home you would have made her buy another evening dress and another fur coat, and thought nothing of it, just so your beloved daughter could wear them for her."

"But she didn't have plenty left, Duke. Clytie went and borrowed everything she had, and I just can't see where she got money to make that journey! Duke, we've got to do something about it. We really have. There's no telling what she'll tell about us when she gets up there with her father's friends!"

"Oh, hang it all! Can't you shut up till this shindig is over? Then we'll all go east and raise the biggest rumpus ever was. The world war won't be in it! But I'll be blamed if I'll stand another whining word about it till after the wedding!" and he flung into his dress coat and slammed out of the hall door to the elevator.

Then, with her eye on the clock, Miriam went at her toilet and got in make-up repairs in short order. And Clytie in the other room fastened on the pearl pin and the darling earrings that matched the ones that she had bought with Astra's stolen money, and went smiling down to the car, en route to the wedding, knowing that the adoring eyes of her parents were upon her uncritically and contentedly.

And at the reception more than one admiring young guest watched her enviously and said: "Oh, what a darling pin and earrings! Where did you get them, Clytie, dear?" and Clytie dimpled and smiled and looked demurely down and said: "They were a present from my darling cousin, Astra Everson."

"What, the one that's been living with you since her father died?"

"Yes, but she's gone away from us now, and we don't know how we're going to get along without her. She was simply adorable! We think she's going to get married. She's gone back to her old home and she must have had a great many admirers there of course. You don't know how we're going to miss her."

But that night when the last of the wedding was over, even to the scrambled eggs in the wee small hours, and everybody herded finally to their beds as the morning began to dawn grayly into the hotel bedroom windows, Miriam and her tempestuous husband lay gravely considering the situation.

"I think," said Miriam, after a long pause, during which only a series of momentous sighs showed that Marmaduke was not sleeping the sleep of the just and happy, "I think that we have got to find out somehow whether Clytie really borrowed that money for those pearl earrings from Astra, or whether she just took it. It's time we checked up on Clytie. She's getting too casual about other people's things. She may, of course, have merely bullied her until she gave it to her, but I wouldn't like to think she took it without Astra's knowledge or permission."

"You *would* bring a thing like that up when we've got Astra on our hands. One girl is enough to attend to at once."

"Yes, but which girl? Clytie is our own, and this is a pretty serious thing."

"Well, if you consider the investigations had better begin at home, suppose you stay home and work on Clytie, and I'll go east by myself, and begin on Astra. Perhaps we'll accomplish more in that way."

"I think," said Miriam after another long pause, "that you better stay at home and work with me on Clytie, and let Astra go her own way. Because to tell the truth, I don't believe you'll get anywhere with Astra. She's too much like her father, and she just adores those lawyers and the guardian her father used to have. You'll just wish you hadn't if you attempt to go out there and argue with an unknown quantity."

The head of the house lay silent for a space and then he said with a deep yawn,

"Well, for Heaven's sake, let's get some sleep!"

So Duke said no more about it that night, but he did a good deal of tossing and angry thinking. The next morning he diligently searched until he found a certain agency that would do almost anything that was asked, for money. Behind closed doors his arrangements were made And that very night an eastern bound plane took aboard a man who understood the plans thoroughly, and knew that action was required in the course of the next few days. For Marmaduke Lester had definite ways in which he could use the comfortable fortune that he knew was left to Astra. He had planned to wait until near time for her majority when her money would soon be in her own hands, and he could use his persuasive powers on her quietly. But her sudden departure had upset his schemes so that force was going to be necessary.

 **12** Astra and Cameron went to church twice on Sunday, and had a precious time. The church that had been Mr. Everson's choice had stayed true to the faith, and while the old preacher was gone, the one who had succeeded him was just as good.

The people were warm-hearted and welcomed them, and they felt at home and happy there at once. To Cameron at least the whole experience was wonderful. He had not known that people who knew and loved the Lord could love others just because they belonged to Him. Moreover the preaching was more teaching of the Word than preaching, and appealed to Cameron in every way. He had never heard such teaching in his life. It was as if the wonderful music they had heard together the night before had come alive in human lives, and they could see its practical working.

Afterwards they came back to the plain little parlor where Astra was boarding, and sat in the farthest corner talking a few minutes, each reluctant to end the day.

"Tomorrow I shall be very busy," said Cameron, "getting things in my office ready to leave. Perhaps Tuesday also. But I'll try to get a little while one of the evenings to run over a few minutes. So if there is anything I can do to help you over the holiday emptiness, just think it up and tell me, and I'll endeavor to save a space for it."

"Oh, that's very kind of you," she said, suddenly realizing the beautiful day was over, and she had but blankness and her own company to depend upon until Christmas was past and she could have the face to call up some of her old friends, and get into familiar life again. "But you mustn't!" she went on, getting the idea that she was becoming a sort of burden on his mind. "It's been wonderful to go to church with somebody who was in sympathy, and the concert was marvelous, but you really must cast me off now. You have more than paid any debt you may have fancied you had to me. And I know you are a busy man."

"Well, I'm not so busy but that I can enjoy real things now and then in company with real people."

Their glances met again, and Astra caught her breath. She simply mustn't let herself be so glad over a simple little sentence like that. He was a wonderful companion but there was no sense in letting herself get all stirred up about him. She wasn't the only young woman he knew.

"Well," she said pleasantly, "you certainly have made these first days in my home town delightful ones, and I shall never forget your kindness."

"Please don't think of it just as kindness," he said as he took her hand in a farewell clasp. "It's been delightful to me. And, good night. I'll be seeing you soon."

As she went up to her room in the elevator she said to herself, "Well, that's been a nice time. Now forget it! Get some sleep, and tomorrow I'm going to work copying dad's article that I brought back with me."

In the morning she woke with a comfortable feeling that she had had a good time, and had made a true friend, no matter how many mink coats there were to the contrary. She went down to breakfast, and while she was eating decided that when she had done a good morning's work she would call up Mr. Lauderdale, and get things fixed up for Tilly, then either today or tomorrow she would take a run out and set Tilly's mind at rest.

She stopped at the desk to see if there was any mail for her, and then remembered that the only address the Lesters knew was care of Mr. Sargent. So, if Marmaduke had written in a disagreeable strain as undoubtedly he would do when he got around to it, it could not reach her until that Sargent secretary forwarded it to her.

So she went to her room quite contentedly.

She had brought her portable typewriter over with the papers from the Albans' house, and she went quite happily to work, cleaning and oiling and putting it in first class order. Then she went at the typing with zeal.

As she read a few pages over she could almost hear the dear familiar voice of her dead father as he dictated them to her. Such a little time before, it seemed to her now. Being back in the home surroundings seemed to bring it so much nearer. All that long monotonous, uncongenial time at the Lesters seemed to have vanished now, leaving little behind to remember. How surprised they would be if they knew she felt that way!

At eleven o'clock she called up Mr. Lauderdale and told him what Tilly's son-in-law was trying to put over on poor Tilly, and received his assurance that nothing of the sort had been said by him, that the young man had done all the talking, and made it very plain that Tilly *wished* to give up the house. He advised her that it would be a good thing if he could have a talk with Tilly. Could she get in touch with her and bring her to his office that afternoon?

"Of course her son-in-law can't do anything to harm her. I'll call Mr. Boyd. He's the head of that pension affair, and fix it up for her. We'll get it all straightened out so she can have an easy Christmas. Now, how about that unpleasant cousin of yours? Have you heard from him again?"

"Not yet," said Astra with a worried look in her eyes. "The wedding they went out to attend was Saturday night. They wouldn't have had time to do much yet. Besides, your letter must have reached them about the time my letter did, and that may have stalled them off a bit. Though if I know Cousin Duke as well as I think I do, it may have only made him angrier. I wouldn't be in the least surprised if he took the first plane he could get and came over here to force me back there!"

"So! Well, that's bad! I'm sorry I arranged to go away. Of course if he arrives before I leave, or you have word that he is coming, I'll put off my departure. But if he should turn up after I've gone, you wire me or call me up, and I'll fly back at once. I'm not going to run any risk of your being annoyed!"

"Oh, no indeed! You mustn't think of doing that! I'll manage. And besides he doesn't know where I am stopping. He sent his telegram to Mr. Sargent's office and the secretary forwarded it to me."

"Oh, is that it? Well, leave it to me then. I'll see that that secretary doesn't give him your address. In fact I think she told me she or her assistant is to be away after tomorrow till the end of the week. I'll look after them anyway. And it will probably take him a little time to find you. You might decide to spend Christmas with friends, and not be immediately available. But be sure to keep me in touch with you all the time. Haven't you a few old friends upon whom you can call if you are in a trying situation?"

Astra thought instantly of Cameron, but immediately put him out of her mind. She didn't want to tell that story of how she came to know Cameron, not just yet. It was all right of course, but Mr. Lauderdale might not understand. Besides, Cameron was to be away over Christmas. Well, she wouldn't need any help, of course. It wasn't in the least likely Miriam would let Duke run away until all her plans were carried out.

"Why, yes," she said after a second's hesitation. "I have plenty of friends, only I didn't want to let them know I was here until after the holidays. They would feel they must invite me, and I'm not ready yet to be invited. If it hadn't been for my cousins' absence I wouldn't have chosen just this time to come, but I thought it would be easier to run away when they were not there. Of course, though, if it came to an emergency, there are several people I could go to. But the Lesters wouldn't be as bad as that. If they should come and insist that I go back with them, I would tell them I must stay till you get back to sign some papers, or something like that."

"You're a smart girl. I believe you'd make a good lawyer. Well, then, run along child, and take things easy. I'll see that you have all the addresses you need, and I'll be right there at the end of the wire whenever you choose to call me. Now go and see what you can do with Tilly. The earlier this afternoon the better. That will help a lot."

So Astra went out to Willow Haven, and dragged Tilly away from a washing she was doing at home for a woman in the village. Made her leave her clothes asoak, promising to return soon so that she could finish.

Poor Tilly was greatly delighted to see her, for after Astra had left she had been regarding her visit in the light of a vision or dream that couldn't possibly be true, and she had even gone on getting her things in order with the probability in mind that she was going to have to leave her home, and go into family servitude.

Tilly was hustled into her best bib and tucker, without any chance to let her recalcitrant son-in-law know what she was going to do. She was taken by the next bus into town, arriving in the lawyer's office almost as soon as he returned from his late lunch.

Mr. Lauderdale was most kindly, and put poor frightened Tilly at her ease at once. And after the matter of the pension and the reduced rent were all fixed up with definite papers to prove it, and fully explained to Tilly so that she couldn't be bullied by her son-in-law any longer into thinking she had lost her home, Astra took Tilly out and gave her a delicious lunch, ending with mince pie a la mode. She also bought her three pairs of warm woolen stockings, and a pair of kid gloves for a Christmas present. Then she gave her a crisp new ten dollar bill, and put her on the bus back to Willow Haven.

She went back to her lodging place with a lighter heart. That matter was settled and she knew that Tilly was a great deal happier. There might be trouble with her family later, but Tilly was well fortified with knowledge now, and could hold her own.

Back in her room Astra did a few more

pages of typing, and wrote a letter to her father's publisher to say that she was trying to get in shape the article for which they had asked, and hoped to have it ready for them to see very soon.

When she went down to the Association restaurant for her dinner she found she was very hungry. She had worked hard and really accomplished something worth while. She felt she was doing what her father would have wanted her to do, and it made her very glad. And so far she had been able to put out of her mind to a certain extent, the vision of Cameron, who had so seemed to possess her for several days. But seated in the restaurant now she felt very lonely, and couldn't help thinking back to the pleasant meals they had enjoyed together. Becoming suddenly aware of how her thoughts were flying back to him again now that her mind was not busy, she hurried with her eating. She would do something to break this up quickly, even if she had to go back to her work on the typewriter. She simply must not get daffy about a young man. A stranger too! Although her heart denied that, even as she thought it. He wasn't a stranger. He never could be, and whether she ever saw him again or not, she would always count him a real friend. Besides, a man who owned such interest in

Christian things *had* to be a friend. If he had taken Christ as his Saviour, and he certainly talked as if he had, then he was a fellow-child of God. That brought a relationship which was not to be measured by human standards. It was the fellowship of those who love the Lord.

Up in her room again her first act was to kneel by her bed and pray for Cameron with her whole heart, that he might truly take Christ as his Saviour; that he might be guided in his life, and that he might be kept safe from harm. And then she prayed for herself, that she might not let her thoughts wander where they had no business to be, and that her life might be a true witness to all with whom she came in contact, that she might be kept safe from harm and danger, and led in God's way.

Then she got up from her knees and went back to her work.

About ten o'clock there came a telephone call from Cameron.

"Sorry to disturb you, but I suggested that I might come over a few minutes this evening, and I was afraid you might wait up for me. So I'm calling to say it is impossible for me to come tonight. I got involved with a man on business, and couldn't get done sooner. And it turns out after all that I am not leaving for the old home in the morning, as I had planned. I can't possibly get off now before Wednesday morning. But even at that I shall be able to spend Christmas Eve with my stepmother, and she will like that, I know. So perhaps I may be able to run in on you tomorrow night and wish you Merry Christmas. Sorry not to have been there to-night of course. I hope I didn't spoil any possible plans for you. Good night. I have to take my man to the train now, but I'll be seeing you again soon, if you don't mind."

The tone was that of a real friend, a comrade, and she felt her own voice had been a bit breathless as she answered him. She hoped he hadn't noticed it. But it was nice to have someone in a whole wide city to say good night when she felt so alone. Tomorrow night! Well, that would be something nice to look forward to, even if it didn't really happen when the time came. It gave a friendly feeling to the world. And of course he was a man of business and couldn't be counted on to keep casual appointments every time. Every sensible busy person had to remember that.

So she curled up on her couch and read a magazine for a little while before retiring, telling herself all the time what a very nice time she was having, away here on her own, getting work done and enjoying herself.

And nearer and nearer came Christmas. That day that means so much in home life, the crowning peak of all the joyousness of the year. Christmas was going to be a lonely day. Really, tomorrow she must take a little time off and think up something nice and Christmasy to do for somebody. If she had a lot of money she would do something for the people in this building where she had found a temporary home. Something cheering that would bring brightness into any life. Say a rosebud, or a carnation, sent up to every room with a tiny label, "From a fellow guest, with Christmas Greeting." Should she do it? Oh, likely all the girls and women who lived here had Christmases of their own, friends who would give them gifts, but a single blossom couldn't do any harm to anyone, and she could put a Christmas text on the flower. Well, that was a thought. If she couldn't find any better way of celebrating she might try that. Of course it would have to be strictly incognito, but it would be fun to watch their faces. Would they wear the flowers? Should she do that? Well, she would think about it. Since there was no likelihood of her having any Christmas of her own except in her heart, why not do something for somebody else?

At least there could be joy in that.

Of course there were other things that could be done. There were little children in some of the city's slum streets, not far away probably. A box of candy, passed around among some of the dirty-faced urchins who would have no real Christmas. A handful of tiny bright little dolls, some red Testaments in attractive covers. Ah! There were ways to spend money. Some day, if all went well, when she came into her own, here were thoughts to put aside and remember. She wrote some of them down idly. She might decide on one plan and try it out, and maybe another year she could try others. Surely there must be some way in which a lover of the Lord Jesus could get the story of His birth, and the reason why, across, to some of the people on the earth to whom God's children were supposed to witness. The great gift of salvation, the supreme Christmas gift, the reason for Christmas, forgiveness of sin. If people knew how to get forgiveness of sin it would make a real Christmas for them. Well, if she ever had opportunity to talk things like that over with Cameron, it certainly would be interesting to see what he thought about it.

And with that thought Astra decided it was time to go to sleep. But definitely she made up her mind as she drifted off to sleep, that she would find some way to bring a Christmas message to someone this year.

And then she dreamed that she was talking it over with Cameron, and the look he gave her fully approved of it all.

 **13** The stepmother's letter reached Cameron late Wednesday afternoon when he rushed back to his room to fling a few things into a bag, preparatory to taking the evening train.

She had written it after due deliberation on Sunday evening and given it to a neighbor the next morning to mail "special delivery," and then she had gone about her preparations for the journey to her sister Nancy's home. But the neighbor had put the letter in his pocket and forgotten all about it until late Tuesday afternoon, when he mailed it just as the postoffice was closing. So it finally came to Cameron's office about the middle of Wednesday afternoon, and halted his preparations at the last minute.

He frowned when he read the letter. It seemed so unlike his stepmother to do things in that way. She hadn't been very close to that sister for years, and it wasn't in the least like her to start up suddenly and run away when she knew he was coming. However, it seemed reasonable.

But afterwards, as he was taking the first leisure breath of the day and wondering what he should do next, the telephone rang, bringing the voice of his plotting sister Rosamond, and then he wondered again.

"Charlie," she said in her usual pleading voice that always took him for granted, "are you in a very kindly gentle mood, and are you going to be very good to your worn out sister Rosamond? Because I'm going to ask a very great favor of you, and in turn I'll be glad to do anything in the world you want. Now be a good brother and say yes, before I ask you, won't you?"

"Not on your life!" said Cameron. "Not till I know what it is you're asking. And if it's anything to do with any of your simpering female go-getters I'll say no, and that's flat!"

"Now Charlie, why do you want to be so coarse and disagreeable? I really don't know what you mean. It's a simple little favor that I'm asking, partly for my sake, but most of all for my three beloved kiddies, who simply adore you, and want you all to themselves for Christmas. You see, Harold and I have been trying to plan for a long time to get away on Christmas Day and go up to see some friends of his who have a marvelous log cabin in the wilderness. It's a wonderful place, with great forest trees all around and plenty of mountains near by, and wonderful skiing. I'm just wild to go. But I can't bring myself to leave the kiddies with just the maids on Christmas Day, of all days. And I've said no so many times that Harold is really cross with me. So I've thought and thought, and the only thing I can think of is that perhaps you will be self-sacrificing enough to stay with them. I know you haven't got any particular fun of your own on hand. You never do have, and so I've figured it all out. Harold says we can start tonight early, and come back late Christmas night. He has to be in his office the next morning in spite of everything, so we won't leave you in the lurch any longer. And of course you'll practically have both evenings to yourself, for the kiddies go to bed at seven, and won't bother you a particle. I know you were going up to see that poor old poke of a stepmother, but that can surely wait a few days. Anyhow, I don't see what claim she has on you now, and I do think on Christmas Day kiddies have the first right to be considered."

She paused and Charles Cameron got in a word.

"Rosamond, do you actually mean to tell me that you are going to desert your babies on Christmas?"

"Charles, they won't care a mite if they have you. They adore you. And I know you'll make them have the time of their lives.

Then when we get home we can give them some extra treats to make up for it. And they will only think Christmas is that much longer and better than ever before. Besides, Charlie, they're only kids!"

"Do you want to know what I think of you?" said Charles in disgust. "I think you are both contemptible to consider a plan like that! Run off and leave your own little children, so you can act like a couple of kids and slide down a mountain on skis! I don't think you have any right to have nice sweet lovely children and then treat them like that!"

"Oh, Charlie dear! I'm so glad you consider them sweet and lovely, because then I know you'll make them have a charming time, and I shan't be missed at all. And besides, Charlie, don't you think I have a duty to my husband?"

"Duty to your husband! My eye! You're doing this for your own selfish reasons, I know. And as for the stepmother, well, I'm not so sure you didn't do something about that. But tell me, Roz. Suppose I say no to your proposition. What will you do? Divorce your husband, or throw your children out in the street and let them shift for themselves?"

"Now, Charlie. You're being too funny. You know you would never let it come to that!"

"Oh, certainly not! You knew you could count on that. But what I want to know is, who is going to look after those children? Dress them and wash them and do all the things that have to be done for them? You know I'm no child's nurse when it comes to that. I can play with them, but when it goes farther than that I'm utterly without experience. You know it isn't as if you had lived at home and I'd had a chance to see what went on."

"Oh, Charlie, you're too funny! But of course I'm leaving the servants. They are accustomed to looking after the children, and everything will go all right, I know. Only Charlie, I wanted you there to make it bright and happy for them on Christmas Day. Play Santa Claus for them, or something. And of course if you feel there ought to be some woman besides the servants, why, I'm sure I could get some friend to come in. It runs in my mind that Camilla Blair is going to be around the neighborhood that day, and I'm almost certain I could get her to come in for a time and play jingles for them on the piano, or sing, or something."

"Yes!" said Cameron savagely. "I thought you had something up your sleeve! And I warn you if it's that Blair woman I won't come within fifty miles of the place. If you dare send her around I'm off you for life! I *mean* it, Roz. I don't want to *see* her, and if she turns up I'll pass right out of the picture!"

"There, Charlie! Don't get upset. Of course I won't ask her to drop around if you really don't want her. But just in case you should change your mind and get lonesome when the day's half over, you'll find her at —"

"There you go! Cut that out! I mean what I said. If you have any ideas like working that Blair person in, nothing doing!"

"Why of course not, Charlie. How silly! If you prefer to be there alone with the children, all right, I'll say no more! And of course I'll arrange that the servants will stay. I'll give them extra days off later. And they will get you a nice little dinner. Only I thought it would be so much pleasanter for you if you had someone else to come in when the children are well started on a good time, someone who would be company for you."

"If I want any company, Roz, I'll select it myself!"

"Well — all right then! And can I *depend* on you, Charlie?"

"I suppose you can, Roz, just as you have been depending on me to do whatever you demanded ever since I was a lonesome little kid myself. I'll do it just because I feel sorry for your lonesome little youngsters on Christmas Day, with no parents to make it the grandest day of all the year. Only, listen, Roz. I tell you if you don't play fair and lay off from the Blair woman, it's the last time I'll do anything you ask, and I *mean* it!"

"All right, Charlie dear. Have it all your own way, only come!"

"When do you want me to come?"

"Could you come this evening? Harold says we could practically get there by midnight if we could start right now."

"Can't do it, Roz. I have to have a couple of hours first to do a few things before I could possibly come."

There was silence for a moment while a hurried consultation went on between Harold and Rosamond. Then Rosamond said reluctantly, "All right, Charlie, but make it as snappy as you can."

"I'll do the best I can, but Roz, this last-minute business isn't very easy to work. I had other plans."

"Well, I know, you sweet thing!" said the honeyed voice of the sister, triumphant now she had her way, "but really I wasn't sure we could do it till a few minutes ago."

"Oh yes?"

Cameron hung up with a snap, and turned about angrily to collect his thoughts.

He felt morally sure that Rosamond was trying to put something over on him, and yet he couldn't figure out what it was. Was he too kindhearted? That couldn't be, could it? Yet even as a child Rosamond was always getting him into unpleasant situations, from which he couldn't extricate himself without appearing to be most unaccommodating.

But he had no time now to think things over. He had promised to go, and of course he had to for the sake of the kiddies. He was very fond of them. He would enjoy giving them a good time. Now, what had he been about to do when Rosamond interrupted?

He whirled around to his desk and went hard at work again. He must get things in shape. If Rosamond didn't get home when she had said she would, there might be delay the next day, and there were some things that wouldn't bear waiting, that were too important to leave to chance. There were a few letters to dictate, a couple of telegrams to send, and several business details that ought to be looked after lest he would be detained Friday. If he had gone to his stepmother's as he had expected, his plan had been to start back Christmas night and be ready for work early the next morning, but now all that was upset. You never could depend upon Rosamond, nor her maids either.

Ten to one they would walk out on him Christmas morning.

One of his last acts before he left his office was to call his office boy and send him with his own portable radio, a neat little accurate affair, to Astra Everson. He had intended to take it himself, and stop long enough to show her the most effective way of tuning it, but there wouldn't be time now. And perhaps it was just as well not to go himself when he could stay but a moment. So he wrote a few words on his card, "I thought perhaps you'd like to borrow this to cheer your holiday, Charles," slipped it in an envelope, and gave direction for the young man to leave the radio if Miss Everson was out or if she was there, to show her how to use it. He also called up the florist and ordered three dozen crimson roses sent to Astra. He frowned a good deal at the instrument after he had hung up. Now, would she think that was all right? She was not a girl one presumed with on slight acquaintance. And yet was theirs a *slight* acquaintance? When one considered it, he seemed to have presumed a good deal already, from the time he had first seen her. Well, he only wished he was free for this holiday to try and make her have a pleasant day. But of course he would be tied up to those kiddies. Perhaps he could telephone her sometime during Christmas Day and give her greetings.

There was one man with whom he had important dealings who had not been heard from yet, and he was all nerves watching for word from him. If it didn't come before the afternoon was over he would have an anxious Christmas Day, for it really meant big things for his business if he got this order.

But the afternoon passed and no word came, and Cameron grew more and more worried. He had been so sure of this order, and it was going to make such a lot of difference in his plans.

Finally a little after five o'clock Rosamond called up.

"Charlie, you haven't fallen down on the job, have you?"

"No."

"You'll surely be here?"

"I generally keep my promises, don't I?"

"Well, but you seemed so unwilling and so uncertain, I was afraid."

"Sorry, sister, but this is making a lot of trouble for me."

"Well, for pity's sake, why don't you come? It can't be so important to stay in an office Christmas Eve."

"You wouldn't understand of course, but it is. However, I'll be there!"

"And I can really depend on you?"

"Absolutely."

"How soon will you be here?"

"In less than an hour now, I hope."

"Oh, *dear!* An *hour!* You know it means an awful lot to us to get started right away. It's beginning to snow, and there may be a blizzard."

"In that case you'd have to consider staying at home, I suppose?"

"No indeed! It's only snowing a little now, but we want to get well on our way before the storm really sets in. Can't you hurry?"

"Not any more than I'm doing now. You see what I'm doing means an awful lot to me. But you needn't worry. I'll be there!"

He turned back to his desk just as his secretary handed him a telegram. He tore it open frantically.

Cannot decide without talking with you. Sorry you are to be away. Shall pass through Philadelphia Christmas morning. Had hoped to get in touch with you between trains, from ten to twelve, Thirtieth Street Station. If you can make it watch for me at train. I may decide to take your offer. Otherwise will wait till spring.

H. A. Burnside.

Charles Cameron sank down into his desk chair again in utter despair. Must he allow Rosamond's whims to upset this great opportunity, which would mean everything to his business? Surely if Rosamond knew she would be reasonable and change her plans!

He sprang to his telephone and called Rosamond's number, and as soon as he heard the receiver lifted he shouted, "I can't possibly make it, Roz! You'll have to make other plans! I have a deal on that will take all tomorrow morning. A telegram just came!"

Then the nurse's voice answered in great excitement:

"Oh, is that you, Mister Charles? Why they've *gone!* They haven't been gone more than two minutes. They said they knew you would be here soon, and we would be all right till you got here but the baby has been that contraptions to see her mommie go, that she's yelling so I can't hardly hear. And both the older children are that upset to find out at this last minute that their parents are not going to be here Christmas! What's that? Didn't she tell them before? No sir, she just told them as she was kissing them good-by! I hope you'll come soon, Mister Charles, because they are all that fractious it seems I'll go wild."

Cameron sat in consternation for an instant, and then in a grim stern voice said: "Very well, Catharine, I'll be there very soon now. Tell Junior to come to the phone. That you, Harold? What's the matter, pard? You feeling down? Well, chirk up. I'll be there in three jerks of a lamb's tail. And tell the girls to mop up their eyes and be ready with plenty of smiles, and we'll have a gay time."

"You mean we'll have a nice time before we go to bed, Uncle Charlie?" asked the woebegone voice of the little boy.

"Sure we will!" came the hearty voice of the dismayed uncle. "Had your supper yet?"

"No sir!"

"Well, neither have I. Just tell the cook to get a slick supper for us, and we'll have the time of our life! And we'll hear Christmas carols, and a lot of other things. Okay, boy?"

"Okay, Uncle Charlie! That'll be swell."

In a daze Charles Cameron hung up the receiver and stared around his deserted office. It was Christmas Eve, and his satellites had crept by his preoccupation, murmuring, "Merry Christmas, Mr. Cameron," without his hearing them.

Now, what was he going to do next? For somehow he *had* to meet that customer! And yet he couldn't desert the children!

 **14** All the afternoon of the day before Christmas Astra had been out shopping. She had worked hard all the morning, and had her father's article, the last one he had worked on before he died, nearly copied. She felt she had a right to go out and play at Christmas a little while by herself.

Of course it was a bit crowded in the shops, especially as she chose the cheap stores, ten cent and the like. For in spite of Mr. Lauderdale's assurance that she was not to worry about money, in spite of that good fat check he had given her, she felt she must spend cautiously, at least until she was located permanently somewhere and knew just what she was going to do.

So she bought rather sparingly, with only now and then a lavish expenditure on something that she felt she would like someone to give her, although she had at present no definite persons in mind for the gifts. Well, it was fun anyway.

She bought a lot of red and green tissue paper, and red and silver ribbon. Also some blue paper with silver stars. Because if there were to be gifts they would have to be wrapped, though she didn't yet know to whom they were to be given. Then she found some charming little ten cent figurines, of tiny shepherds with crooks, and little white sheep and lambs. She bought a handful of those, and a package of white cards. A few small tan velvet camels with wise men atop. Ah! She would have a Christmas decoration in her room perhaps. It would help to occupy the day that seemed so lonely to look forward to.

And then she made a discovery. She found a Christian book store where they had charming books, and lovely Christmas cards with real Bible verses on them. They also had large illuminated hand painted texts for the wall. There was one in blue and silver she must have for herself. And then she discovered the Bibles and Testaments and she was delighted. She could hardly tear herself away from them. At last she came away with an exquisite Testament, luxuriously bound, thin and pliable, and just the thing for a man's pocket, if she had any man to whom she dared give it. There was Charles Cameron of course, but she could not give him a Christmas gift. Of course he had been very kind to her and taken her to a concert, but a girl could not offer a gift to a stranger, a man, whom she knew so very little. Yet if she had been going to give him something this was what she would like to give. It looked like him, refined and quiet, and endurable. It was so soft and small, yet clear in print, that it seemed the very last word as luxury goes in Bibles. She also found some lovely little gospels, — a few bound in blue leather, and some in Christmasy red.

She went to another store and bought a handful of very tiny dolls, in case she carried out some of her ideas about doing things for others, and also, three beautiful ones. And she bought a few other inexpensive trifles just because they would be nice sometime for somebody, and when she went back to her lodging she felt she had been very silly indeed. Such a great stack of bundles little and big, that she had been forced to purchase a couple of big paper shopping bags in which to carry them! Silly, that was what she was! Well, sometime she would find somebody who would enjoy them, and anyhow she had had a good time. This was her own Christmas, just making believe.

She came into the hall with her burdens, just as the boy from Charles Cameron's office had about decided it wasn't any use to wait for her any longer, and had arisen to leave the leather case which contained the radio with the boy at the desk.

"There she is now," said the boy pointing down the hall. "You can give it to her yourself if you want to."

The boy from the office looked at Astra with admiring eyes. She was a lovely girl, but then his boss *would* pick out a lovely girl, of course. He came smiling forward to greet her deferentially.

"Is this Miss Everson?"

Astra looked up astonished.

"Yes," she said, and took the little note he held out, a pleased pink color glowing in her cheeks. Then she looked at the leather case questioningly.

"Mr. Cameron thought you might enjoy using this Christmas Day," said the boy. "He told me to show you how to use it. Can we go over to that table? I'll show you how it works best."

So they went over to the table and Astra was inducted into the method by which this little machine brought tales of the world out of the atmosphere. And other girls coming in to get their mail from the desk looked and listened, and cast envying glances her way.

The boy understood what he was doing, and made it very plain to Astra, and when he went away she carried the leather case proudly to her room, the glad color in her face, a pleased light in her eyes. Her new friend had been kind again. He had not forgotten her even though he had gone away without the half-promised call. Well, she had been away all the afternoon, even if he had called.

She put down her bundles and laid aside her wraps and started the new radio. How thrilling it was that she was to have this pleasure tonight and tomorrow.

Then it came to her that she had a great deal to do, and should begin at once. She had ordered carnations enough for one for each person in the house, and had bought very tiny Christmas cards, each with a Scripture text. So now she sat down to write on the cards "Christmas Greetings from a fellow house guest," and to slip a bit of ribbon through the fold of the card. Now it wouldn't take her long to tie the cards on the flowers. She would take them to the desk the last thing before she retired, ask the boy to put them back in the refrigerator, and deliver them to each door very early in the morning.

She was glad she had stopped in a drug store and taken a cup of coffee and a sandwich, because she didn't want to take the time to go out again in the snow, and the restaurant belonging to the house would be full and noisy tonight, everybody having company. Besides, she wanted to stay with her radio and enjoy it.

But she had scarcely turned it on when there came a tap at the door, and the boy handed in a large florist's box. At first she thought it was her own carnations, and wondered why he had brought them before she told him, but then she saw the name of the florist and knew it was not the near-by place where she had bought hers. And there was the card of greeting.

Christmas Greetings and all Good Cheer,
                    Your friend,
                    Charles Cameron

She opened the box and exulted in the gorgeous crimson roses. Such a wealth of them! She buried her face against their coolness, and her heart thrilled at the kindliness and friendship that had taken all this trouble for her. If she only knew where to get him how she would enjoy calling him up and thanking him. But he was likely on the train now, speeding to his old home and his kind dull stepmother.

Well, she would just ask God to tell him how glad he had made her. She would thank God for the flowers. So she went down on her knees with the open box beside her, and one great crimson rose drawn close to her face, its perfume stealing over her senses like a precious caress. Then she arose and went to work.

She assembled her collection of shepherds and camels and sheep in a box by themselves. She wrapped the little dolls in red tissue paper and tied them with gold ribbon. She put the cards she had bought together so she could use them at a moment's notice should the need arise, and she laid the prettier things in an empty bureau drawer till she should decide what to do with them. Now would be the time to tie those cards on the carnations.

She went out and told the bell boy about her plan, and found ready assent and help in her scheme. He himself would see that the flowers were properly delivered quite early in the morning, and he promised utmost secrecy, smiling gratefully when she presented him with a small leather Testament and thanked him for helping her. And she hadn't the slightest idea what it meant to the boy to have her lovely face smiling at him, with its soft frame of gold hair, and her beautiful blue eyes. He hoped some day he would have a girl as beautiful as this one. Only of course he wouldn't, because she was a real lady, and he was only a poor boy.

When Astra came back into her room with the box of flowers she felt very happy, and her radio welcomed her with Christmas Carols being sung all over the world:

"Night of Nights, so calm, so pure, so holy!"

She sang with the radio as her deft fingers tied the little cards to the gift flowers, and she prayed as she sang that the little verses on the cards might each bear a blessing.

She had finished tying the ribbons, and stood looking down at the completed full box when the bell boy knocked at her door.

"There is someone on the phone wants you. Is your box ready? I'll carry it for you. Say, aren't they swell! That's great of you to do that for the folks. I bet they'll appreciate that!" he said.

He put the cover on the box and carried it away, and Astra hastened to the telephone booth at the end of the hall. How glad she was that no one was about just then.

It occurred to her that perhaps this was her cousin Duke, and she took a deep breath and prayed that all might be well. And then it was Cameron's nice friendly voice greeting her.

"Is that you, Astra?" and she never noticed till afterward that this was the first

257

time he had called her by her first name.

"Oh, yes —" she gasped. "I — you!"

But Cameron was talking.

"Say, good friend, I'm in a terrible hole, and I'm wondering if you will come to my rescue and help me out? Now don't say you will if you have other plans, because it might not be pleasant, but I'd be all kinds of obliged if you can see your way clear to help."

"Why, of course!" laughed Astra, and her laughter rippled over the wire with heartening cheer. "Of course! I'll be *delighted* to do anything I can for you! Where are you?"

"Why, I'm in Philadelphia."

"You haven't gone yet?" Her voice was like a glad chime of bells.

"No. I had to change my plans. My stepmother wrote she had to go and see her sick sister, and I'm to come later sometime. And then my sister wished her three children on me for over Christmas, because she and her husband thought they had to go away. I foolishly promised to stay with them. They've gone, and I've at last got those three wild little hoodlums to bed and quiet. But the catch is a telegram from a business man I've been trying to contact for two years, saying he is passing through Philadelphia tomorrow, and if I will come down to the station

258

he will talk to me between trains, and perhaps be ready to sign a contract. It means a very great deal to my business if I get it, but I can't go away and leave these children, even for an hour. I promised to stay here and see that they had a good time for Christmas. Their nurse is here, and the cook, but I don't trust the cook. I think she drinks. And the nurse asked leave to go to church in the morning and she may not come back. There's no telling. I don't think my sister trusts either of them. Now the question is, would you be willing to come over, say, by nine o'clock in the morning, and stay till I get back? I can't promise when that will be, but it ought not to be over two or three hours at most, and *may* be only a few minutes. I know it's a big thing to ask, but you've always been so willing, and I'm learning to presume on that."

"Oh, I'd be charmed!" said Astra, her eyes shining. "I love children, and we can have the grandest time together, I'm sure. How old are they?"

"The boy is seven, the girls are five and half past two. I don't know how spoiled they are. I haven't seen so much of them lately. But we always manage to get on together. I thought if you could come as early as nine I could introduce them to you and ease out without their realizing it. You see they are pretty sore at their father and mother deserting them on Christmas. They weren't told till just before they left. Do you think you would mind telling stories or playing games or something with them till I can get rid of this important man and get back to you?"

"Why of course not!" said Astra. "I'll have the time of my life. It will make a real Christmas for me. Now don't you worry any more. Go get yourself some real rest, and I'll be there by nine o'clock sharp!"

"Well, I knew you were that kind of girl or I wouldn't have dared to ask. But I am grateful with all my heart. Are you sure you hadn't planned to go to dinner with some old friends?"

"Certainly not. I told you I intended to keep away from them all until Christmas is over. I don't want to barge in where I'm not wanted at any family gathering. If my guardian had been at home that would have been different. But I was being very happy in the thought of hearing your radio all day long. And oh, those roses! I can't thank you enough!"

"Please don't! I'm glad they pleased you, but I'm thinking you'll be only too glad to get back to your quiet room with the radio and roses, after you get through with my assignment tomorrow. I must warn you that these are very strenuous kids."

"Oh, that's all right! We'll get along. And I'm just so glad to help. I hope you have great success and get your man. I'll be praying you will."

"Thanks for that more than anything. I'll be remembering that. Now get to your rest for you'll need it. And in the morning take a taxi. Those are *orders!*"

He gave the address very clearly, made her write it down, even gave the telephone number, and asked her to call him when she was starting.

After she had hung up Astra felt a happy glow in her heart. It was as if he had been visiting her. And tomorrow would be fun! No matter what the children were she felt sure she would get along. Of course she mustn't expect to see Cameron much. He would be leaving as soon as she got there, and when he returned it would be her place to depart as soon as she could. He wouldn't want her hanging around. But she would have the radio and the roses, she remembered gleefully, to come back to.

And now here was her chance to do something for somebody. Could she possibly get those children to listen to the Christmas story? Well, she could try. If she failed in that there would be some other way. Perhaps they already knew the Christmas story so well that it was old and worn out to them. But wouldn't they be intrigued perhaps if she built Bethlehem for them? That was what she had been going to do in her own room, just to be Christmasy.

She went to her store of things she had bought that afternoon. The green paper! That would make the hills and valleys where the sheep were pastured. Hadn't she some cotton? She could run out to the drug store that was in the same block with the Association and get a roll. That would make the stuffing for mountains.

Slowly she gathered the things together, put them in one of the shopping bags, threw her coat about her and ran out to the drug store after the cotton, and a pot of paste. The snowflakes stung her face and powdered her hair, reminding her of the night she started on her journey.

Back in her room again she took out some of the little white cards and began fashioning small flat-roofed dwellings, with outside staircases, and a general air of orientalism about them. She stuck them together with paste, and packed them all in a tiny box for safe keeping.

When she had the makings of Bethlehem packed she went to her store of gifts again and selected several things to take along. There surely could be no harm in giving gifts to little children, even if you didn't know their mother, and she selected two of the prettiest little dollies, which any little girl could not help but love. For the boy she chose the little pony. It wasn't but five inches tall, but so perfect in every detail, covered with real hide, a silky brown coat of hair, a tail and mane, "all saddled and bridled and ready for the flight." Surely any boy would enjoy having that. His mother of course might extract it from him sometime and use it for a bridge prize, but it surely would delight him for the time being.

So she packed her gifts, slipping in the lovely Testament, and a few of the little ones. Perhaps there would be an opening for them somewhere.

A gay little mossy green jersey dress with buttons like red berries seemed the proper frock for the occasion, and a scarlet ribbon for her hair. Or was that too coquettish? But no, not for Christmas Day, and for children. Especially since the young man was not to be a part of the picture permanently.

She laid everything out, deciding she would wear three at least of her wonderful roses, tucked in her dress.

So she packed a little overnight bag with everything it seemed she could possibly need for the day, including a clean apron. She didn't know much about the care of children but an apron didn't seem an unreasonable requirement, even on Christmas. Supposing the cook got drunk and she had to finish the dinner?

And when everything was ready, even to the hat and coat laid out to be put on quickly, she got to bed, the radio by her side, and one lovely rosebud where her cheek could touch it on her pillow beside her.

She laughed to think as she lay down, how nicely her program had been arranged for her. Now if Duke should come to hunt her up, he could not spoil Christmas Day for her anyway, for she was going for the day. And she would not leave word where to find her, either.

By and by she grew weary of listening to singers, and radio announcers. Even Christmas speakers seemed tiresome, and presently she turned the radio off. She didn't want to have it going all night while she slept, and she wouldn't want to wake herself up to turn it off when she was just dropping off.

She opened the window just a little for a

cold wind was blowing, and she could hear the snowflakes splashing on the window pane. The spicy breath of falling snow; the cold air touching her cheeks and forehead; sleepy comfort stole about her. Cameron had called her up, had called her "Astra." Had asked her to help him! It didn't mean anything special, but it was nice.

Softly up to her window floated the sound of carolers singing "Silent night! Holy night!"

But the thick carpet of snow muffled any sound of footsteps on the street below, and Astra would not have recognized, had she heard them, the steps of a certain man who walked away from the building to his hard earned rest, well content with what he had discovered.

 **15** Astra awoke early Christmas morning and swung the radio dial around until she had a clear response from it. She had taken a minute or two the night before as she came through the hall to pick up a newspaper and look at the list of stations and what they were offering, and she knew that there was a devotional program on at seven o'clock. So while she was hurrying through her preparations for the day she had the pleasure of hearing some sweet and most unusual Christmas singing, a tender prayer, a real message that seemed to strike a keynote for living through the day, and make it more than just a holiday, a *holy* day! And her own prayer that morning was for grace to live that day through as unto the Lord.

At eight o'clock she went to the restaurant and got a hot breakfast, though she didn't waste much time over it. At the newsstand she bought a newspaper to leave in her room so that she might more intelligently hunt for stations on her radio when she returned.

At half past eight she summoned her taxi, called up Cameron to announce her soon arrival, and started on her way, carrying her bag of ammunition with her. The roses pinned to her coat gave her a festive appearance, and she felt as if she were going to have a wonderful day.

Cameron himself opened the door of the pleasant apartment where Rosamond Cameron Harrison lived, and welcomed her eagerly.

"You've come!" he said in a low eager tone as he gripped her hand in greeting. "I was afraid that something would prevent you, but I might have known you'd carry through any amount of handicaps."

"As a matter of fact," said Astra gaily, "I didn't have a single handicap! I've just been anticipating coming all night! Although you did crowd my life so full of luxuries that I found it difficult to concentrate on getting ready."

Then a small girl approached with great dark eyes upon her.

"Are you a sup*prise?*" she asked looking up at Astra.

"Why, yes, I guess I must be," said Astra giving a quick look at Cameron.

"This is Mary Lou," announced Cameron in a tone of a gentleman announcing a lady's entrance. "She's the baby of the family, and has been mourning my imminent absence, till I told her I had a surprise for her while I was gone."

"Thanks for giving me a hint," said Astra

smiling. "I'll do my best."

"I fink you'll do pwetty well," said Mary Lou. "You have a coat made out of a gray kitty! And you have pwetty hair all sunshine!"

"Well, thank you, little lady. I appreciate the compliment."

"But I didn't think that *you'd* go off and leave us with a new stranger, when our mother is away!" put in a new voice, as Brenda, the next little girl stepped forward, giving her uncle a withering glance. Her eyes were still darker and her black curls longer than Mary Lou's.

"This is Brenda," said Uncle Charles. "She's inclined to consider herself somewhat of a queen, and exercises a mild female dictatorship in the home."

Brenda solemnly considered the newcomer.

"I *may* like you," she said with a haughty chin raised, "but what can you *do?*"

Astra laughed.

"Suppose you answer that question after I've been here a while," she answered gaily.

"Well, *I* shall like her," said the boy stepping up and helping her off with her coat. "That was a pretty good answer to give you, Miss Smarty."

"This is Harold," said the uncle.

"I'm glad to know you, Harold," said

Astra putting out her hand with a warm clasp. "I think we shall get on pretty well together, don't you?"

"Swell!" said Harold.

"Well, *I* might like her too," said Brenda in a relenting tone. "She's got pretty clothes, and mother says that's half! Mother might like her too, perhaps."

"Well, I like her first because Uncle Charles likes her," said Harold.

"How do you know Uncle Charles likes her?" demanded Brenda.

"Because he brought her here for a pleasant surprise," answered the boy gravely, "and I think you're pretty sappy to treat her this way when she's come to help us have a good time."

"Has she?" asked Brenda. "How?" The child stared at Astra scowling.

"Well, when you get this matter of whether we like each other settled," laughed Astra, "perhaps you'll find out. Anyhow I'm staying while your uncle is away, and I guess you'll have to put up with me. But you know I never can really do my best for people who don't like me."

Brenda looked a little troubled.

"What is your best?"

"Well, that's another thing I'll let you answer after we've been together awhile."

Cameron was standing just outside the door of the guest room where he had taken Astra to lay off her wraps, and his face was a study in mingled disgust and amusement.

"Well, I must say, if I had known how rude you were going to be I wouldn't have brought you a nice surprise at all," he said. "I'd have brought you a disappointing surprise. I declare, Brenda, I've a notion to take you into the bathroom and give you a good sound spanking!"

"*Me?*" screamed Brenda. "I'd have you to know my mother never *allows* me to be spanked! Not by *any*body!"

"Well, this is one time you'll find your mother hasn't anything to do with it," said her uncle. "I'm left in charge, and I'm going to spank if you can't behave yourself and act like a civilized child."

Suddenly two great tears gathered in Brenda's big eyes as she surveyed her uncle.

"I — don't think — I *like* you — any more Uncle Charlie!" burst forth the child with quivering lip, and then she broke down with a big sob.

"Well, now, this is no way to begin a Merry Christmas, do you think it is?" said Astra diplomatically. "Suppose we just put all this nonsense away, and play it didn't happen. Shall we? Suppose we start out *in-*

tending to *like* each other, whether we do or not. Won't that be nicest?"

Brenda sidled over to Astra and slipped a skinny little hand into Astra's, looking up at her with a watery smile.

"I guess I *do* like you," said Brenda.

"Why of course, and I'm going to like you a lot! Now, suppose you bring me a nice drink of water and then we'll call ourselves friends."

Brenda bloomed out in another smile and hurried away to get the water.

"I call that rare cleverness," said Cameron in a low tone. "I guess you'll win out. Now, come out here and sit down a minute while I give you a little idea of the layout, and then I'll have to be getting on."

The children stood across the room and watched them as they talked, finally sidling nearer, and slipping down at Astra's feet.

"I do hope this isn't going to be an awful bore to you," said Cameron. "I meant to get some kind of games outlined, but somehow there were so many buttons to fasten and faces to wash that I didn't get around to it."

"Oh, that's all right," laughed Astra. "That's more in my province, don't you think? I've been sort of planning out a program for us in my head. I think we'll get along. I wonder if they have ever built Bethlehem? Do you know?"

"Built Bethlehem?" questioned the astonished Cameron.

"Do you mean the big steel works?" asked Harold suddenly interested. "Do you have to have one of those sets of steel blocks and things to build it? Because I don't have any."

"Oh, no," said Astra. "I don't mean that Bethlehem. I mean the Bible Bethlehem, where Jesus was born?"

"Why I didn't know there was any other Bethlehem," said Harold.

"All right then, we'll build Bethlehem pretty soon, and I'll tell you all about it," said Astra smiling reassuringly.

"Do *girls* build Bethlehem?" asked Brenda wistfully.

"Oh yes, we'll *all* build Bethlehem. But first we have to sing some Christmas songs, so we can sing as we work. Don't you think that would be nice? Do you know any Christmas songs?"

"Oh yes," said Mary Lou, "vee can sing!"

"Good-by," whispered Cameron from the shelter of the doorway, "I'll get back as soon as I can. You're all right!" and he eased out into the hall, and silently into his overcoat and hat that were waiting for him. He hurried out the door shutting it noiselessly behind him.

Cameron hadn't introduced the servants to Astra because when he went in search of them the nurse was nowhere to be found, and the cook said she had gone to church.

"She said you said she could go to church."

"Well, yes, I said I would see about it, but I didn't think she would go so early."

"Yes, her church meets early," said the cook sulkily. "Oh, she'll be back sometime when she gets good and ready."

"Well, you had better come in and meet Miss Everson," said Cameron.

"An' why shud I hev ta ga in an' meet her? Ef she want's ta see me she c'n cum oot here!"

So Cameron felt that the better part of valor was to retreat and leave the grouchy cook to her own domain. There would be time enough to fight when he got back from meeting his man.

So Astra started out on the new consignment with one disgruntled servant in the kitchen, and three uncertain little belligerents in the living room. But nothing daunted she took life as it came and started in on Bethlehem.

"Where shall we build Bethlehem?" she asked, looking around on the possibilities

"How about our kindergarten table?" suggested Harold.

So he and Brenda brought the kindergarten table from the nursery, and arranged several small stools and benches.

"Is Bethlehem in Philadelphia?" asked Harold.

"Oh, no, it is away over the sea in Palestine, and it was built many many years ago before you were any of you born."

"Is it a city?"

"No, it's a little town. I wonder if you can't sing that song about it that the world has been singing for a good many Christmases. 'Oh, little town of Bethlehem.' Do you know it?"

"Wes. Vee have 'at in our kinnegarten Hunday Toole!" asserted Mary Lou eagerly.

"So do we all," said Harold.

"Yes," said Brenda. And suddenly they were all singing, mostly on different keys at first. But finally Astra got them started off together, and the young voices really sounded very pretty. The grouchy cook stole through the pantry and peeked angrily through the swinging door, and then retreated with a cunning look in her eye. That golden haired girl with the red ribbon couldn't do much. *She* wouldn't be bossed by *her!* So she stole up to her room and brought down a big black bottle which she hid in the pantry. But Astra was engaged in

274

making Bethlehem real to her young audience and she wasn't caring about any cooks.

"Now," she said eagerly, "Bethlehem is among little hills, and we have to make the hills first. We'll make those with the green paper."

She took out a pair of scissors she had brought, cut off several generous pieces of the green tissue, and began crumpling them in her hands. Then she unrolled her package of cotton and tore off good-sized pieces.

"We'll stuff the cotton under the hills to make them stand up nicely," she explained gaily, as her deft fingers twisted and patted and stuffed the hills quickly into shape across the back of the low table, slipping a pile of magazines under one hill, with the green paper smoothly over the top.

"This will be where we shall build the little town of Bethlehem," she explained to the watching children. "We have to have a smooth firm base to put the houses on so they won't fall over."

"What are we going to build the houses of?" asked the boy. "We've got a lot of stone blocks."

"Oh, have you? That will be lovely. Can you get them?"

"Oh, yes," said the boy springing up eagerly. "They're right in the nursery on the shelf."

He came bringing the box, but the cook, already cross from the "wee drap" she had taken from her bottle, stuck her head out of the kitchen door, saw him coming along the hall, and began to object.

"Hey, you boy you! Take them toys back where they b'long! Don't ya know the nurse got them all picked up and put away nice? And didna she tell ya ta let 'em alone? Yer mommie'll smack ya good fer gettin' them toys out an' clutterin' up the livin' room fer Christmas. Don't ya know ef yer a bad boy Santie Claus won't give ya nothin' when he comes?"

"Aw! Santa Claus!" sneered the child. "He ain't coming *here*. My father and mother are gone away. Thur won't be any Santa Claus *here!*"

"Well, shut you up an' tak them toys back where they b'long!"

"No!" said Harold "We need 'em. She wants 'em fer something she's makin, for us," and he vanished into the living room excitedly.

"The cook's mad," he remarked calmly, as if it were a common occurrence. "But I told her you wanted 'em."

"Well," said Astra soothingly, "after a

while we'll invite her in to see Bethlehem and then she'll understand."

A gleam of relief and triumph came into the boy's eyes.

"O.K.!" he said with a sigh of pleasure.

By this time the region round about Bethlehem was taking form and shape, and the children were fascinated, watching it grow.

Astra went to her box of things she had found in the ten cent store and brought out some trees, lovely fuzzy green things, and a few palm trees with stiff metal backs that stood up beautifully Then she began to build tiny white houses out of the stone blocks, three or four blocks to a house; now and then an arched doorway, or a tiny crack of a window between two larger blocks, with a wee one below; one or two larger houses with flat roofs, and one with a tiny outside staircase. It all looked very real. And then some of the little cardboard houses she stuck here and there between the others. Astra was as much interested in her work as were the children. And presently the cook swung the pantry door open halfway, and peered in scowling, but stayed to watch also, gradually edging in and standing behind Astra, emitting a strong odor of whatever was in her black bottle. But Astra went steadily on with her work.

"Bethlehem had a hotel," she said, "they called it an inn."

"That's what they call our hotel out here," announced Harold excitedly. "It's right over there on the next street. It has big piazzas and flower beds all around in the summer. Sometimes we go there to get ice cream."

"Yes?" said Astra. "Well, now we'll put this inn over here on the left. Perhaps it didn't have piazzas, but it had a flat roof, and people could go up there and sit, and walk. We'll build it with these big stone arches, because down under these arches was their stable. Or at least we'll play it was. The real Bethlehem might have had a separate building, but it must have been near the inn. They kept their cows there. The sheep were off on the hills with their shepherds, but the cows would stay around the stable probably. Here are two or three little cows I brought with me. We'll stand them here by the stable, and here are some guards for the hotel. We'll stand them up here on the housetop."

Deftly Astra placed the tiny figures she had bought, an Arab in a long white robe, with a sword lifted over his turbaned head, two or three other figures in oriental garments.

The children watched her breathlessly,

and old Becky edged nearer and peered with her near-sighted eyes.

"And now off here in the valley at the foot of these hills," went on Astra, "the sheep were out in green pastures, eating grass, and drinking water out of this little silver stream. We'll put this little looking glass down here to show where the drinking water is, and we'll put the sheep and the little lambs around it."

The children's eyes were round with surprise as one by one the sheep and the little white lambs appeared and took their places in the setting. And the shepherds came and guarded their sheep.

Then Astra began to tell the story.

"Once a long time ago God felt very bad about the people He had made to live on this earth, because they were very naughty. They had all sinned, and God had told them that they would have to be terribly punished if they sinned. Their punishment was to die forever. And God had to keep His promise because He was God, you know. Do you know what sin is?"

"Yes," said Brenda, "it's doing what daddy says not!"

"No, it's what mothah says not," interrupted Mary Lou.

Suddenly there came an interruption.

The hall doorbell rang!

The cook gave a wild look toward the door and scuttled away to the kitchen.

"Wasn't that the doorbell?" asked Astra, just as she went out the door.

"It ain't my business to go to the door," mumbled the cook.

"*I'll* go," said Harold.

"No, *I'll* go!" shouted Brenda.

"*I* go!" said little Mary Lou, and they all three scrambled up and rushed to the door. The boy reached the door first and swung it open on a lady.

Astra called out to the children. "Oh, but that's not a nice way to meet a caller. Quiet down. It doesn't take but one to open a door, you know."

And then she looked up at the caller, and the lady wore *a mink coat!*

**16** The pleasant welcoming smile she wore as she came forward to quiet the children was still on Astra's face as she looked up and recognized Camilla Blair, but her heart suddenly felt like a little frozen thing, out of its right place.

But there was the lady regarding her with belligerence and assurance. Astra's trained mind immediately brought her smile into a dignified about-face, and gave the lady questioning attention.

"Isn't this Mrs. Harrison's apartment?" asked Camilla.

"Yes," said Astra, as a lady would say it.

"Well, is Mr. Cameron here?"

Astra opened astonished eyes.

"Oh, did you expect to meet Mr. Cameron here?"

Camilla's chin went up in affront.

"Why, yes. I supposed he would be here. How soon is he coming?"

"Well, I really wouldn't know," said Astra, with the detached air of a servant.

Camilla surveyed her with eyebrows slightly lifted.

"Aren't you one of the regular servants here?" she asked, almost insolently.

Astra gave a merry wicked little grin.

"Oh, no," she said, "I just came in to help with the children while their mother is away."

"Oh!" Camilla looked Astra over again.

"Are you a professional nurse?"

Astra's face dimpled amusedly.

"Not exactly," she said. "Won't you come in and sit down?"

The children gave little suppressed gasps and looked at Astra with frowns. They didn't want their playtime interrupted.

"Well, I'd like to know first what time you think Mr. Cameron might get here."

"I wouldn't be able to tell you that," said Astra clear-eyed, looking at the visitor steadily. "If you would like to come in and wait a while I should think it would be all right. And now, I'm sure you will forgive me if I go on with the story I was telling the children. You see, that's what I'm supposed to be here for."

"Oh, I see," said Camilla haughtily, looking at the girl in astonishment. Was this sort-of-a-servant girl attempting to dismiss her, reprove her?

She settled down in the easiest chair in the room and observed what was going on somewhat scornfully. But Astra went right on with her story.

"Now, let me see, just where did we leave

off, Harold?" she said, trying to think back, and greatly annoyed by the presence of the mink coat in the room. Its rich luxurious folds fell over Camilla's chair with an oppressive air of affluence which did not fit with the simple town of Bethlehem and the grazing sheep beside their tiny wooden shepherds.

"I know what you were saying!" said the boy. "It was about sin. You said everybody had been naughty, and God had said if they were naughty they had to be punished. He had to keep His word because He was God, so everybody was going to die forever 'n ever."

"Yes," said Astra, "but you see God so loved people that He made a way for them to be saved from eternal death, if they wanted to be saved. He promised to send a Saviour who would die in their place. He had to be a sinless One who had no sin of His own to die for, so He could take the sin of the whole world upon Himself. There wasn't any ordinary person who hadn't sinned, so God sent His own Son."

"Did He die for our sin, too?" questioned Brenda who had plenty of such to her own small account.

"Mine too?" asked Mary Lou. "Wouldn't my mamma hafta spank me any more?"

"Oh, you don't understand, baby. It wasn't our mother's spanking. It was God making us die if we didn't be good!" said Harold in a superior tone. "Did you say it was for everybody? That lady's sin, too?" and he pointed a speculative finger at Camilla.

"Yes. God says everybody. They all have a chance to be saved. All they need do is believe it."

But the lady in question arose in annoyance and came over toward the table with its mountains and its little town.

"What ridiculous stuff are you teaching these children?" she said bending over and fingering several sheep and upsetting a little tan cow.

"You *stop* that!" said little Mary Lou in a disturbed tone of voice. "You spoil our picture and our town. You *must*n't touch our fings."

But the guest paid no attention to the baby, and continued to pick up one and another shepherd, and lamb, and look them over.

"I beg your pardon," said Astra in a cool voice. "I'm telling the Christmas story. Would you like to take my place and tell it?"

"No, indeed!" said the guest coldly, withdrawing to her chair. "I have no desire to descend to story-telling. But I was just wondering what kind of foolishness was being stuffed down the children's throats. I shall take pains that my friend Mrs. Harrison knows what has been perpetrated during her absence. You seem to have a certain amount of cleverness with children. It's a pity you couldn't have gone to college and found out that the sort of thing you are teaching is nothing but folklore and tradition, mixed up with a lot of dogmas. It's not the sort of thing to tell children. However, I don't suppose they understand enough to hurt them, and what they do understand they'll soon forget!"

Astra twinkled her eyes at the children and smiled quietly, wondering what the lady would say if she mentioned the two noted colleges that she had attended at different times when she and her father were abroad, and if she could see the diploma carefully packed away, of the still more noted college where she had graduated. However she closed her pleasant lips and said nothing. Then suddenly she saw that Harold had stalked over to the guest and was standing indignantly before her, his feet wide apart, his chin up in the air, his eyes flashing.

"I won't-*not* forget what she says! I will-*so* remember every word! And I do *so* understand what she says. I guess I'm old enough to know *all* peoples are naughty. You are *yourself,* you *know* you are! And maybe you've got to die, too — because you don't sound to me as if *you* would believe! But I wish you'd go home and not bother us. We were having a nice time until you came. And you've no business to talk that way to our Astra. We all like her! Now, get out. I don't care if you are my mummie's friend, you're not nice, and I don't *like* you!"

Astra looked at the boy aghast!

"Harold! Stop talking! You're being very rude indeed! You're being naughty now, and you certainly must know it. What do you think God thinks of such conduct?"

Harold drooped his eyelids, and looked ashamed.

"You'll have to apologize to the lady before we can go on," said Astra, with a grieved note in her voice.

The child looked up with fury in his eyes:

"What, 'polagize ta *her?* Not on yer life! She hadn't any business ta come here and spoil our Christmas Day when our mother and father are away! And she's saying bad things. I know, because we learn those same things in our Sunday School where we go, and I know they're good things. Don't we, Brennie?"

"We cert'nly do!" affirmed Brenda, as if

she were a referee in an international con-
test.

"There! I told ya!" said Harold. "An'
you're a bad lady. She's *our* Astra, an' we
won't let you talk bad to her."

Brenda was standing a little back of the
angry boy, shaking her head, flashing her
eyes, stamping her little foot, and saying,
"No! *No!* NO!"

And little Mary Lou was sitting in her
small chair with her mouth all puckered up
into a quiver, her eyes wide with anguish,
and great tears rolling down her pink
cheeks.

Camilla arose with haste.

"Mercy!" she said. "What a household!
Deliver me from ever having any children! I
don't wonder their mother wanted to get
away for a day!"

Then she turned on Astra, as if she were
to blame for it all:

"I hope you see the effect your teaching
has had! And now I want to know *whose* servant you are! I certainly shall report you. It
isn't fair to other customers to have a nurse
like you around, posing as a child spe-
cialist."

But Astra just then had hold of Harold's
arm with a firm and masterful grip, her eyes
were sorry and troubled, and her lips shut

firmly together. She was not hearing Camilla.

"Harold, you have been a very naughty boy to speak that way to your mother's friend, and I want you to go over there and sit in that chair by the door and think about what you have said and how wrong it was. Your mother and father would have been ashamed of you; I am ashamed of you; and I am sure God must be ashamed of you. Just go and think about it, and see what you think God feels about it. And when this lady goes out I want you to apologize to her. You said very naughty things to her."

"Well, they were all *true!*" said Harold lifting honest eyes, still angry.

"Look here, little boy," said Astra, putting her arm around the angry young shoulder, "don't you know that you are not that lady's judge? God is the only One who has a right to say what she is, not you. Even if she were very wrong it would not be your business to judge her."

The boy hung his head, and would not lift his eyes to the contemptuous eyes of the lady in the mink coat. But he finally lifted them to Astra's.

"Okay," he faltered dejectedly. "I'm willing to let God judge her, — but I'll bet if He does, He'll be harder on her than I was!

On Christmas Day, too, and we are only children without our own mother!"

With a motion like a tender caress Astra led the little boy over to the appointed chair and sat him down gently.

"Try to think how you have made God feel about this, Harold," said Astra in a low tone. And then she turned toward the angry woman who had made all this disturbance.

"I beg your pardon," she said quietly, "you asked me a question, I think, and I wasn't quite sure what you said."

Camilla flashed back importantly to her question.

"Yes," she snapped. "I asked you whose servant you are! I shall certainly report you to whomever you work for."

Astra stood utterly still and looked at the woman for an instant and then she said with a sweet humility, and yet with a proud note in her voice:

"I am a servant of the Lord Jesus Christ. If you report me to Him I am sure He will help you to understand."

"You are blasphemous!" said Camilla. "If you didn't need reporting before you certainly do now. And those children deserve a thorough spanking! I would be glad to administer it to them right now!"

She made a motion as if to take off the

mink coat for a time, and suddenly Mary Lou gave forth a great sob like a shout of terror, "Not me!" and rushed over to Astra, flinging herself in her arms to be taken up. And Brenda slid over to Astra's off-side, and hid herself in Astra's skirt.

Astra took little Mary Lou up in her arms and cuddled her close, and put one hand on Brenda's dark curls comfortingly, facing the interloper with a steady gaze. She was very white but otherwise she was entirely calm, and she stood her ground almost as if she were protected by an unseen army.

And then the little boy got up from his chair and walked over to stand before Camilla, his proud little head raised defiantly, his young lips a-tremble, his fine eyes flashing.

"I'm sorry I made God feel bad," he said, every syllable clear and distinct. "I thought maybe He wanted me to tell you what you were, but I guess I oughtta uv let Him do it! I hope you'll excuse what I said, but if God is going to be your judge after this I'm just sure *you'll get yours!* And it won't be just a little old spanking either, I'll tell the world! It'll be real! I'm just tellin' ya for your own good."

Then with a low bow which Harold had probably learned at dancing school, the little boy backed away and sat down in his chair of punishment, with a satisfied look as if he had done his best to set himself right with God.

Astra, standing there with the warm arms of the little girl about her neck, the hot baby tears splashing on her face, and the small girl Brenda cowering against her, felt a sudden desire to sit down and laugh. The whole situation was so ridiculously tragic, and on Christmas Day! What was wrong? Was it her fault? And what ought she to do now? Of course she wasn't the lady of the house, and perhaps her responsibility was ended. And yet it seemed outlandish to let the occurrence end like this.

But suddenly Camilla settled the matter for her. She turned to the children collectively, as much of them as she could see, and addressed them.

"You have been very naughty children! Every one of you! And I shall take care to see that your mother and your father hear all about it. I'm quite sure they know how to give you all the right kind of spanking, or even something worse. And now I'm going home before any more insults are heaped upon me. And *you* —" here she turned to Astra with her imperious chin in the air, "when Mr. Cameron comes you will tell him that I couldn't possibly wait for him any longer. I have duties at home, and I am utterly exhausted with the reception I have had here. Tell Mr. Cameron I wish he would call me up at once as soon as he comes in. And as for *you,* I shall certainly see that you get your just due. I consider this all your fault, and I shall not lose any time in telling a lot of other people so."

But Astra's head was bent down to the baby in her arms, and her lips were touching Mary Lou's cheeks with soft kisses, patting the little heaving back that was still quivering with sobs. With the other hand she smoothed the tumbled black curls of Brenda, who was still sobbing.

And stanch and true in front of them stood the little boy, his fists clenched, his chest heaving, and big boy-tears rolling down his furious young face.

And then he suddenly gasped out in a high sweet voice, "My Uncle Charlie told me ta take care of you, and I'm gonta do it, no matter how many bad old women come around!"

Camilla went out quickly with a slammed door, and a minute later they heard the elevator go down.

Then suddenly the door from the kitchen swung open, letting in the sound of loud gutteral snoring from the back of the kitchen, and there in the doorway stood Uncle Charlie!

He had a great bunch of white chrysanthemums in a tall glass vase in his hands, and his face was stern with astonishment and anxiety.

"What in the world is the meaning of all this?" he demanded of nobody in particular. "Has something happened?"

17

What Charles Cameron saw first as he stood there in the doorway with his great sheaf of gorgeous chrysanthemums, was Astra with the baby in her arms, nestled so comfortingly in her neck as if she might be the child's own mother, and her other arm around the little Brenda. It was a sweet tender picture and it stirred his heart deeply. Astra! How lovely she was! Her cheeks were scarlet now, like the ribbon on her hair, and it was plain to be seen that she and the children were in entire accord, and had all been through a hard experience. There was something basically masculine and protective about Harold. And it was he who answered his uncle, as if he, being the man, must account for all that had happened while he was the head of the house.

"There certainly *has,* Uncle Charlie," he gasped, with almost a manly sob at the end of his phrase. "We've had a bad lady here, and she got us all haywire! We were having a swell time, building Bethlehem, and she just barged in and tried ta run us all. She called our Astra a *servant!* Imagine that! An' asked who she worked for! And told her she was stuffing lies ur something down our froats, and she oughtta gone ta college, an' a lotta rotten stuff. An' then she squared off an' offered ta *spank* us! Imagine *that!* An' I hadta tell her where ta get off! Only Astra said I wasn't her judge, an' I hadta 'polagize. But I guess God'll have His time with her 'fore He gets her ta do anything. But anyhow I 'polagized, an' that's the first time I ever did, too! But I'm *glad* I said what I did, anyhow, and I guess God is too! She needed it, she really *did,* Uncle Charlie, an' I don't mean *maybe!*"

Cameron's eyes suddenly met Astra's and in spite of themselves they grinned covertly, ducking down their faces to hide their mirth.

"Well, who was this lady, Harold?"

"You oughtta know. She said she came here ta meet *you!*"

"To meet *me!*" exclaimed Cameron frowning. "Who in the world is she?"

"Yeh, she said you expected her ta meet-cha here!"

"That's absurd!" said Cameron, much annoyed. He gave a quick glance at Astra but she was occupied in mopping up Mary Lou's tears, and meditating on whether he had been in the kitchen during the last two or three minutes while Camilla was there discoursing. Then she spoke.

"She said she had something very important to tell you, and she was sorry she couldn't wait any longer for you, she had some things to do and must hurry back. She asked that you would call her up at once when you came, but I doubt if she has reached there yet unless she lives close by."

"In a pig's eye you will, Uncle Charlie, *will* ya? You wouldn't call up a thing like that, *would*ya?"

"Well, from your description it doesn't sound as if she was the kind of person I would care to call up. Did she leave her telephone number?"

"She thought you'd know what it was," said Brenda suddenly barging into the conversation.

Her uncle put out his arms.

"Come here, little girl," he said, setting down the great vase of flowers and taking her on his lap. "You look all stirred up. Did they get *you* into the fight too?"

Brenda nodded and snuggled into her uncle's arms.

"An' on Chris'mus Day, too!" said Harold indignantly.

"Yes, it was a shame!" said Cameron. "I shouldn't have gone and left you. But since I had to go I'm glad I had such a good substitute."

"Yes," spoke up Astra. "He was fine. He

really told the lady where to get off most effectively, though I'm not so sure his mother will be pleased when the lady gives her account of it. However, it's over, and he really did his best as far as his frame of mind would let him, to apologize, so I guess we won't spoil Christmas Day any further. Now, I wonder if we shall finish Bethlehem, or would you rather play something else?"

"Oh, finish Bethlehem!" begged the children. "Uncle Charlie, you come play Bethlehem too!"

"Sure," said the smiling uncle, divesting himself of his overcoat, and settling down. "How do you play it?"

"Oh, you just watch, and wait till she tells you."

"Don't you think it should be a good thing for you to call this lady Miss Everson?" said Cameron.

"No," said Brenda firmly, "it makes her too far-offy, and she said we might call her Astra."

"Very well," said Cameron. "What the lady says goes. But when you call her that, remember her name means a star, and you must be very polite to her, and respectful, just as you would be if one of the silver stars in the sky should come down and play with you a little while."

The little girl giggled, but Harold looked at his new divinity solemnly, and after a while he smiled.

"I see what you mean, Uncle Charlie. She's like that — ! That's why I told that other lady to get out."

"It appears to me, Harold, that more and more you are revealing that your language to the other lady must have been rather reprehensible! But let's forget it now and go to Bethlehem."

"That bad lady got the sheeps an' the shepherds all mixed up," said Brenda who had been looking over the work so far done.

"We'll soon set that right. While we are doing it, Harold, you can tell your uncle the beginning of the story."

Willingly the boy began:

"Well, Astra told us how we were all sinners c'ndemned to death, and the bad lady didn't like that, because that meant her too. But God loved everybody He had made — Say, Uncle Charlie, ya don't suppose He loves her, too, do ya? Because I don't see how He can."

"For God so loved the world," said Astra in a low tone.

"Oh yeh, we had that in Sunday School. That's John three sixteen. We learned that in the beginners' room. But how could He love

298

her? And why did He make her, anyway, horrid-acting like that?"

"Well, it seems He did," said Cameron thoughtfully, "although He didn't make her act that way. She did that herself. But I guess we've got to be polite to her at least."

"Even if she's rude to us?"

"How about that, Astra?" asked Cameron, their eyes meeting in that glance that seemed to bring them so near together.

"Who when He was reviled, reviled not again," said Astra smiling.

"Well, that sort of sounds as if that was what people should do, if we want to do the right thing. It seems as if Astra knows nearly all the Bible, doesn't it? You and I will have to do a lot of memorizing if we want to keep up with this lady, Harold."

The child gave Astra a slow sweet smile that showed he adored her, even on such short notice.

"Now come on," she said, "and let's finish our story. Will it bore you to listen, Uncle Charlie?" and she gave Cameron a charming smile.

"I should say not," said Cameron, his eyes resting on the girl's lovely face. "Go on. I'm all eagerness!" So the little audience gathered around the table while Astra straightened out the sheep, and began.

And then the old story lived there before them. The walls of the quite modern living room faded away, and blue heavens, star-pricked, came in their place. A great light grew and angels came winging their way down. It was as real to those children, and to the young man, as if they had been looking through a window and actually seen it all. They saw the great angel step forward with his message, and thrilled with the wonder of it, as it came home to each that the story was meant for them too, as well as the shepherds. They watched with reluctance as the other angels went back up into Heaven, and the night grew quiet again. Then they went to Bethlehem to "see the thing which had come to pass," and saw in a word-picture the baby Who was born for them that Christmas Day.

"Well," said Harold at the end, "I'm glad you told us about that. I always wondered how Christmas Day happened, and now it's a lot nicer than I thought it was."

"But I'm awful *hongery!*" suddenly wailed little Mary Lou. "Don't we have any Chris-sum dinnee?"

"Well, I should say!" exclaimed Cameron, glancing at his watch. "It's after half past two! Rosamond said she had ordered dinner for us at exactly one. I wonder where that snoring cook is!"

He went into the kitchen and found disorder, and a great black empty bottle on the floor beside the chair where the cook had reposed when he entered the apartment, but no cook, and not even a smell of dinner anywhere. Further investigation showed the turkey in the refrigerator with its hands helplessly folded, not even a smell of fire on its cold dead skin, and the cook on her bed in the maid's room sound asleep.

There was another black bottle on the floor beside the bed and it was plain to be seen that there would be no Christmas dinner in that house that day, if it depended on Becky to cook it.

Cameron frowned, stood watching old Becky for a minute or two, then he stepped out of the room, removed the key from the inside of the door and put it in the lock on the outside, locking the door with decision. This was no creature to be allowed to waken in the night and go madly about the house among the children. She was dead drunk and there was no mistake about that. By and by when he had time to think it out he would decide what to do with Becky, send her to a hospital, or to the lock-up, or get a doctor and try to get her sober. But for the present she was safe and so were they.

He came back to the kitchen, locking the

door that led from kitchen to the maids' quarters, and studied the possibilities of an immediate dinner from the standpoint of the refrigerator and pantry. There was a large fruit cake in the cake box, several mince pies ranged on the pantry shelf, another tin box of fancy cake. They wouldn't starve of course, but that was no dinner for three healthy hungry little children, cake and pie; not a Christmas dinner. So he stalked into the front hallway and took up the telephone.

"Oh, Uncle Charlie, you're *not* going to telephone that old egg, are ya? I'm off ya fer life if you do." This in a wail from Harold.

"Uncle Charlie, we're *hongery!*" sobbed Brenda.

"When we gonta have dinnee, Unca Sharlie?" wailed Mary Lou.

"Right away, kitten. Hush a minute! I'm telephoning."

"Not to that nassy woman, Unca Sharlie! Her not gonta come here 'gen, is her?"

"No, no, Mary Lou! *Hush!* Is this the restaurant? Send a boy up with your Christmas dinner menu right away to Apartment C. How soon can you serve a dinner for five? All right. Send the menu at once."

Then he hung up and catching up the little girl pranced into the living room.

"How about you ladies and gentlemen setting the table in the dining room? The cook seems to be sick. She's been drinking too much medicine out of a black bottle, and she's in her room asleep now, so we're not waiting on her. The boy is coming up with the menu from the downstairs restaurant, and you are each to pick out just what you want, so be ready to decide right away and not keep him waiting."

"I want turkey," said Brenda, "with stuffings, an' cramb'ry sauce, an' smashed potato, and green peas! No 'pinnage, an' no carrots t'day! It's Christmas! Then I want punkum — no, *mince* pie, 'n' ice cweam!"

"Okay, that goes for me too!" said Harold.

"Me too," said Mary Lou, "an' I want my dwink o' milk."

"Well, I shouldn't wonder if you could have that right now," said Uncle Charlie, making a quick raid on the refrigerator and producing a glass of milk.

Then the boy came up with the menu and took the order, while Astra was helping the children get the dining room table ready for the dinner.

"Aren't we having fun?" said Brenda with a radiant little face lifted to Astra. "I wish my muvver would ever do this wif us."

"Oh you're crazy, you silly!" scorned the

little boy. "Our mother would never have time. She has too many old bridge parties."

"Well, there might be some time, somewhere," said Brenda wistfully.

They had a very gay Christmas dinner. It was quite new and delightful to have strange different things sent up from the restaurant and the children enjoyed it immensely.

But at last their keen appetites were satisfied and they lagged with the final spoonfuls of ice cream.

"What'er we goin' ta do now, Astra?" asked Brenda. "When daddy an' mothah are home they always have presents and we can play with 'em, but we didn't have any presents yet."

"No, but your father and mother are going to give you their presents when they get back, so you'll have another Christmas tomorrow," said Uncle Charlie hopefully, and wondered, as he looked at the slow lazy flakes that were going idly past the window, whether they really *would* get back when they had promised.

"Okay!" said Harold with a deep young sigh.

"Oh," said Astra, "I brought some little presents. Perhaps they will do for today! There is one for each of you."

"Yes," said Cameron, "and I think I have

some packages too. I had forgotten them but since you've mentioned it, I guess I can contribute to the gift-bringing performance too."

"Oh! Oh! Oh! Aren't we having a lovely time!" squealed Mary Lou.

Then the boy from the restaurant came to get the dishes, and Astra gathered up the crumbs from the tablecloth, folded it nicely and put it away, and they all adjourned to the living room.

They put the presents in a pile in the center of the room, and Uncle Charlie distributed them. The first one was for Mary Lou! A lovely dolly, looking like a real baby, with a soft pliable body, big blue eyes and a sweet little cap of gold curls. Mary Lou was wild about it. Her other dolls had been freak rag dolls that were unbreakable, and she slung them around and was always trying to get Brenda's dolls which were more sophisticated. But she recognized this as a doll of the upper classes and duly appreciated it.

"You know what a little girl wikes!" she said with a sweet grateful glance toward Astra. Then as second thought, with the new dolly in a careful arm, she came and climbed into Astra's lap, kissed her, and then made the doll kiss her.

The next was Brenda's turn. And she had

a delightful little croquet set that could be played on the carpet. This from Uncle Charlie. Brenda promptly took the whole box in her arms and tried to climb into her uncle's lap to kiss him.

Then came Harold's turn and he opened a big box that looked like a hat box, and said "From Uncle Charlie" on its top, and there was a pair of boxing gloves for him. He shouted with joy and all but broke up the gathering by his demand to have a boxing match then and there.

"Not till all the presents have been given out," said Uncle Charlie.

Then Brenda had a lovely doll, not very large, but with a beautiful piquant face, and eyes that moved sideways, and turned, and made her look very real and human. She wore a lovely blue dress the color of her eyes, a little knitted coat and cap, and real little mittens. Brenda took her in her arms and cooed and kissed her, and then frantically rushed to Astra and kissed her. It was a very loving time indeed, and Cameron, watching Astra, noted how lovely she was, and how delightful with the children!

There was a little swing for Mary Lou from her uncle, which he promptly set up in the corner, and Mary Lou retired to it to swing her new dolly, and presently to fall asleep quite happily, while the rest of the program went on without her.

Then came the darling little pony for Harold and he was wild with delight.

"I shall keep this on the mantelpiece in my own room," he announced. "Mother needn't think she can have it in the parlor. It's my own horse. And some day when I get grown up I shall have a live one just like it!"

He went over and took Astra's hand and kissed it with the low bow that he had learned in his dancing class and then he retired to get acquainted with his horse.

But there were two more packages on the floor. One of goodly size for Astra, and a small neat package for Cameron.

He made her open her package first. A large fine box of candy in all sorts of shapes and sizes. So after she had thanked him she made him take the first piece out and then passed it around to the great delight of the children, and they sat there enjoying everything, till Harold discovered that his uncle hadn't opened the little package yet.

Cameron opened his package slowly, with many comical remarks about what it could possibly be, and who would send it to him.

He untied the ribbon slowly, turned back the paper very deliberately, stopping for a word between each turn, and then just as he got to the last soft tissue paper cover, he fixed Harold with a stern eye, and said, "Boy, I'll bet you know who gave this present to me."

"Uh huh!" said Harold with a grin.

"Well, boy, I'll just bet it is from that person that you described a little while ago as a bad lady! If it is you can just take it out and put it in the trash can!"

"Oh, no, Uncle Charlie. It isn't from her! She didn't bring any presents for anybody. And she didn't send anything!"

"Then who can have given it to me?" asked Cameron with great curiosity written on his face.

"Whyn'tcha open it 'n find out?" asked the boy.

"Well, that's an idea! Do you suppose it will tell inside?"

"I'll bet it will," said the boy.

So at last Cameron opened the paper, and disclosed a neat little box, and inside the beautiful Testament. Suddenly his eyes went to Astra's shy watching eyes, and a great light came into his own. She needed no other thanks than that look he gave.

But the children gathered around as he turned to the fly leaf, and read, "Charles from Astra," and below, "To help with the next assignment."

The day went quickly after that. Harold had to try out his boxing gloves, and Brenda insisted they should all play croquet — excepting the sleeping Mary Lou. And then it suddenly grew dark in the room, and they turned the lights on and found it was quite a bit after the children's usual bedtime.

They fed the sleepy Mary Lou a glass of milk, and Astra got her into her night clothes, and tucked her in bed with a kiss, and a bit of a prayer she was too sleepy to say herself. Then Astra made some nice hot cereal and fed the others and got them to bed.

"We've had a wonderful Christmas," said Harold as he sank down gratefully into his pillow. "We'll have another one tomorrow, perhaps, but it won't be half as nice. That Bethlehem was great! Can we keep it here a few days?"

"Oh, yes," said Astra, smiling. "That is your Bethlehem. And when the holidays are over you'll find a nice box in the guest room under the bed in which you can pack Bethlehem away for another year. I'll leave that to your care, Harold."

"But won't you be here, Astra?"

"Well, I couldn't be sure of that, Harold. But you won't forget, will you, little boy?"

"No, I won't forget. But, Uncle Charlie,

won't she be here again?"

"Well, if you ask me, boy, I think she will! Now good night!"

So they kissed the children good night and went out into the living room.

"And now," said Astra, "it's time for me to go home. I've had a lovely party, mister, and I thank you for inviting me. I hope you have a pleasant evening, and your children all behave well. But I'm sure they're all just about asleep, so I'm safe in leaving you. Good night!"

He looked at her so tenderly that the tears almost came into her eyes, but she blinked them back hard and managed to smile.

Then his hands went out to her shoulders, and lay gently there for an instant while he looked deep into her soul, before he spoke.

"You *dear!*" he said softly, as if the words were too precious to be heard aloud. "You've been just *wonderful!*"

Then suddenly he put his face down closer to hers.

"I love you!" he said most tenderly. "I love you with all my soul! I know I ought not to tell you yet, because you've had so little time to know me, you wouldn't be sure if you could ever love me or not. But it has seemed to me all day that I had to tell you now, even if you won't ever marry me. I had to let you know how deeply I love you! I had to tell you on Christmas Day! Even if I have to go lonely all my days, I had to have the joy tonight of telling you how much I love you, and want you for my own — Astra, will you marry me?"

Astra looked up with a great wonder and joy growing in her face.

"Oh, *my dear!*" she breathed softly.

And then his strong arms went round her and drew her close, and he stooped and laid his lips on hers in a kiss that seemed to unite their souls!

He had her in his arm, drawing her face close to his breast, and she rested her head against his shoulder, closing her eyes to let the beauty of his love roll over her.

"Oh, my love! My precious little love!" he whispered.

And just at that moment the telephone rang out sharply. They both started and drew apart, as if an alien presence had entered the room, and then they laughed. But Astra came to her senses at once and pushing open the door of the guest room snatched her hat and coat from the bed where it had lain, and began to put them on rapidly.

"It's likely that woman who came this morning, and she mustn't find me here, you know," she said with a twinkle of her eyes.

"I shall not answer the telephone if you think she is there! Don't go yet. She couldn't get here right away."

"Oh, but I *must*. She might be only downstairs in the office. What will she think of me, staying here with you alone?"

"I shall not answer that telephone!" he said with dignity.

"Oh, but you'll *have* to. It might be your sister, you know, calling to say they were detained or something. Good-by!" and she lifted her lips for a quick kiss and drew away from his detaining arms, her happy face full of a joyous light.

He sprang to the door and shouted along the hall:

"Call me up the minute you get there and let me know you are all right!" but his answer was the clang of the elevator door as it slipped its way down to the first floor, and when he pressed his tense hands on his burning eyeballs he had the vision of a twinkling merry face framed in golden hair, laughing back at him. When he got back into the room again the telephone was ringing more madly than ever.

But the room seemed desolate and empty, for Astra was gone. And the worst of it was he was tied down here, and couldn't even get away to take Astra home. He had to stay here and take whatever came. That dratted telephone! Why didn't it stop ringing?

He stepped out into the hall and walked up and down. Finally it seemed to have stopped. But when he went back into the room he caught a vision of his young nephew in blue and white pajamas stumbling sleepily back into his bedroom.

"Harold, is that you?" he asked in a low tone so the other children would not be wakened.

"Yeh, Unc' Charlie!"

"What were you up for, boy?"

"I was answerin' the phone."

"Who was it?"

"That bad lady."

"What did she want?"

"She wanted ta know, was you here, an' I said *no*. You *wasn't*, you know, you was out in the hall, but I didn't hafta tell that. I didn't want her comin' back."

"What else did she say?"

"She said, was we here alone, an' I said no, the cook was here. Uncle Charlie, I want a drink of water."

"Okay, boy, run and get it. No, lie still, I'll get it for you."

When he brought the water the child drank eagerly, and then, as he handed back the glass, he opened one eye at his uncle and said:

"Unc' Charlie, she said she'd probably call up later. I tol' her okay, only we might not answer, for we'd probably all be asleep."

"Good work, Sergeant, I'll maybe be promoting you soon."

"Okay, Colonel!"

Cameron stood there quietly until he heard the steady breathing of the child. Then he stooped down and kissed the young forehead.

18 Astra, as she hurried down in the elevator and took her seat in the hastily summoned taxi, felt as if she were running away from a lovely dream, and yet she could not have stayed and run the risk of having that girl come and find her still there after Cameron had arrived. She had taken her for a servant, let it go at that.

All during the drive she would not let herself think, yet her lips were thrilling still at the memory of his kiss, her very soul was filled with ecstasy at the memory of his arms about her. But it was too sweet, too precious to be formed into actual thoughts, out in the open among common things. She knew she had done right to come away, and she felt that Cameron would agree with her about it when he stopped to think, but how she had hated to leave!

Then she walked into the office to find that there were a letter, two packages and a telegram for her.

She was fairly annoyed that all these things of the outside world should interrupt her thoughts now, for she had wanted to call Cameron as soon as she arrived, and he would be expecting her voice. In a moment more she would hear him speak again, and her heart was thrilling with the anticipation.

She tore open the telegram because that was what telegrams did to you. They forced themselves upon you in spite of anything else, with the sudden terror of what they might contain. But when she saw it was from Duke she slid it quickly in her purse. Here was another person whom she did not wish to have mingle with her pleasant thoughts. She would read his telegram later. It did not belong in this dear moment of this precious day.

The packages of course could wait. She did not even look to see the names of the senders. She must call up Cameron.

But before she could go to the booth the boy at the desk called to her:

"Someone on the phone for you, Miss Everson!" and there was Charles Cameron! He had grown impatient waiting.

"Yes? Yes, Charles, this is Astra! Yes, I just came in and was on my way to the telephone. Yes, I am safely back, and glad to hear your voice again so soon. Nobody knows how I hated to leave, but you know it was the right thing. Has your sister come? Oh, of course, I knew it wasn't time yet. Let us hope that they had as good a time as I did. Thank you, I'm glad you were pleased with the way I amused the children. I loved them all. They are adorable, and I hope I'll have another chance to play with them sometime. Now, I must get off this wire. There are some people outside the booth waiting to use it. Yes, there really *are!* Good night!"

With glowing cheeks over his last tender words, Astra came out of the booth, and hurried to her room carrying her packages with her. As soon as she had removed her wraps she sat down to open her mail. And first came Duke's telegram.

Deeply grieved at your attitude. Was about to suggest to you a new investment which will net you big profits, and was only waiting till my return to tell you about it. Please don't do anything about investments until you hear from me. Kindly send address where I can reach you personally. Dislike to contact you through lawyers, or the man you call your guardian. Am flying east in the next few days. Wire address immediately.

Duke.

The letter was from Mrs. Albans, saying that the doctor had been talking with them again. He felt that Mr. Albans ought to have another two or three weeks at home before he attempted the long journey. Would Astra like to come to them at once and make herself at home while they were slowly getting ready? It would help them very much if she could see her way clear to doing that.

The packages were from Miriam and Clytie, charming little sophisticated gifts, expensive, and unique in their way, but not at all in Astra's line. Miriam had sent a bracelet, noisy with ugly little charms that rattled, though she knew Astra was not fond of bangles. And Clytie had sent a compact with special emphasis on lipstick, although she well know that Astra didn't use it.

Astra laughed a little bitterly when she laid them away, and thought how very little she had in common with her cousins after nearly two years of daily contact.

But now Christmas was over, and the crowning joy of it an utter surprise, something to remember always! It wearied her beyond expression to have to turn her mind back to the trivialities which made up her cousins' world. Oh, how many things there were to decide, and how she did not want to think about any of them tonight! And yet some of them *had* to be thought about. Mrs. Albans had asked an immediate reply. And there would have to be some decision about Cousin Duke, or he would arrive and create all sorts of a scene. What should she do? Get out and hide, and escape Duke? No, Mr. Lauderdale would be at home tomorrow at the latest. She would wire Duke to meet her at his office. That would settle that difficulty.

Then, about Mrs. Albans. Perhaps it would be a good idea to go there for the present. It would be convenient for the work she was trying to do.

So she laid her perplexities aside, and knelt to thank God for the joy He was sending into her life. Though now, at the distance of only about two hours it seemed so unreal, just as if she had dreamed it. Did Cameron really love her, a little stranger, when there was that handsome lady of the mink coat? Why, she hadn't remembered to ask if she had telephoned again! And another thing, she had forgotten to ask how Cameron's morning expedition came out with the man who was so important that she had to take his place with the children! How it thrilled her again as she remembered that she had been able to help him with his own business affairs!

So, hovering on the border of her own great joy she at last fell asleep.

She was awakened in the morning by a knock at her door. Someone wanted her on the telephone!

She made a hasty toilet and hurried down to the telephone booth, and then was thrilled anew by hearing Cameron's voice.

"Sorry I had to waken you," he apologized, "but I had a call from my man of yesterday. He has stopped over in Washington, and wants to double his offer of yesterday if I can assure him of certain conditions. He wants me to run down to Washington early this morning and meet him and another man. It will take the principal part of the day, but it's worth it. Do you mind?"

"Why, no, of course not. I'm glad for you!"

"Well, *I* mind a lot. I wanted to come and see you the first thing this morning, and be with you as much as possible all day, but I guess this is something I ought to do."

"Of course," said Astra. "And *I* mind, *too*. But I'm glad for you. And by the way, I may be moving today. I'm going to my own house. I think I told you about it."

She gave him the address, and the telephone number.

"So, if you don't find me at the Association, you'll find me there! And I'll be listening for your voice."

"You dear! Well, that may be a solution for the time being anyway. Does the cousin know that address?"

"I don't think he does. I don't intend to tell him. He has sent another telegram. Is coming on by airplane in a day or two. Says he wants to advise me about investments!"

"I *thought* so! What did you answer him?"

"Nothing yet. I'll give him Mr. Lauderdale's address."

"Well, I'll hope to be back and have a good talk about all these things before he gets here. Now I must go to my train. I love you, Astra!"

The last words were added under his breath, but she heard them like a chime of lovely bells.

Then she hurried happily to her room, and made ready for the day in a more leisurely way. The aspect of the whole world seemed to be changed with those last words of his ringing in her heart.

She went to Mr. Lauderdale's office and found he had just arrived and would see her. She told him the latest developments, and showed him Duke's second telegram.

"Does Mr. Lester know the date of your majority definitely, or just that the time is near at hand?" he asked.

"I'm not sure. Of course his wife knows the date of my birth, that is, if she hasn't forgotten it. However, if it interests him for any reason he will lose no time in finding out."

"I think we can conclude that this man has definitely made plans to get at least some portion of your inheritance in his hands, and he wishes to get the transfer made before it comes to the notice of your lawyers," said Mr. Lauderdale.

"Yes, I was afraid of that," said Astra. "Once father said something about not trusting him too far. And so in case I have to talk to him alone sometime, just what should I say to him? He will undoubtedly make a way to see me alone somehow. He is not easily foiled."

"Yes, of course," said the lawyer thoughtfully. "By the way, does he know just how much your inheritance amounts to?"

"I don't know. I do not see how he could find out. I have never told him. I do not think his wife knows either. Except perhaps by jumping to conclusions, remembering how we used to live when she was living with us as a little girl. She has never said anything to me about it. I do not think she is interested unless she had been ordered to find out. She couldn't have found out from me, because I only know in a general way, that I am supposed to get an increase when I come of age. My father never told me definitely how much it all would be. He did write down for me a list of investments that he had made for me, but they meant nothing definite to me. My father wrote out things that he wanted me to know, and asked me to read them over occasionally, but I'm afraid I never paid much attention to them. Here is the book."

Mr. Lauderdale took the little black book and went hurriedly through its pages. Midway in his examination he looked up.

"Did your cousin have access to this book?"

Astra looked surprised.

"Why, not that I know of. He never asked me about financial matters after the first few days when I went to live with them. Just a few questions, and I told him father had written out for me what I needed to know about my affairs."

"Where did you keep this book? Was it in your bank?"

"No, it was in my desk in my room."

"And your cousin could have found it sometime when you were out of the house, and looked it over, or copied it?"

"Yes, I suppose he could. But it never occurred to me that he would."

"Perhaps not. But I'm afraid he knows something, or he wouldn't take all this trouble to pursue you. I would suggest, if he talks any further to you about your possible investments, that you simply tell him your father arranged all those things for you and you do not wish to make any changes. Let it go at that and don't allow yourself to discuss it. You can avoid a great deal by just smiling innocently and saying nothing. It won't be many days before you will be mistress of your own affairs. Now how about your old friends here? Have you got in touch with any yet?"

"Well, no, not with many. I didn't want to barge in till Christmas was over, you know."

"Of course. I see. But who are your closest friends? I can't just name them, except of course the Sargent crowd."

"Why, there are the Washburns, and Jennings, the Baldwin girls, their brothers, the McLarrons, and all that young crowd I used to know in school and college."

"But aren't most of them married?"

Astra smiled.

"I guess they are. I haven't kept in touch with them all. But there will be Rose Ashton, and Tom Eldridge."

She paused and looked at the lawyer with sudden hesitation.

"And there is Charles Cameron. Do you know him, Mr. Lauderdale? I haven't known him so long as the rest. He moved to the city only a couple of years ago, about the time I went away. But Charles is a good friend of mine."

"Cameron? Cameron! Why, you don't mean the young man who is owner of that remarkable new patent that there is such a stir about? The government is talking of taking it up in defense work. Is that the one? He has an office in the Faber building. Why, is *he* one of your friends? I didn't know that. Yes, surely I know him. That is, I've met him, and admire him very much for a certain stand he took in a legal matter I had to do with not long ago. If he is a pretty good friend of yours I should say you are well fixed in the way of friends."

Astra was listening with downcast eyes, rosy cheeks, and a pleased demure smile on her lips. She had only thought to bring Cameron's name into the conversation in that first hesitating mention of it, just to keep her friends from asking by and by how long she had known Charles, and just where and when she met him. She had no desire to announce to the world that he was somebody she had picked up on a train. Her intimacy had advanced so far that it now seemed to her as if she had known Cameron for years. But it had occurred to her that perhaps her other friends didn't know him yet, and might question annoyingly and become indignantly insistent to know all there was to know about her friendship with him. Therefore it was a relief to hear Mr. Lauderdale's favorable comment upon him. After all, according to the formal rules of social life, the rules in which she had been brought up, she had not been introduced to Charles Cameron in the regular way. Yet her heart and her common sense both told her what he was, so it was welcome to her ears to hear this unqualified praise of the man she loved.

When she left the lawyer's office she went straight to Mrs. Albans and made the necessary arrangements for going there at once. She found to her delight that already the old people had planned to put the most of their goods in storage, ready to be shipped wherever they decided to go after getting to California. They had already talked with the storage people, and their living room could be cleared of their belongings that day.

So Astra called up some working people she used to know, and some movers, and by early afternoon the living room of the old house was emptied and being cleaned, and ready for the Everson furniture that the movers brought downstairs and set in place before they left. Astra had also arranged for the movers and cleaners to return the next day and complete the work of bringing down what furniture she would need for her bedroom and study.

It was wonderful to her to walk into the dear old living room and see the big old Serapis rug that her father and she had both admired so much, again spread the length of the room where they had had so many happy times in the past. To drop down to rest for a moment in the big chair where she had so often sat reading by the hour. To set her father's chair in its place by the fireplace, where he had so loved to sit! How could she have borne it to stay away from her beloved surroundings so long?

She was glad, glad that she was back. It almost seemed as if her father might walk in pretty soon, and her heart was greatly cheered by the thought.

And now what pleasure she was going to have showing all her treasures to Cameron! Perhaps he would come that very evening and they would not have to sit distantly on a dismal public course with strangers coming and going, laughing and talking. It was going to be wonderful to have a real chance to get acquainted with her lover!

She hurried back to the Association building and hastily gathered up her belongings. She had brought a couple more suitcases from the house so that her packing would not have to be done so carefully, nor take so much time. She was eager to have everything cheerful and ready to receive Cameron if he came.

So she folded her garments very hastily, almost carelessly. In a few minutes she would take them out again and hang them in her own closets. They would not be mussed in such a short journey.

She stowed her Christmas flowers in the great pasteboard box in which they had arrived, got her baggage in a neat pile, with the radio to carry in her own hand. Then she went down to the office, paid her bill, and told them she was checking out. She left Mr. Lauderdale's office address if anyone should inquire for her, and then summoned her taxi and was gone. And if anyone was watching her depart, standing across the corner by the public square not far from where the busses had their station she was not aware of it. She was overwhelmingly happy, and anxious to be back before Cameron would be likely to come.

But Cameron did not come that night. Instead he called up and had a long telephone conversation. He had great things to tell her when he got back about how business matters were coming out, but he could not tell it over the telephone. Neither could he come back for another day or two. The whole thing had something to do with government orders, and it was all very exciting and interesting. But he longed to be back, and to know just what she had been doing all day, and she told him, hour by hour. It seemed they went many leagues in their acquaintance, and heart experiences, through that conversation. Miles apart and only a long wire stretched between, yet they could almost see the light in one another's eyes, could almost feel the pressure of the hands across the distance. There were many many things they wanted to say to each other that had to be covertly said because others could hear. But oh, it was a happy conversation, and no room for sorrow or foreboding of any kind, no eyes out across the street where an idle straggler had just come to stand, walking casually up and down now and then as if waiting for a bus.

The Albans invited her to supper. They were having vegetable soup that had been simmering all day on the low burner at the back of the range, and was rich and piquant with vegetables and herbs, and fluffy boiled potatoes, and succulent beef. There was an apple pie, gummy with juice and spicy with cinnamon, and little squares of mellow cheese on a thin china plate, and coffee of the real amber tint, for they had all been working so hard all day that even the old people felt that nothing could keep them awake. It all tasted so very good. Not even the smart dishes that Cousin Miriam used to serve could begin to compare with this home food, delicately cooked by a master hand that had been cooking for years.

And when Astra went up to her own old room that night her heart felt at rest for the first time since she had gone away. This was home. Home without the dear ones, it is true, but still the place where home had been, and she wondered if perhaps her father and mother were not looking down upon her that night and rejoicing with her that she had come back, and that she had a lover who was going to cherish her.

She looked out of the window on the little park across the street, white in its Christmas snow, with a real Christmas moon shining down, and loved it all, and was grateful God had brought her back again.

19 The next day Astra brought down her pictures and some of her ornaments that she and her father had gathered up in their travels from the ends of the earth. And they hung the wonderful portrait of Astra's father over the fireplace, such a speaking likeness, done by one of the great painters of the world. The picture had an arresting quality, as the painted eyes looked straight into the eyes of all who entered. It was as if the man himself were there.

"He brings a blessing, just to look at him," breathed Astra softly as she stood back and looked up into those dear eyes.

Astra had much pleasure in arranging everything as it used to be. They brought back her piano too, from the house where it had been stored, and she sat down and touched the beloved keys with tender fingers, playing the sweet old melodies her father had loved.

Oh, she had played the piano at her cousins', but the Lesters did not love her kind of music, and she soon ceased to bring it out to be laughed at by those who preferred modern jazz.

Upstairs in her father's old study she had arranged the desks, his bookcases, and chairs just as they used to be. She was going to enjoy so much working here where everything was so familiar. And she felt so sweet and safe, and so set apart from all things that could trouble her. The days of pleasant work, and the evening talks with Cameron made up a whole that was most satisfying.

Astra sat down and thought about it, and was thankful. It did not seem that anything just now could break up her content. Even Duke and his absurd menace of police seemed idle and far away. Surely he would never bother to come this way and trouble her. Strange she had been so disturbed.

And then, the third day back in the old home, the annoyances began.

Cameron had telephoned that he was coming home that night for sure. He would come straight to her, and her heart was happy, happy, happy! She was singing all day long.

"O, little town of Bethlehem, how still we see thee lie!"

And over across the city the three children were standing by the sadly wrecked remnants of their beloved Bethlehem, and singing too, at the top of their young lungs and off the key. Badly off the key.

"Oh wittle town of Bef'elum," sang little Mary Lou, and her mother in the living room entertaining her friend Camilla Blair, sighed and said:

"Oh, dear me! I don't know what I shall do if those little naughty kids of mine don't stop singing that same old song. I've threatened, and ordered, and implored, but sing it they will! Because their beloved 'Aster' sang it, whoever she is. Some unknown whom Charles dug up to take his place when he went off traipsing in search of business on Christmas Day. Can you imagine it? Business on Christmas Day!

"But I haven't asked you, Camilla, whatever became of you? I thought you were coming to solace Charles' lonely hours, and when I asked about you Charles only said he hadn't seen you, and that he had to catch a train at once. So I don't know anything. Only from the children, and they talk of nothing but Astra, Astra, Astra from morning to night, until I think I shall go crazy. I certainly shall never ask Charles to take care of my family again. He pretty nearly broke up housekeeping for me. The nurse never did come back. She sent her brother to get her bags and say that she had taken another place. And as for the cook, poor thing, Charles locked her in her room all night. Of course, she'd been drinking, but then you know they will do, a drop at

Christmas time. You can't blame them. Oh, I know she drinks at times, but she is such a wonderful cook, and I can't ever get another as good. I don't know whether she's going to be appeased and come back or not. I suppose I'll have to raise her wages if she does, and goodness knows I was giving her enough as it was. Some of my friends say I'm making all sorts of trouble for them by paying my cook so much. But Camilla, tell me, didn't you come at all? I've asked the children several times, but they shut their lips tight as if they were sealed and I can't get a word out of them. Only little Mary Lou said once, 'There was a bad lady here,' but I couldn't make out what she meant. I suppose it was that Astra, although she seems to adore her. Well, tell me about it. Why didn't you come?"

Camilla, thus exhorted, shrugged her shoulders.

"Oh, I came!" she drawled. "But I wasn't encouraged to stay. In fact they were all perfectly insolent. I suppose it was really the fault of that girl. She was impossible. She was actually trying to poke an old-fashioned religious tale down the children's throats, and they were wild about it. They kept clamoring for Bethlehem. That girl was making some kind of a movie of an old-fashioned Bible story, building Bethlehem."

"Oh, don't I know!" sighed the mother. "When I attempted to clear the house up, and sweep all that tangle of green paper away there was the most awful howl from my children I ever heard in my life! I actually had to attempt to put it all back the way it was, only they said I hadn't done it right, and cried buckets full of tears about it, till I finally carried the table into their nursery and left them to their own devices. Then I had the only peaceful hour of the whole day while they attempted to set things right. They just about worship that miserable little city, and talk about it all the time. But I will say whoever that girl was, I'd give a good deal to get hold of her. My nurse is gone, and I just dread trying to get another. If I could find that girl I'd hire her for a while, for she certainly has gained a tremendous influence over the children. They even mind her now she's gone. Harold will say, 'Now Mary Lou, don't you remember what Astra said about that? Don't you know about the star that came?' And Mary Lou will stop crying and smile. I never saw the like. I really mean to get hold of that girl if I can and hire her. Do you have any idea where she came from? Charles is away now, down in Washington on business, so I can't ask him, but I'd give anything to get this fixed up before Charles comes home! Did she say anything that would give you an inkling of where she's to be found?"

"Why, no," said Camilla, "I don't remember that she did, but I'm sure I can find her for you if you want me to try. She's quite unusual looking. Gold hair and big eyes and all that. If you want me to, I'll see if I can find her. In fact I thought I saw her on the street the other day, over in the north section of the city. She probably works there — they are all fine residences there. I'll ask around. A good many of my friends live there."

"Well, I certainly wish you would. I'm worn to a frazzle, and since she's taught them one song, perhaps she can persuade them to give it a rest for awhile and teach them another."

So that was how it came about that Camilla Blair started out in search of Astra Everson. Only all she knew about her name was that it was Astra.

But it happened that Astra had found a little book that her father used to buy by the quantity to give away to young people he wanted to help, and she felt it was the very thing that would help the boy at the desk in the Association House. So that morning when she went out to post a letter to Mrs. Sargent expressing sympathy for Mr. Sargent's illness, she thought she would take the book along. She came in her brisk walk along the snowy pavement, to the corner across from the Association where it happened that Camilla Blair was waiting for a bus.

Astra was wearing the same little dark green wool dress, and the bright scarlet ribbon on her hair that she had worn on Christmas Day. She had on a scarlet tam that showed the hair ribbon else it might not have caught Camilla's eye. And then the bus came along, but Camilla did not get into it. Instead she lingered as if she were waiting for another bus, and kept watch. She saw Astra go into the Association door, and she waited near the restaurant out of sight until Astra had given her book to the boy, and came out. Then, Camilla, afar off, followed Astra home, thinking to herself how clever she had been to find the girl. Meanwhile she lingered afar, and studied the lovely fur coat that Astra was wearing over her green wool dress. Where did she get that coat? It was really too nice for a servant to wear. Maybe her mistress had given it to her. Or she might have saved up her wages and bought it. Ridiculous that people who had to work for a living should be so extravagant with their hardly earned wages!

And when they came to the substantial stone house in the unmistakably desirable quarter of the city, and Astra, now quite a distance ahead, ran lightly up the *front* steps of the beautiful old house, applied a key to the lock and let herself in, Camilla paused in amazement to think out this problem. How did the girl called Astra belong in a house like that? Well, it must be she had a job there, and had borrowed that coat from her mistress while she went on an errand.

Camilla wasn't the only one watching the Everson house. There was a young man, slim and sallow, with averted eyes, watching the upper windows of the house, watching the front door, and then turning away as if he had no interest at all in it. But Camilla did not see him. If she had she might have paused longer to work out her romantic theories of the servant girl who wore squirrel coats and sang Christian songs, and had a key to the front door of a house like that. She would certainly have taken the sleuth across the road to be one of Astra's lovers! And how she would enjoy finding a disreputable lover or two to parade before Charles. Charles who had brought this girl to his sister's home to take care of her dear little children. (She had called them brats to herself on Christmas Day after she got home from her visit with them.)

So Camilla, carrying out a carefully arranged plan, took her way up the street a block, crossed over and came to the Everson house, mounted the steps and rang the bell.

And it happened that it was Astra herself, fresh from her walk in the snowy world, her cheeks still glowing from cold and exercise, who opened the door and saw the gorgeous mink coat, worn by the lady of her great dislike. And as once before, on Christmas Day, Camilla stepped inside the door and confronted her adversary.

"You are the girl Astra, I believe?" she said, haughtily, chin up, eyes smoldering.

Astra laughed a little trill of a laugh.

"Yes?" she said gaily. "And you are the girl Camilla, isn't that right?"

"You are still impertinent, I see?" said Camilla.

"Was that impertinent? Why, any more than for you to call me Astra?"

"But you are a servant!" said Camilla, contempt in her whole manner. "You told me yourself you were a servant. Although you certainly were blasphemous when you answered my question about whose servant you were. But that is neither here nor there.

My friend Mrs. Harrison, is very anxious to get hold of you again and I volunteered to try and find you. Can we sit down somewhere and talk about it?"

Astra stared at her, and then she grinned for an instant, sobering into an amused smile

"Why certainly, come right in and sit down," she said and swung open the wide door into the newly restored living room, with the wonderful eyes of Dr. Everson, the great scientist, looking down and dominating the room.

Camilla stopped short on the threshold and looked about her, then stepped back.

"Are you quite sure your mistress would be willing *you* should take a caller into *her* living room?"

Astra's eyes danced, but she answered gravely:

"Oh, yes, I'm quite sure she wouldn't object. She is quite broad-minded. Won't you sit here by the fire? It is quite cold outside."

Camilla sat down on the edge of the great chair offered her.

"I will come to the point at once," said Camilla. "I don't wish to take any more of your mistress' time than is necessary. Will you tell me how long your engagement here is supposed to last? Is it merely for a short time, or an indefinite period? Because my friend would like you to come to her as soon as possible as a regular nurse for her children."

Astra's eyes were dancing again but she still answered quietly. "I couldn't possibly take another situation. I am very busy and cannot leave what I am doing, and while I like children very much I would not be able to take care of anybody's children."

"But Mrs. Harrison is willing to pay very high wages if she can be suited."

"That wouldn't be the point," said Astra. "I'm sorry. I can't do it. I have obligations here."

"Then I shall have to ask to see the lady of the house. This is quite important to me, or I should not venture to appeal to her. If she should give you up I suppose you would be willing to come to my friend."

Even Astra's eyes grew sober now, though the grin still lingered and fitted in the corner of her mouth.

"No," said Astra. "I would not be willing to come under any consideration. I have other work to do. I think there are agencies where you could probably find servants to please your friend, but I cannot come."

Camilla considered Astra's firm young mouth, and reflected that after all it was her friend's affair. She had found the girl for her and from this point Rosamond Harrison was fully capable of putting on her own siege, so she arose.

"Well," she said stiffly, "I must say you are a very foolish girl, for if you suited my friend you would perhaps be engaged for your lifetime. However, I suppose you feel you are well fixed here. This is a very nice home, of course. But I am sure you would like my friend's place as well. I think you will see her sometime soon, for she is a very determined woman."

"Yes," said Astra with dancing eyes again, "I shall look forward to seeing her sometime. But as a matter of fact, I am already engaged for life!"

"And how!" she giggled softly to herself as she closed the door behind the departing mink coat.

But the furtive man across the road slunk out from behind his tree and presently overtook the mink coat.

"Lady," he said in an apologetic tone, "would you kindly tell me something. I saw you go into that house across the way, and would you kindly tell me if there is someone there named Astra?"

Camilla Blair faced the young man with an appraising eye:

"Yes, there is," she said coldly. "I suppose you are in love with her or something. But I may as well tell you since you have asked about her, that you will be wasting your time going after her. She is a very determined and opinionated young woman, and you really wouldn't have a pleasant life with her. She's a servant in that house, you know."

The man gave Camilla a startled glance.

"Thank you, lady," he said. She had told him all he needed to know when she told him Astra was living there.

"I would advise you to go away and forget her. She really is not worth wasting your time on."

"All right, lady. Thank you very kindly, lady," and he slouched off in the opposite direction.

Late that afternoon the same man could be seen making his way toward the Philadelphia airport, and hovering about until a plane from the west came in. Marmaduke Lester with great pomp and ceremony and many bags, deposited himself on the ground and walked away following the general direction of the sleuth.

20 An hour after the arrival of the airplane, Marmaduke Lester attired himself inconspicuously and entered a shabby old automobile parked in a desolate spot on the outskirts of the city. The man who had watched outside the Everson house and held conversation with Camilla was driving, and the third passenger was one Tom Hatchley, the unworthy son-in-law of the meek little woman living in the Willow Haven stone cottage that Astra had so lovingly provided for her use in her declining years. Oddly enough this son-in-law, still intent upon the purchase of a new car, and ready to take up with anything that would further that end, had been an easy subject of Duke's henchman, who had rooted out the facts and had sought out his man in a tavern, had watched him awhile, and them approached him with a proposition.

"I don't want no killin' job," said Hatchley with a shift of his cunning eyes, "understand that! I'm connected with good respectable people, an' I wantta live right!"

"Oh, no, it's nothin' like that!" said the sleuth from the west. "This is only a little persuasive matter, for her own good. To work it right we have to isolate her for a little and get a chance to make her see reason. Then everything will be jake. Now what we want of you is to make the contact. In the early evenin', sometime when there won't be nobody on the street to holler. We want ya to go to the door and put up a story, and then before she can say a word, quick snap a black cloth over her head and carry her down to our car we'll have parked handy. There'll be two of us besides you to watch out and tell ya when ta go, and there won't be scarcely a bit o' risk. O' course there's plenty o' dough in it fer ya ef ya do the job right. What's that? Jail? Naw! You look like a bird who could do a slick job, and there's no cops around in that neighborhood at that hour of the night. We'd liketa pull it off very soon if possible, and we'll be back of ya and pertect ya. You can vanish as soon as ya get her in the car. There'll be another fella waiting in the car. He's the agent from out west, and he's some bird. He knows his onions, an' I guess there's no law he don't know how ta trip up. He's a member of one of the biggest racket gangs on the west coast. Now, can we depend on ya? Take it or leave it, we gotta get goin'. The bird that's bossin' this comes in on the plane tomorra mornin'!"

"What's this here girl's name?" asked

Tom cautiously just before he gave his word he would take the job.

"Everson," said the other man, "but doncha breathe it to a soul. She's got high up kin an' ya might get inta trouble."

"You don't mean Miss Astra Everson, do ya?" asked Tom in astonishment, "because my mother-in-law usedta work fer her mom, and I gotta personal grudge against her. She done me a mean trick. Spoiled my plans. Boy, I'd liketa get even with her all right. Sure I'll take the job. How much you say you'll pay?"

And that was the way Tom got into the matter.

"I got a plan all righty!" he told his new employer the next day. "I'll tell her my wife's mother is awful sick, and she sent me ta ask, would Miss Astra come and see her. She's near ta die, and has ta tell her something she oughta 'a' told her long ago. We cud take her right up ta the old lady's house. It belongs ta Miss Everson, ya know, an' give her the works right there. I'll have the old 'un outa the way. Nobody'll ever find out where the girl is till it's all arranged!"

Thus did the fertile brain of Tilly's son-in-law help to plot the way for Duke Lester. And so it was that Duke found himself in this sordid company riding along from the airport in the shabby car. To tell the truth this whole job was a little out of Duke's line. He wasn't used to taking part in what he called the "dirty work" of his own crooked schemes. He usually hired deeper-dyed crooks than himself to carry out his purposes, so now he felt distinctly uncomfortable. What would his persnickety wife and spoiled daughter say if they could see him now riding away like this, through the city, and out into the pleasant suburbs on such a mission?

So that was the ancestral mansion of the Eversons? Not so bad. Then Astra's money must be a tidy sum, to carry a house like that on its list! She was established there already! Well, he'd soon spoil her plans!

And so they drove on out of sight of the house and into a world of their own to wait for evening shadows to gather when their plans could be carried out.

Meantime, Rosamond and Camilla were having a telephone talk.

"Well, I found her, but that was all," Camilla was saying. "She's a servant all right, and she's working in a swell house in a swell neighborhood, real old substantial people, I should judge. I'm afraid you'll have a time getting her away even if you pay a criminally enormous sum. But you'll have to do the getting yourself. I've exhausted my efforts in finding her, and I did my best to get her to come and see you, but she practically laughed in my face. She said she wouldn't leave where she was and what she was doing for anybody or anything. And I warn you, if you do get her you'll be sorry. She's an insolent piece, and you never will stand for her."

But Rosamond took down the address and determined that she would go tomorrow and find out about the girl. She couldn't go today because she had a very important meeting of a committee belonging to her club. But she thanked Camilla, and laid aside her worries on the score of no nurse for the present. She was sure she could coax any living girl away from her employer if she went about it in the right way. And she always knew the right way.

After Astra had closed the door behind her disturbing guest, the day went forward more calmly. She took time to go by herself and snatch a Bible verse to live by through its hours, and to talk to her Lord, and ask help and guidance in every happening.

The verse she came upon in her hurried reading startled her, because she had been so upset by Camilla's visit. It was, "No weapon that is formed against thee shall prosper; and every tongue that shall rise against thee in judgment, thou shalt condemn. This is the heritage of the servants of the Lord, and their righteousness is of me, saith the Lord."

She said it over to herself several times as she went on through the day, glad to rest the matter of this disagreeable enemy of hers entirely in His keeping, and just forget it.

So the day came to evening, and evening brought another message from Cameron. He had to take a later train than he had planned, and would not get to her house until a little after nine. Might he come to her then?

And the hours crept slowly, happily by.

The shabby car came to find a parking place among a dense patch of shrubbery in the little park across from the Everson house, and Cousin Duke in another car which he had hired for himself, and driven himself, took up his stand at a curb in front of a vacant house a short distance from the point of immediate interest, yet where he could view operations without being observed. He arranged himself in the shadow, with a hat drawn down over his eyes, and a collar turned high about his chin.

From where he sat in the darkness he could see Astra sitting near the window reading. She looked so bright and happy that his fury rose. She was going to be a hard customer to deal with, he was afraid. But of course she would yield to reason if he worked the thing in the right way. And it must be done quickly, for it wouldn't do for Miriam to find out about this. Miriam could be pretty determined at times, and make the world most uncomfortable for him. This must be done thoroughly and done tonight, for tomorrow was Astra's birthday. He ought to have started sooner. It was all Miriam's fault that he didn't because she was so slow to remember dates and things.

Once he noticed a police car drive by and turn into the park, but listening, it seemed to him he heard it drive away far in the distance.

And then he saw the Tom Hatchley person steal across the road and mount the steps of the Everson house, with something dark like an overcoat over one arm. Then he saw two other shadows detach themselves from the darkness and blur into the shadows of the Everson place, quite near the front steps. The time had come then. It seemed to be very still on that street at the moment, as if the vicinity were waiting for something. Then he heard the soft purr of a bell. It must be they had rung the doorbell.

And now he could see Astra rise, and lay down her book. She was going to answer the door herself. They wouldn't have to wait to ask for her. That was making it easy.

He could see the light on her gold hair as she passed under the chandelier in the middle of the room. He watched and listened keenly, and he felt his heart beating too rapidly. He hoped they wouldn't be too rough with her. After all she was related and had been in his house almost like another child of his family. He wouldn't like to have Clytie in such a position. Although of course they had promised not to hurt her.

Then he saw the light stream from the front door, and the quick motion of the black cloth being thrown. The light in the hall was snapped out suddenly, leaving the view in utter darkness.

Then a confusion of sounds. A bus stopped at the next corner behind him, one block over, and there came brisk steps walking down the street. Oh, they must hurry. Someone was coming! There might have to be some rough work after all. But one of those men had said he was an expert at such things. He could put that man out of commission with a swift blow. It was no one that Marmaduke knew, so what was the difference?

And now they were coming down the steps, swiftly, a great black bundle in their arms. There was no outcry. It was not like Astra to cry out. Astra always took everything quietly. Now the man who was carrying her was running, swiftly and silently, down the stone flagging to the street. There were other sounds breaking on his consciousness, a muted car with piercing lights, a red car. The police! The sudden sound of a gun, a flash down low by the feet of the man who was carrying the black bundle, the quick collapse of the struggling bundle. The kidnaper had been shot in the feet!

In sudden panic Marmaduke flung wide the door of his rented car, and plunged out on the sidewalk! Straight into the arms of a sturdy policeman who had been silently standing there, no telling how long. Duke had never thought to hear handcuffs snapped onto his aristocratic wrists, but there he was, fettered! Caught in this net by which he had hoped to catch Astra! Oh, he mustn't be caught! He had papers in his pockets that would incriminate him if he were searched! He *mustn't!*

He struggled, he tried to protest. He was only a private citizen waiting for a friend to come out of a house. He had nothing to do with this affair that was going on. This shooting! He knew nothing about it!

But the policeman paid no attention to him.

"Come along with me. You can explain all that and prove it down at the station house when you get there!" and he marched the elegant Marmaduke firmly back to a police car waiting around the corner.

But the swift steps that he had heard coming from that bus had broken into a run, and almost as soon as the man with the bundle fell, the young man was there, lifting up the frightened girl, asking if she were hurt.

Another officer who had appeared from out the shadows spoke to him.

"Hello, Mr. Cameron! You here? You didn't get hurt, did you? We had word there was a bird here trying to pull off a little something on the side, and he happens to be a bird we've been watching for a long time, a killer, so we came quick!"

There were more bullets flying now. Tom Hatchley was down and out, and no chance of that new car for sometime ahead.

There were other patrol cars coming, and quite a disturbance in the quiet street.

But Astra was in the arms of her beloved, and over and over again in her mind ran the words "No weapon that is formed against thee shall prosper . . . the heritage of the servants of the Lord!"

"Better take her in the house, brother!" advised Cameron's policeman friend. "There's goin' ta be plenty of action before we're done. One pretty bad bird is still at large, I'm afraid."

So Cameron bore his beloved into the house and closed the door on the outside world, and Astra looked into his dear eyes with joy and gladness, and for some minutes Cameron could not put her down. He just stood there holding her close in his arms, his face against hers.

And then the Albans came in to find out what all the noise and shooting was about, and they looked in amazement at the handsome young man standing there holding Astra as if she were the most precious thing in all the world.

Then Astra roused to the occasion and introduced Cameron, and they had a happy little rejoicing and thanksgiving together, till by and by the Albans retired, and the street got quiet. Astra and Charles had a real talk, with their arms about one another, sitting in the deep chair where Astra used to sit sometimes with her father when she was a little girl growing up.

"And now," said Cameron, when he at last got up to go, "you've got to get some rest, and tomorrow I think we had better be married. I can't stand the strain of not knowing what is happening to you, with things like this going on."

He looked pleadingly down at her, but she laughed gaily up into his eyes.

"All right," she said. "Tomorrow is my birthday. I shall be of age, and I can do as I please, so I'm willing, but you'll have to excuse me from having a swell trousseau or a big wedding."

"That's all right with me," he smiled. "I only want you, not an impressive wedding. We could get our wonderful minister from the little church, or have it in the church, or here at this place. This is a lovely house. Would the people here, the Albans, mind?"

"They'd better not. It's my house," smiled Astra. "But I know they'll love it. They are sweet people. And these are my own things, mine and father's. I've been getting it ready for you to see."

"It's wonderful!" said Cameron, as he looked all around with eyes of deep appreciation. And then he looked up at the picture. "And is that father?" he asked gently. "How great to have a picture like that!" Then suddenly he took her close in his arms, and bowing his face against hers he closed his eyes.

"Dear God," he prayed, "help me to guard and care for this dear child as her own earthly father would have wanted me to do, and help us both to walk in Thy ways, till we come Home to You and father and mother, and my father and mother. Amen."

The kiss that sealed their promises was sweeter than anything that either of them had ever known.

It was the next morning quite early that Cameron had his talk with his sister Rosamond. She called him up very early.

"Charlie, I want you to tell me where you got that servant you had to look after my children Christmas Day while I was away. I haven't any nurse, and I can't stir an inch anywhere without one. These children just clamor for that girl they call Astra. So as you seem to have been the means of my losing both cook and nursemaid, I think it's up to you to dig her out and secure her for me. Who is she? Did you know anything about her? But anyway I want her, no matter who she is. I never saw Harold so amenable to reason as he has been since she was with him that one day."

"Astra?" said Cameron coming out of a deep sweet sleep of happiness to answer her. "Yes, I know who she is, and where she is, but I'm afraid I can't secure her for a nurse-

maid for your children, because you see I'm marrying her tonight. Do you want to come to the wedding?"

"Marrying! Why Charles Cameron! You're joking! You can't marry her. She's only a servant! You can't disgrace our family by marrying a servant. That's worse than even our father did, for his second wife. She at least was of good respectable family! Charlie, you wouldn't make all your sisters a laughing stock to all their friends? You can't marry her!"

"Oh, but I am," laughed Cameron joyously. "Eight o'clock is the hour, I believe, and the wedding supper just after. My only stipulation is that you bring all the children."

"But Charlie! You'll break my heart. To have you marry a servant, when I had found such a good suitable match for you, so capable, and so beautiful and so wealthy! And you to take up with a poor little servant girl who has worked for a pitiful wage."

"Are you referring to that poor pasty-faced Camilla as the girl you so kindly provided for me? Well, if you were, just think again. I wouldn't marry her if she was the last woman left on the earth, and I had to go lonely all my life. Money and beauty don't count unless you love, and I never could

love her. But you're woefully mistaken about Astra, dear sister, she never was a servant in her life. She's the daughter of the great Dr. Everson, the noted scientist, and she's traveled all over the world with her father. She's a graduate of three colleges, and she's done some rather notable writing herself. We're going to be married in the house that her grandfather built, and where her father and she herself were born, and if you don't agree it is a nice house after tonight, I'm off you for life. Now, will you help me get ready for this wedding or have I got to do it all myself?"

"Oh, Charlie! You simply take my breath away! Why do you try to have it so soon if all this is really true. Why don't you make a real affair of it?"

"Because neither Astra nor I care a red cent for 'affairs' of that sort. We're just having a plain little wedding. I have to go back to Washington tomorrow for a few days, and I want to take my wife with me. We're not waiting to accommodate the general public. We're getting married, and if our relatives would like to be present they can come, otherwise we'll go on without them. I'm calling up my stepmother, and a few of my friends. Mr. John Sargent, Astra's guardian, is on his way home from Florida

by plane, and expects to be here. So will Astra's lawyer, Mr. Lauderdale, and his wife and a few others of that ilk, and if that isn't enough for you then stay at home and sulk, for I'm getting married tonight. Now, could you call up our sisters and brothers for me, and inform them what's going on and that they are invited, or must I take time out and do it?"

"Oh, I'll do it of course, Charlie. But Charlie, I'm going to invite Camilla. I think she has a right to come after the way you've treated her. Besides, I would like to have her see that everything is all right, if you really think the house will be fine enough. Anyhow I'm going to invite her."

"Help yourself, Roz, only get to work quick and invite the others who live at a distance first. So long! See you tonight and don't forget to bring the kids or else we won't let you in."

So Rosamond had the time of her life inviting people to a wedding of which she would have highly disapproved but a short time before, and when she finally reached Camilla, she certainly enjoyed herself telling the story.

"Not the daughter of that famous Dr. Everson! You don't mean it, Roz! Well, I think that's about the meanest thing Charles

ever did to play a joke like that on you, letting you think she was a servant."

"Oh, but he didn't, Cammie, it was you who said she was a servant. I haven't ever seen her yet, remember! The joke is on you this time, my dear!"

"Well, that explains that marvelous portrait I saw then. And of course the house is unique. Everything about it is real. It explains too why I was so puzzled about a lovely girl like that being a servant, but I thought she was just a nightclub dancer, or a fashion model or something like that!"

"Well, I thought perhaps you'd enjoy coming to the wedding, and seeing the whole show. I understand she's fabulously rich, my dear! Of course Charlie didn't tell me so, but from other things he's said I imagine it's true. But how do you suppose she'll manage a wedding with only a day to prepare?"

"Oh, well, I don't imagine it'll trouble her much. She's that kind. She'd just as soon wear a sports frock, or even a bathing suit perhaps, although, no, I think she's prudishly modest. She may have an old wedding frock salted away. Her great grandmother's or something. If she were not so frank and free from airs I'd be frightfully ashamed to go after having asked her, really begged her,

to be your maid servant. However, wonders never cease. I wonder how Charles will get along with such a frightfully religious person. I never thought he was particularly religious himself."

"Well, I'm not sure," said Rosamond. "Maybe that's what has always been the matter with him. Maybe he was religious and didn't know how to express himself. Maybe that's what has made him so kind to that old frumpy stepmother! He's even asking her to the wedding himself."

"Oh, is she coming? Well, that settles it. I always wanted to see her. I'll come. And really, after this, Roz, I've got to get busy and polish up some of my old discarded sweethearts, for Charlie's deserting me this way leaves me high and dry. Do you know, Roz, I really was almost fond of Charlie!"

"Oh, yes?" said Rosamond significantly. "Well, good-by, I'll see you tonight."

And so there was a hasty gathering of the Cameron clan, and of the Everson friends, invited by telephone, some by telegraph. They came one and all with very few exceptions. By train and trolley and bus they came, by plane and car and one even by bicycle.

Astra wrote a sweet little note to Miriam and Clytie.

Dear ones: It is my twenty-first birthday, and I am going to be married tonight at eight o'clock to Charles Cameron. It was very hastily arranged, too late to get you here even by plane from so far. But I'll be thinking of you, and I hope you will be thinking of me as very happy indeed. Will write you later. We are leaving for Washington tonight for a brief honeymoon, and then back to the old family home. Loving wishes to you all.

Astra.

And then after it was written she decided to send it as a telegram. They would feel more as if they had not been entirely left out. They received it about the time the ceremony began. Clytie read it sullenly with smoldering eyes.

"Seems as if some people have all the luck!" she remarked to her mother in a sort of wail.

But Miriam as she read was taken back through the years to the time when Astra's mother had taken her, a motherless little child, into her home and made her happy, and there were tears upon her cheeks. For a great trouble rested upon her heart. She did not know just where Duke had gone, — in an airplane one night without warning —

nor what he had gone to do, and she was greatly worried about that. Sometimes she had suspected that Duke's ways were not always the ways of righteousness. If she had known that he was at that moment sitting forlornly in a cell by himself, reflecting upon the ways of the wicked as he had never done before, and realizing that the incriminating letters that had been found upon his person when he was arrested would probably keep him in confinement a good many of the best years of his life, she would not have been any happier.

But the wedding was going on, and nobody of the family so far realized anything about him.

The guardian had come home by plane to be present at the coming of age of Astra, and his presence filled her with great delight.

The stepmother was there and beamed upon Cameron, and pressed the bride's hand tenderly, saying, "I hope you'll have a happy life. Charles always was a good boy!"

The lawyer, Mr. Lauderdale, and his wife were there, smiling happily over it all. Lewis Sargent, and Will were both there, apologizing because they hadn't been on hand to greet her when she first arrived, and even old Tilly was there, peering out from the pantry door where she had so many times been queen of that kitchen. Even the office boy at the Association was there, because he had brought her the flowers and messages on Christmas. And Rosamond's three children were present with glee. They even had to be restrained forcibly from bringing what was left of Bethlehem to be used as table decorations.

They had a charming wedding supper served by a caterer. Astra had gotten out her mother's treasured dishes and silver to add to the occasion. It didn't seem that there was anything more that could have been done even if they had had six months in which to prepare.

Astra had no ancient dress of family lore to wear, but she found in the shops a little simple white satin, quite plain and sweet, its only decoration a bertha of lovely old Honiton lace that had been her mother's. Even Rosamond said how wonderful she looked.

Afterwards, when it was all over, and they were alone at last on the train that was bearing them to Washington, Astra said with a sweet thoughtful look:

"Wasn't it wonderful that God showed me that verse yesterday just when all that was coming to frighten me?" She repeated it:

"No weapon that is formed against thee shall prosper, and every tongue that shall rise against thee in judgment thou shalt condemn. This is the heritage of the servants of the Lord."

"Yes," said Cameron. "We have a wonderful God, and a wonderful heritage, and it's going to be grand to live our lives together, for His glory!"